A Creature of Smokeless Flame

Applied Topology Book 5

Margaret Ball

Galway Publishing

*For Scot, my invaluable go-to guy for ballistics,
urban warfare, and other military matters*

1. Black site

At first sight, the room was grey, dingy, and unspeakably depressing. On a second look, it was worse. There were no windows, and a metal plate bolted over the small barred opening in the door prevented any possibility of getting a glimpse outside of the room, even the sight of what was probably an equally dim and dingy corridor. The plate and bolts were on the outside of the door, which would have prevented most people from trying to loosen them. I didn't bother because I had little hope that the view on the other side of the door was any better.

The air hissing through the ceiling vent was cold and smelled stale. This was the end of a long hot Texas July, a time when I am normally pro-air conditioning, but from where I was now – lying on a clammy cement floor – the coolness was decidedly unwelcome.

Since I was already lying on my back and staring at the ceiling when I came to, I spent some time contemplating the ceiling air vent. It was about the size of half a sheet of typewriter paper. Even if I got the grille off I wouldn't be able to fit through that opening, and Colton would have had to be fed through in pieces. I lay quietly and considered our other options. Besides the one that they were probably expecting, that is.

Whoever "they" were.

Colton had been working on a topological application that would demolish abandoned, ramshackle outbuildings for his father and other farmers, but I didn't know how much control he had; he had taken his experiments out to a field of prickly pears off Highway 183, where there was plenty of room for error. In any case, I wasn't sure it would be a good idea to use his application on the door of a cell that had no other outlet for the resulting blast. Then, too, Ben and Ingrid and I weren't up to date on that project. Colton would have had to blow out his own cell door, then find each of us – and that was assuming we were all in the same building – and free us individually. Before any of the nice people who'd locked us up noticed any unusual goings-on.

Fortunately, as researchers at the Center for Applied Topology we had one very obvious way of departing the scene. I just wasn't sure it was time for us to use it yet. The way we'd been treated so far suggested that our captors had some serious misapprehensions about the limits of our abilities. It might not be wise to give them any more data than we absolutely had to.

I'd been the last of the four of us to be captured. It had happened when I was leaving the office – this evening? Yesterday? After being drugged twice and having lost my watch, I wasn't at all clear on the passage of time. I remembered making a gesture towards cleaning my desk – well, okay, piling the papers in neat stacks. The office had been very quiet, but I hadn't thought much of that. Mathematicians aren't very noisy, and it was late enough that our receptionist and the rest of the support staff had probably gone home. It had been quite a while since lunch; I thought I'd just check out the break room, in case there were any leftover doughnuts to help fuel my trip home. But when I walked the Möbius strip through the blank wall between the research division and the public side of the Center, there had been no one in the outer office but two strange men, and the double doorway to the stairs was wide open. We really need to replace that lock one of these days.

One of the men grabbed me while the other slapped my arm with something sharp. Oh, hell. I've been sedated like that before. I don't like it. I had just enough time to think *Dammit, not again* before I fell into darkness – not the clear darkness of the in-between, shot through with intersecting lines and spiraling shapes of brilliant color, but a cloudy and stifling darkness that suffocated thought.

When I came to, there was something around my wrists and my arms ached from being forced into a strained position. I was in a dark place that roared and vibrated alternately; if it hadn't been for the pain, I wouldn't have been absolutely sure I *was* conscious and not having a nightmare. A couple of tugs convinced me that I wouldn't be able to free my hands by any normal techniques. It was probably safer, just for the moment, to pretend I had no other options. I sat still and tried to feel out the darkness around me.

After a few minutes I could sense other people. No, nothing paranormal about that; there were subtle shifts in the not-quite-total darkness, movements of the air from someone's breathing, other tiny cues that we don't normally rely on.

"Thalia?"

It was Ben's voice, barely audible over the noise around us.

"Ben! Are you all right?"

"Sssh. Yes. All three of us are okay."

"Who else?"

"Colton and Ingrid."

So, not Lensky. Of course not. He hadn't even been in town.

"Mr. M.?"

"Haven't seen him. You've been out the hell of a long time. What did they do to you?"

"Drugged, I think." That made me aware that my mouth was dry and my head was pounding; not things I really wanted to focus my attention on. Well, maybe they were; it was better than thinking about the strain on my arms and shoulders or the nauseating bouncing of the vehicle we seemed to be in. "You?"

"Same, except it wore off faster."

I tried to focus. It wasn't easy. "Well, I'm smaller than the rest of you. If they gave everybody a dose geared to people Colton's size, I'm surprised I'm not dead. What happened to you guys?"

Ben, Colton and Ingrid had stories almost identical to mine, except that Ben and Ingrid had been snatched when they left the building. Colton, like me, had been caught on his way to check out the doughnut tray. They had no idea what had happened to the support staff, and that was worrying them too. Ingrid, who was supposed to be marrying our computer expert Jimmy in six weeks, was being very carefully *not* hysterical in a very controlled tone of voice. As she said, we had to get ourselves out of this before we could do anything to help the others, so there was no point thinking about them right now.

Her voice hardly even quavered when she said it, so we all emulated her stiff upper lip. Unfortunately, that didn't help us come up with any creative ideas.

We were, we thought, in the back of a windowless van that was on a highway. Probably not I-35, we didn't hear that many trucks and semis blaring to right and left of us.

We couldn't use our best escape option while cuffed to rails that seemed to have been bolted to the inside of the van. Colton tried to pull the rail on his side loose, but he couldn't get enough leverage on it. And even if we had been able to get loose, I didn't really want to try teleporting out of a speeding van. Too much chance of winding up smeared across our destination point.

"We could try the way you got out of Balan's trap in January?" Ben suggested tentatively.

"Umm. That was rope I burned, that time." And it hadn't been a pleasant experience; my hands and wrists got burned too. This time could be even worse, because it felt like I was confined by plastic zip ties now. "I don't specially want to melt plastic onto my skin. Anyway, I didn't have to generate all the heat by myself; the carpet caught fire quite well. I don't think there's anything in here that we can burn." Not to mention that while Riemann fire might free our hands, it wouldn't solve the problem of teleporting while moving at high speed.

"Nothing we can reach, anyway," Colton said grimly, "and maybe it's not such a good idea to demonstrate the Riemann technique to them if they don't already know about it."

And there was something I should have thought about earlier. "They could have this van bugged. Was that why you were practically whispering, Ben?"

There was a brief pause, then he said, "Yes. I thought we'd better not talk about anything they don't need to know."

That pretty much restricted us to disjointed trivialities for the rest of the journey. I guessed that during the long silences my colleagues were doing the same thing I was: mentally running through the things we might be able to do to escape, or failing that, to give our attackers some grief.

One very small bright spot did occur to me. "Colton, did they carry *you* down both flights of stairs?" Our offices were on the third floor of a Victorian mansion with no elevators.

"Probably. Although having been out cold at the time, I don't really know. Why?"

"I'm just hoping they have permanent back injuries from trying to carry somebody your size." Colton was an extremely large and athletic young man. He'd played football for his high school and could have gone through college on a football scholarship if he hadn't developed an interest in mathematics and a corresponding distaste for repeated concussions.

After another half hour of being shaken and stirred, I thought of something else. I just wasn't sure how to convey it to the others without conveying the same information to our hypothetical listeners.

"I expect it wouldn't be a good idea for anybody to go to the office just now."

"Well, *duh*, Thalia," Ingrid snapped. "I may not go there ever again. Thanks to the Center I have now been defecated on by grackles, shot at by terrorists, transported back..."

"LA LA LA," I singsonged to drown out what she was about to say. After a minute Colton joined in with his high school fight song and Ben contributed an off-key rendering of "The Eyes of Texas." It's hard to get that one wrong, but Ben is especially talented.

"Very well," Ingrid said when we ran out of breath. "I get the message. All the same, I don't mind telling you that *this* time I am feeling *permanently* fed up with the Center for Applied Topology."

The residual drugs must still be dulling her mind; I couldn't think of any other explanation for her saying "fed up" instead of "disenchanted" or "surfeited." Well, that was another reason not to try anything now, when we desperately needed to be working with perfect clarity. Access to our stars would have come in handy, too. I could sense that mine were in the front righthand pocket of my jeans, like always, but that didn't do me a lot of good right now; no contortion was going to get my fingers and that pocket together. I didn't want to ask the others about theirs. The stars were something our captors wouldn't have noticed, and I really didn't want them to start thinking about invisible stuff we might have. Invisible to them, anyway.

"I understand," I said now to placate Ingrid. "I'm just thinking about the interesting times we've had, the places where we've *all been together.* Remember the giant water moccasin?"

"You mean at—"

This time Ben was the first one to start singing.

"Yes, *there*," I said when he stopped. "I wonder if we'll ever be free to visit that place again. It was... really beautiful... apart from the snake. I bet it's even beautiful *in the dark*." And the water moccasin was dead now. Shot by our worst enemy, actually. One of several miscalculations he'd made.

"Colton wasn't with us then," Ingrid said helpfully.

"But he knows the place I mean, don't you, Colton? It was where we *went fishing* in May."

There was no chance to escape, or even to make trouble, when the van finally stopped; the guys who'd snatched us came in through the back of the van and repeated the drug treatment. When I came to this time, I was on the floor of this dank gray room, looking up at a depressing bluish-tinted light fixture.

On the good side, my hands weren't tied, and there was a chair. After I had contemplated the bejesus out of that air vent in the ceiling, I got up and seated myself. Now, instead of having my whole body in contact with a cold concrete floor, it was just my butt on a cold metal chair. A slight improvement. I was stiff from lying on the cold floor and sore from being bounced around in the back of a van with my wrists cuffed. I did creak slightly on getting up, but I don't think it would have been obvious to any observers. I'd grown up with two older brothers, both on the large side; they'd given me lots of good practice in not wincing when I got hurt. It had often stood me in good stead with Lensky, who tended to overreact when he found out I was even slightly injured.

I had plenty of time to sit on the folding metal chair and contemplate the situation. There wasn't anything to look at that could take my mind off it. There was a bucket in one corner, next to a bottle of water, but I didn't want to think about what that implied. If I had to use that bucket in a room that as likely as not had hidden cameras, the light was damned well going to be off first; I could do that much small object manipulation without making it obvious there was anything paranormal going on. Let them try to get their twisted kicks out of watching my heat signature through night-vision lenses.

The next phase started without warning: the door slammed open with so much force that it hit the wall with a loud *clunk*. If the demonstration of that much kinetic energy was meant to intimidate me, it was working. I hadn't liked being manhandled by my kidnappers, and I liked even less being at close quarters with the man who swung the door shut behind him now. He was big like Colton, though much older: tall, stocky, with thinning brown hair and big meaty hands. I shivered involuntarily. It wasn't just the size of him that frightened me; his eyes were worse. They looked like doorways into a chaotic, gray hell.

"Where are they?" he demanded.

"If you mean my friends, I'd like to know that too!"

"Don't worry about your friends. Worry about yourself."

Oh, I was already doing that.

He prowled around the narrow room. I didn't much like it when he was behind me; I could feel the short hairs on the back of my neck bristling. Too bad. There was only one chair in the room, I was seated in it, and I wasn't going to give up that paper-thin symbol of superiority for anything short of actual violence. I did stick my hands in my jeans pockets. They'd taken everything away from me except the one thing, or properly speaking *set* of things, that I was most likely to need. That wouldn't have been out of generosity, or even carelessness: like most people who can't apply topology the way we do, they wouldn't have been able to see that I had a pocketful of stars. Even Lensky had been known to refer to that collection as a handful of nothing.

If the gray-eyed man got violent with me, though, he just might encounter the effects of those stars and the way they enhanced our other abilities. I thought wistfully of using Ben's trick with Riemann surfaces to ignite his pants, but it wasn't time to show my hand. Yet.

"We've spent enough supporting you jokers," he growled eventually, "it's time you made yourselves useful."

Ah.

That told me a lot. He must be a representative of the secretive three-letter agency that funded the Center for Applied Topology in the hope that our paranormal abilities would eventually develop into useful tools for them. In fact we'd already been quite useful to them, but I decided not to bring that up. I didn't feel at all secure that the CIA was going to treat us any better than any other bunch of unaccountable bullies. The one thing about our captors' identity that gave me hope was that this was *Lensky*'s agency. If anybody could find out what had happened to us and where we were being held, he could. If anybody would storm the gates of a CIA black site to free us, he would. And he'd succeed, too.

"It might help," I suggested mildly, "if you explained what it was you needed our help with." Being polite about asking wouldn't have hurt, either, but it seemed that bridge was already burned.

"I told you. We want you to find them."

"Find who?"

He stopped prowling and glared at me. "You're supposed to have been told."

"Nobody has told me a damned thing."

He raised his hand in a threatening way and I said hurriedly, "Look, it's not in my interest to lie to you about that. You can check up easily enough. I was unconscious when your goons threw me in here and you're the first person who's been here since I regained consciousness."

"Damned incompetents. They really didn't brief you?"

"No. Would you like to tell me what this is about?"

"I... My..." He stopped, glanced up at a corner of the room, and started over. I'd had conversations with Lensky that went wrong in exactly that way.

What was this guy not telling me? "The bombing," he said eventually. "Last week. We have reason to believe that the bombers used paranormal means to effect their entrance and exit. You need to find out who they were and where they went."

"And you think I'll be better able to do that from a cell in a mystery location than from the comfort of my own office?" I laughed at the expression on his face. Though it wasn't all that funny, really. "And without the benefit of knowing what you spooks have already figured out about the bombing?"

"Why did you call us spooks?"

"You'd prefer me to say spies? Okay. You spies, then."

"How did you —"

"You did begin this conversation by bitching about funding us," I pointed out. "Do you really think we still haven't figured out where our grant comes from?"

"Your funds are passed anonymously through the Moore Foundation for Mathematics Research."

I shrugged. "That may have been the intention, but placing one of your own case officers in the middle of the Center kind of blew the anonymity bit, don't you think? You know, you're as bad a liar as I am. I do hope, for the sake of our country's security, that your colleagues are a bit better at this spook business."

His face went through two or three contortions before he settled on a sternly commanding expression. "Certain of my colleagues require a demonstration of your capabilities before opening up a classified investigation to you people. You will demonstrate what you can do, then we will decide how we wish to use you."

I had a strong feeling that things should go the other way around. We should decide what use we would allow them to make of us, and then we should demonstrate only those paranormal abilities that would support such use. I had absolutely no inclination to write a blank check for this man with the crazy gray eyes.

"There are a lot of things we can't do alone," I tried. Coming up with a unified strategy against these nuts, for instance. Too bad we'd never developed an application of topology that would enable telepathy. "It would work out better for everybody if you allowed us to get together and work as a group." Better for us, mostly.

"First," he said, "we're going to explore what you *can* do alone."

I shrugged. "Fine, but that doesn't amount to much."

The back of his hand slammed against my cheek without warning. I nearly fell out of the chair. My eyes watered, my face hurt and I *really* wanted to introduce him to the concept of Riemann fire.

"That was a lie. Do not lie to me again; you will regret it. We already have evidence that you, at least, can do quite impressive work on your own," he said. He resumed pacing around my chair; I resumed consciously *not* turning to keep the bastard in sight. He might be making me nervous, but I didn't have to let him see that. "Last fall you removed materials from a locked safe and then teleported yourself and Lensky from San Antonio to Austin."

Okay, that much would have been in Lensky's report. But he wouldn't know – not from official reports, anyway – the full extent of our teleportation range, or the fact that on occasion we had teleported through both space and time. The second wouldn't do him much good anyway. It wasn't like I could teleport myself to the time just before the bombing. Only the years before I was born were open to me, and of those years I'd already made a dent in 1957 and 1941.

As for the range, I felt it was highly desirable that they continue to underestimate us.

"That jump from San Antonio to Austin nearly killed me," I said with feeling. "Didn't Lensky put in his report that I passed out on the floor when we came through in Austin?"

He looked smug. "No, but it doesn't matter. We've already determined from other evidence that you can't teleport as far as a hundred miles, and that you can only go to places you've already seen."

I wondered what other evidence that would be. The second part was true enough, but as for the range – apparently they didn't know about our travels to Britfield, well over three hundred miles from Austin. Or about Colton's impromptu visit to the family farm in the Panhandle.

Good.

"And for your information," he said smugly, "this facility is nearly two hundred miles from Austin. Since you were brought here in a closed van, there's no place you have seen that's close enough for you to teleport yourselves to."

He thought that? Fine, let him think. I could go along with that theory as long as it was convenient for me.

"If there's no place we can teleport to, how are we supposed to demonstrate it?"

"Come with me."

***

"Of course you haven't seen any results yet," Harrison answered the staff members he'd brought with him. "We already know that they cannot teleport any great distance, nor can they teleport to a place they haven't seen. That's why we brought them here in a closed van and knocked them out again before carrying them into the facility. The *only* place within two hundred miles that any of them has seen is the room where they're being kept." He flashed a grim smile. "Except for the Kostis girl. She has now been shown the alternative room. She'll go there soon enough."

"What makes you so sure?"

"It is significantly pleasanter than her current accommodations. By contrast, it's practically a luxury hotel suite. How long do you think she'll be content to sleep on the floor and piss in a bucket when there's a bed, a private bathroom, a mini-fridge and a goodie bag of grooming supplies waiting for her just a short teleport away?"

"I'm surprised you didn't put a chocolate mint on her pillow," Dean sneered. "Seriously, now. That wouldn't break any of our people."

"Our people are tough, and they have excellent training. This Thalia Kostis is a kid just a couple of years out of college, and she's never been anywhere or done anything beyond reading math books in a comfortable office."

"If she takes the bait," Torres said cautiously, "good, we'll know she can teleport – at least a short distance. If she doesn't, though, how will we know what that means? Could mean she's tougher than you think. *Or,*" he paused significantly, "could mean she can't teleport at all and the earlier reports were lies."

"If the carrot isn't enough, we can use the stick," Dean said.

"Don't be too eager." Harrison said sharply. "We would prefer these people to cooperate willingly."

"That's why you hit the girl?"

"No, that was because she tried lying to me."

Torres started shaking his head. "You two really believe these kids can do magic? What universe are you living in?"

"The reports—"

"Sure, if you trust Lensky. Maybe he's exaggerating their potential to keep himself in a nice comfortable Stateside posting without the usual pay cut."

Harrison shook his head. "I know Brad; we've worked together since his first posting, in Romania. He'd be more likely to pooh-pooh their achievements so he could be free to go overseas again. The man was born to be a field officer. It must be driving him crazy to be tied to a dinky little outfit in Texas, with nothing else to do but interview professors and oil company executives about their foreign travel." He gave Torres a hard stare. "Maybe you've spent too long with the analysts. I've made a career out of interrogating and evaluating people who are highly motivated to lie to us. I'd stake my professional reputation that Lensky's reports are, if anything, *less* than the full truth about these topologists.

"There's something there, and we need it. You know why I believe the terrorists used paranormal means in this attack."

"Ye-es," Torres said reluctantly. "It's – a classic locked room mystery, isn't it?"

"Exactly. Without paranormal abilities, they would have needed an extremely clever way to come and go. One that left no trace and that none of our analysts can figure out."

"The distraction of the bomb blast—"

Harrison shook his head. "Evidence is that they pulled this off *before* the bomb exploded. The bomb *threat* was what they wanted. The bomb threat caused us to put everybody who might be at risk into the safe room. Ergo, they had a way into the safe room and that's where they wanted their... targets..." His speech slowed for a moment and he shook his head violently, as if to clear it. "Where they wanted them to be."

"That doesn't prove anything," Torres argued. "Yes, in retrospect it seems they were herding the targets into the safe room. Yes, that implies they had a way in and out of the safe room. It *doesn't* prove that their methods were paranormal."

"Except that none of our people have been able to come up with a coherent explanation for how they infiltrated and exfiltrated the very heart of our own facility while leaving no evidence of their passage. *And* the eyewitness account supports the notion of paranormal activity."

Torres shrugged. "Absence of evidence is not evidence of absence. And as for the witness... she's under suspicion, and properly so. If she was involved, she probably had that story ready to trot out as a distraction."

"There's precedent," Harrison insisted. "During the Cold War, we tried everything from telepaths to storefront psychics, trying to figure out how the KGB selected their dead drops."

Torres said nothing more, but he shook his head again as he and Dean walked away from the meeting room. "Just because the Company wasted time on so-called telepaths and psychics during the Cold War – with no result – is no reason to waste even more time on the woo-woo stuff today. I think Harrison's losing it. No shame in that, he's holding up amazingly well under the circumstances. But he really shouldn't be in charge of this operation, his personal involvement is screwing up his head. Paranormals, hah!"

"Except that the analysts have come up blank on other leads to the bombers," Dean said. "And we *are* going to get those bastards."

"With the help of a bunch of math majors?" Away from Harrison, Torres felt free to let his incredulity show in his voice.

"With whatever it takes. Maybe we won't get on to them soon enough – not for Harrison, anyway – but we *will* find them. And I'll use whatever I can get to find out where they've gone to earth. If the math majors are good enough tools, yes, I'll use them."

"Tools," Torres muttered after he and Dean went their separate ways. "Tools, sure. Just like a teaspoon is, technically, a tool for excavating a canal. But who'd want to use it for that?"

2. American citizens on American soil

The light in my cell went off without warning. Would the others be in darkness too? I had hopes. These jerks seemed like the kind of people who would think it efficient to run all the cell lights on one master switch.

The unbroken blackness was probably supposed to be upsetting and disorienting. What it was, was a gift from God. Any ordinary hidden cameras wouldn't betray my disappearance. If they had infrared cameras as well, they might wonder why they didn't see my heat signature, but with any luck whoever was on night duty would waste some time cursing and banging the equipment. Especially if we all left at the same time; a minor glitch in their camera system was much more probable than a mass disappearance from four cells at once. I hoped Lensky's felonious colleagues were familiar with Occam's Razor.

I also hoped all the others' lights were out; I hoped they would realize, as I had, that this was our best chance to meet without giving it away to our captors that we could do more than they thought we could. I hoped they had gotten my hints about operating in the dark. But I couldn't be absolutely sure of any of that. Oh well, if they didn't show up I'd just have to do everything myself. I stuck one hand in the pocket with my stars and pictured Mayfield Park in Austin.

I couldn't quite firm up the visualization of two curved surfaces intersecting at the single point that represented me; the drugs weren't completely out of my system yet, and the throbbing of my cheekbone was a

15

distraction. The others should be slightly better off, though. To help me focus, I used the keyword we'd practiced with. *"Brouwer."*

Swirls of light, points of brightness scattering as if startled, impossible angles and curves; I slid through the black space of the in-between and felt the gritty sand of the path around the lily pond under my feet. A sliver of moonlight let me make out shapes and – after a moment – movement. The air was heavy and warm and smelled of flowers and green plants and water; a big improvement on the stale mix in the CIA site. The two-hundred-mile jump had been long enough for me to taste the elation of traveling through the in-between, and that was a big improvement, too. Colton arrived beside me with a heavy crunch onto the sand; he tended to teleport to a couple of inches above where he actually wanted to be. Calibration problem. Happens to all of us from time to time, but almost always to Colton.

A moment later, Ingrid joined us. I had just time to work up a good worry before Ben came down the path from the parking lot.

"Why'd you jump to over there?"

"Why not? You didn't exactly specify a location. There's a lot of Mayfield Park; you should be happy we all came through in sight of one another and at the same time."

"I'm happy, I'm happy. I'm *ecstatic.*"

"Why the secret meeting in the park?" Colton wanted to know. "Yes, I figured out that's what you wanted to do, but why couldn't we all just go home?"

"They probably know where we live." In my case, of course, they definitely knew. "We can't go to our homes, any more than we can go back to the office and carry on with our lives as if nothing had happened."

"Well, we can't stay here all night!" Ingrid complained.

"No, of course not. We have to go back."

"*What?*"

"Eventually," I pointed out, "they'll turn the lights on again. Then – if we aren't back — they'll notice they're four topologists short, and come looking for us."

"You sure about that?" Colton said, "They only had one *short* topologist."

Ingrid snickered. I glared, but it probably wasn't very effective in moonlight. Tall people are the bane of my existence, and here I am stuck working with three of them. "Look, this is serious. Either we decide now to abandon our jobs and families and spend the rest of our lives in hiding from the CIA, or we go back and find some better way to get out of this mess. This jump was just an emergency measure for us to get help."

I did wish we'd worked out some version of telepathy. It seemed that in every crisis we realized anew how useful that would be; then, as soon as the crisis was over, we went out for beer and nachos and forgot about the telepathy question. The thing is, you can't rely on a bunch of introverts like us to come up with a way of destroying what little privacy we retained inside our own heads. That was how I felt about telepathy when we weren't in the middle of a crisis and too busy to experiment, and I was willing to bet the others felt exactly the same lack of enthusiasm for the concept.

"What makes you think it's the CIA?" Ingrid wanted to know now.

"It doesn't seem probable," said Ben. "If *they* wanted our help, all they had to do was talk to Lensky."

"The big guy gave it away when he tried to interrogate me."

"Who?"

I described the jerk. Apparently he hadn't yet questioned any of the others. Typical government inefficiency.

"As for why they didn't ask politely, I have no idea. Except this bombing last week seems to have affected them like kicking an ant hill affects the ants. They yanked Lensky off to help with one aspect of the investigation, and I guess they thought that without him to manage us, they'd have to get their way through brute force and terror." Or else they simply preferred the force and terror approach, and thought they could get away with it because Lensky was temporarily out of touch.

"It's a huge embarrassment for them," Colton, always excruciatingly fair, observed. "A bombing in the heart of their own headquarters. I expect lives – careers, anyway – are on the line here."

He understands these big organizations somewhat better than the rest of us; apparently modern cotton farmers like his father have to work so closely with the government that they sometimes feel like an unpaid branch of the Agriculture Department.

"The thing is, all we need to do is get word to Brad that his agency snatched us. He *will* find us, and he *will* get us out of this." In the aftermath of the terrorist bombing that shook Washington last week he'd been called back to the home office. Now he was at an undisclosed location, helping his colleagues to interrogate the bomber Sandru Balan in the hope of getting some leads on this latest attack. It hadn't been that bad in terms of injuries; what had everybody shaken up was that it had happened right inside the CIA headquarters.

"How do you propose to do that? We don't even know where he is, and they took our phones."

"Classical methods." I explained what I had in mind and couldn't resist adding, "People *did* manage to communicate before cell phones, you know." You'd think Ben would have more appreciation of that fact; it had been just barely over a year since Annelise had persuaded him to get one himself.

We didn't have time to chat longer; there were things to be done before we all returned to sit innocently in our cells.

***

"So much for gentle persuasion," said Torres after two hours of total darkness in the cells and no movement at all in the room that Harrison had set up as a lure for the Kostis girl. "Or maybe – just maybe – those reports were great works of fiction." They'd turned the lights back on without warning but hadn't surprised the topologists in any interesting activity.

Dean shrugged. "Maybe he should have started with the other girl."

"The ice princess? No way. You can tell that one's tough as nails."

"Well, *I* think we need to step up the pressure. Lean on all four of them at once, and not with anything so gentle as a mildly uncomfortable cell."

They studied the grainy images on the video feed. The equipment badly needed an upgrade; what had been good enough for a prison was barely adequate for serious intelligence work. The little dark girl was seated cross-legged on the floor of her cell, staring into her cupped palms as though she could see something very interesting there. The blonde was sitting bolt upright on her metal chair, betraying no discomfort. The larger of the two men actually appeared to be asleep. The tall skinny guy who needed a haircut was tracing invisible patterns on the wall with one finger.

"At least we're getting a good feed now," Torres commented. "Did you ever figure out what went wrong with the infrared?"

Dean shook his head. "Some power glitch, probably. All the cells lost the feed about the same time, and then a few minutes later it came back. It's a crappy retrofit; we need to lobby for a completely new video system. Oh well, I hope it doesn't happen again. We need to move on."

"Move on?"

"We can't wait for them to give in to mild discomfort," Dean said. "It's time to move on to phase two, and make them so unhappy they'll *have* to teleport. You get a couple of guards and show the other three the nice room we have waiting for whoever is the first to break, while I set up the sound and light effects. For this, it won't matter that we have to use the lousy prison broadcasting system."

"Did Harrison okay this?"

"He is in more of a hurry than anybody else for results, and no wonder. He won't object."

Not if they got results, Torres thought. What if they didn't? They would have four royally pissed-off American citizens on their hands and nothing to show for it.

But he kept his misgivings to himself and followed Dean's orders. Just like in any big organization, there was nothing to be gained by bucking the hierarchy.

*****

The lights didn't stay off long; allowing for the time we'd spent taking care of things in Austin, I was guessing it had been about two hours. A different man came in this time. He didn't slam the door, which earned him a couple of points. And he looked less scary than the first guy: younger, longish black hair, steady brown eyes, no crazy twitches going on in his face. For just a moment, I was fool enough to feel relieved.

"You should have responded to gentle persuasion," he said softly, and a shiver of fear ran down my spine. Sandru Balan had spoken softly, just like that, when he told me that I was wearing a bomb that he could detonate at any moment. "I am afraid that now we will have to be more… convincing."

My mouth was dry. Fortunately – or perhaps unfortunately – that's never been enough to stop me giving people grief. Only when they deserve it, of course.

"You must be pretty damned desperate if you're going to torture American citizens on American soil," I said. "What do you think that's going to do for your agency's image?"

"No torture," he said. "Nothing that leaves marks, anyway. And the sooner you teleport to the other room, the sooner it'll be over."

He left the room as quietly as he had entered.

It didn't start for several minutes, maybe as many as ten or fifteen – they had taken my watch, of course, when they grabbed me, and I hadn't been stupid enough to replace it in Austin and give them hard evidence that I'd been out of this cell. From what I'd read, this was standard procedure for disorienting people: no watch, no windows, lights on and off in unnatural patterns. I began to hope that this disorientation, with occasional threats, was their entire repertoire.

Then it started.

The dim little overhead fixture went out. My eyes were just starting to adjust to the darkness when they were assaulted by a powerful white light that strobed on and off in a migraine-inducing sequence. I couldn't find a safe dark corner to look at, and when I closed my eyes the jagged, arrhythmic strobing translated to red flashes stabbing through my eyelids. I started counting; maybe I could distract myself by figuring out what number series determined the timing of the light system. These people were *way* too dumb to come up with a good random number generator. I was betting on digits of π, but even that might have been too sophisticated for them.

Then the noise began.

I don't remember all the sounds now. There was an air raid siren swooping up and down the scale, just like the ones they used in England during the second world war – and yes, as a matter of fact, I would know. 1941, remember? I happen to have up-close and personal experience of the Blitz, which is something not many people my age (I was born in 1994) can boast of.

Next they added bits and pieces of the kind of rap rock that only someone as young as my kid brother could love. Then screams, very realistic – a most unwelcome addition to the mix. I didn't want to think about how they'd gotten those recordings. They sounded like something that could have been the soundtrack to an ISIS torture video.

And then, just in time to save my sanity, "Ride of the Valkyries" joined the rest of the cacophony, and I started laughing. Possibly laughing a tiny bit harder than the situation warranted; I might have been closer to hysteria than I like to admit. But – *that* music? Sure, there were people who considered Wagner at high volume a kind of torture. Before this night, I might even have been one of them. But at least one of the four of us was going to have her spirit cheered and her spine stiffened by her favorite fight song.

The light and sound effects stopped abruptly and the dim blue overhead light came back on. A moment later the dark-haired man shoved the door open. "*What's so damn funny?*"

Touchy, touchy. "You idiots *really* haven't done your research, have you?"

"What do you mean by that?"

If I told him that they were arousing Ingrid's alter ego as a Viking shield-maiden, I'd be pointing them right at her. I hoped I would never do something like that, but I wasn't too certain how well I would resist actual torture. Noises and flashing lights weren't going to do it, though.

"Trying to make us teleport with your sound and light show? You don't understand anything at all about applied topology. It's just like any other mathematics; we can't do it if we can't concentrate. You're doing the one thing that guarantees we won't be able to help you at all. With whatever minor and limited capacities we may have," I added, belatedly realizing that – as usual – I might have said too much.

"Oh, *really?*" he sneered. "You seem to be very good at coming up with excuses for not producing. I'll just have to try harder to motivate you. Tell you what – the first two of you to teleport, we'll let them stay in the nice room we showed you. The other two can stay in these cells and think it over. They are not," he said, "going to be very pleasant places to stay."

"And you're not very consistent, are you? If we can teleport, how do you propose to keep us here? And if we can't, what's the use of torturing us to do something impossible?"

Something ugly flickered in his expression, but he smoothed his face out almost immediately. "You won't be so chatty in a few minutes."

Almost as soon as the door closed behind him, the sound and light show began again. Still heavy on the Wagner; I grinned, thinking of the effect that would be having on Ingrid. I wasn't sure that, even with the augmentation of the stars, she would be strong enough to retrieve her latest accessory and get it into her cell. But I wasn't sure she *wouldn't*, either. And I did like the image of Wild Man and Menacing Dude being chased around a small cell by a shield maiden wielding a Viking axe.

The air was beginning to smell funny. For just a moment I almost panicked, imagining that they'd found some way to bring fire into the cell. Then my eyes stung, my nose burned, and I sneezed violently. OK. Just pepper spray.

So far.

I wondered if these maniacs had any limits at all. The nastier they got, the more dedicated I felt to frustrating them. But I was uncomfortably aware that this dynamic could reverse quickly. I'm not a superwoman, nor am I stupid. If they kept escalating, there was some point at which they could inflict enough pain and fear to make me desperate to avoid more. I would then become more interested in pleasing these bastards than in thwarting them.

I was actually surprised that we hadn't reached that point yet. I'm not all that brave. But they seemed to be all that inept.

I groped my way to the corner, took off my T-shirt and soaked it with water from the bottle. Then I tied it over my nose and mouth. By the sleeves, so the body of the shirt hung down in front of me and preserved a little modesty.

I hoped Ingrid did have her axe.

I hoped even more that Dr. Verrick had seen my message and contacted Brad already, unlikely as that seemed.

3. Corralling cats

He was just leaning against the wall, looking menacing, while Patel questioned Balan. It wasn't difficult; all he had to do was remember what the son of a bitch had tried to do to Thalia and the urge to tear him into small pieces, *slowly*, resurfaced.

His expression got slightly harder as he reflected on the fact that frightening Sandru Balan into compliance was in fact his only role in this interrogation. The hotshots from DC had made it very clear that they and nobody else would ask the questions. Never mind that he'd tangled with Balan twice in the last year and had actually been responsible for his capture. Never mind that thanks to his posting in Romania, he could actually say, "You're a dead man walking," and other chatty tidbits in Balan's native language. None of that counted against the fact that he'd been seconded to Domestic Operations for the last fifteen months.

His scowl must have suddenly become more alarming; Balan started talking faster and more fluently than before. Over the last two days the contract bomber had gone from sneering at them, to dickering over a possible release, to pretending memory problems, and – remarkably quickly – to this last phase of babbling about anything and everything. The problem now was keeping him to the point.

He had to admit that his colleague's idea seemed to be working. It was hard to frighten Sandru Balan. If they'd taken him to a black site the man might have become worried, but the Deputy Director of Operations hadn't wanted to take the time required nowadays to get permission to take custody of a prisoner and transport him out of the country. Instead, he simply told Patel, who was running the interrogation, to borrow Lensky from Austin.

When Balan laughed in their faces, Patel had told him there was a possibility he could be repatriated.

"Is that a threat or a promise?"

"Unless you start cooperating," Patel said, "you can consider it both. Oh, one thing I forgot to mention; if repatriated, you'll be escorted by this gentleman." He nodded and Lensky moved out of the shadows so that Balan could get a good look at his face.

Up to that point Lensky's chief worry had been that he would start laughing at his own impersonation of the ultimate bad cop. One good look at Sandru Balan removed that concern. Memories of the last time he'd seen Balan flooded him. For a moment he was back there, in Allandale House on a bleak January day, while the man before him gloatingly described how his own call to Thalia's cell phone would have detonated the bomb that tore her to shreds. There was a sour taste in his mouth, a rushing noise in his ears, and he took two more steps towards Balan without thinking. The man flinched and Patel laughed. "I see you don't care for the prospect," he said to Balan. He nodded at Lensky. "Stay back behind the taped line from now on, okay? I don't want him too scared to talk."

Every time Balan resisted the questions, Lensky stepped forward.

"I didn't actually think I had a face that would frighten hardened killers," he had said, a trifle ruefully, after the success of the first day's interrogation.

"Ah, man, it's the sincerity that gets them," Patel reassured him. "You really do want to tear him into little pieces and set them on fire, and he can sense that. *Way* more effective than a standard bad-cop routine. And he knows you've got good reason to hate him, after what he tried to do to your girlfriend."

"Wife," Lensky corrected him.

Patel's eyebrows shot up. "Nobody told me that… Was it in your report?"

"We weren't married then. We are now." And that was as much as Patel, or any other colleagues, needed to know about his personal life. His marriage changed nothing about the agency's arrangement with the Center; they funded the place, he ran the four topologist-mages as his assets. He passed on agency requests to them, and they reported their results to him.

At least that was the theory. In practice, he'd discovered that managing mathematicians was more like corralling cats.

On the evening of this second day, Patel was getting very excited about Balan's revelation of a possible German connection for the bomber. Then Lensky took the call from Dr. Verrick, the titular director of the Center for Applied Topology, and minor matters such as bombings and German terror cells ceased to mean anything to him.

"What? When? How long… I'll be there as soon as possible." He ended the call but didn't put the phone away; he had an airplane ticket to buy.

"Sorry," he told Patel when he'd finished his business. "I have to be on the next plane back to Austin."

"So much," Patel said sourly, "I gathered from your side of the conversation. But you can't leave now. We're just starting to get useful information out of him."

"Tell him I'll be back if he stops cooperating," Lensky suggested.

"Will you?"

"If possible. It may not be possible. Someone has kidnapped my topologists."

"Who?"

"That's what I plan to find out."

He didn't reach Austin until quite late that night. Dr. Verrick was waiting for him at the Center's offices on the top floor of Allandale House. The old man looked – well, *old*, in contrast to his usual look of ageless preservation. His hands were shaking. But he had news for Lensky. Something had happened while he was flying back to Austin.

"You have a note." Lensky shook his head in disbelief. "What, Thalia left a note to explain where everybody went, and you didn't happen to find it until I was on the plane?"

"It was not *here* when you boarded the airplane," Dr. Verrick said. "I had left the office briefly; when I returned this was written on my whiteboard."

Thalia's distinctive, angular capital letters slanted downwards from left to right on a board that had been unceremoniously cleared with a couple of quick swipes. They were all well. They were being held in a CIA black site approximately two hundred miles from Austin. TELL BRAD!!!

Dr. Verrick told him that there were similar notes on the whiteboards of all the support staff.

"Miss Kostis underrates me," the Director sniffed. "It had already occurred to me to inform you of their disappearance. Once she failed to meet me for our dinner engagement, and then not only she but also all the other topologists proved to be unreachable by telephone, it was the obvious next step. Especially after Miss Wilson, Mr. DiGrazio and Ms. Melendez told me of their experience."

At the moment, the experience of the non-research staff was not Lensky's primary concern. "So. They're not stopping her from teleporting; she was able to come here long enough to leave a message. Messages."

"I presume," said Dr. Verrick, "that they *believe* they have stopped my researchers from teleporting, but that they do not fully understand the powers and limitations of applied topology."

"But if she could get out, where is she now?"

"She has probably returned to her pseudo-captivity to avoid alarming the fools who kidnapped them. She knows that you will sort out this idiocy."

Lensky sat, hard. For some reason he was feeling shaky. "I wish she had waited for me. No, no," he held up a hand to stop Verrick, "I get it. If they found her missing, they would have taken it out on the others. And even if all of them were able to teleport out of the facility, where would they go? They won't really be free until I make it clear to – whatever moron dreamed this up – that they can't treat my agents this way."

He still wished Thalia had waited for him. Seeing the message on Verrick's whiteboard had given him an almost painful pulse of hope, but nowhere near enough to counter the fear for her that consumed him.

"Can you do that? Can you *find* them?"

"Oh, yes." He felt confident of that much. "There aren't that many possibilities." The CIA didn't actually maintain black sites within the country, but Thalia wouldn't have known that. He trusted her estimate of where they were more than the label she'd put on their location. They *did* have a facility she might have taken for a black site right here in Texas. It was just about two hundred miles from Austin, an abandoned and outmoded prison generously put at the agency's disposal by Concho County in return for their help in getting appropriations for the new prison. He could be there in three hours. Fly to Washington first? No, that would take time, and he probably wouldn't even be able to get a flight until tomorrow; they'd been turning out the lights at Bergstrom Airport when his plane landed. He had his boss's cell phone number, he could talk to him while driving up to Concho County.

"What about the others?" There was nobody in the office with them.

"Free, but indignant," Verrick told him. "Apparently someone pretending to be with the University administration persuaded them to come with him for some kind of petty paperwork, and then lured them into a little-used storage facility where they were locked in for several hours. They were finally released when a security guard heard them yelling and banging on the door. I felt there was little more they could do tonight, but if you require their aid…"

Lensky thought it over. There were only three people involved: a receptionist, a robotics engineer, and a computer jockey. "No. It's conceivable that I'll need Jimmy to hack into somebody's computer, but I doubt it. Just in case, though… Here's where I'm going. If I disappear too, you need to call my boss at Langley. Steve Harrison. Here's the number. He's a good guy; he'll sort this out. I'll call him while I'm on the road."

4. A darkness in the air

Harrison didn't even have the decency to look surprised or ashamed when Lensky stormed into the room he was using as a temporary office in the old Concho County prison. "Ah, Brad. I assume you're here to complain that I've poached your assets?"

"No wonder you're not picking up my calls. And I thought I was calling you to get *help*." Lensky wanted to spit. He'd just told Verrick that Steve Harrison was a good guy. Now he found out that his own boss was behind the disappearances.

"You want your assets back?" Harrison grinned. Bared his teeth, anyway. "Get their cooperation, and you can have them. They've been nothing but trouble up to now."

"Yes. I want them back. And I want my wife freed. Immediately!"

Harrison picked up his phone and pushed a button. "Tell Dean to stop the experiment and bring the topologists here." He looked back at Lensky. "Okay. You can see your agents in a few minutes. As for your wife, I'm afraid I can't help you out there; I didn't even know you had married."

"Last month," Lensky said between his teeth. "One of the topologists. Thalia Kostis. Your intelligence gathering abilities must be slipping. Badly."

"Wasn't it up to you to report that? I don't remember even getting your 'close and continuing relationship' statement."

"Not required. She's an American citizen."

"I wonder why she failed to tell us that she was married to you. We

29

certainly wouldn't have handled her like the others if we'd known that."

Knowing Thalia, Lensky suspected that was exactly why she hadn't enlightened Harrison and whoever else he was using for this mission. She wouldn't buy special treatment for herself that way.

"How *have* you handled them? Do I need to call an ambulance?"

"No need. They're essentially undamaged."

Essentially, in Harrison's mouth, covered a nightmare range of possibilities. Fortunately, before Lensky could give in to his impulse to throttle the man into giving details, the door opened on four tired, angry, disheveled, red-eyed, coughing and sputtering topologists followed by a couple of armed guards and Harrison's stooge Dean.

"Pepper spray," Harrison murmured apologetically. "The effects won't last, now that they're out of the sprayed area. I told you they weren't really hurt."

That was clear; even while they coughed and scrubbed at their eyes, the topologists were *arguing*.

"I told you we needed to modify the shields to keep out poison gas!" That was Ben. "We need to define them at the molecular level. Now, branching covers on a three-manifold—"

"Yes, but the only algorithm you ever came up with also shielded against oxygen!" Ingrid said. "Read my – aack! – lips: humans need oxygen. If—" Whatever she'd been going to say was drowned in a fit of coughing.

"*And* your model kept the carbon dioxide in, which is even worse!" Colton contributed through a bout of sniffles.

Lensky barely registered the argument. The small, dark-haired woman who'd come in last had cut through her colleagues like a logician through philosophers to reach him. Once he had his arms around her and knew she was safe, nothing else mattered for a moment. Then she sneezed. "You godda hadkerchief?"

He produced a folded white square and she buried her face in it for an explosive few seconds. He noticed that the damp T-shirt clinging to her body was on back to front.

"You must have got an extra dose," he said, comparing her red eyes and husky whisper to her companions, who appeared to have recovered completely from the effects of the pepper spray by the time they got into the second stage of their theoretical discussion.

"I wouldn't be surprised," she croaked. "For some reason these guys don't seem to like me."

"You've been giving them grief, haven't you?"

"Of course, it's my..." She started coughing again. Lensky saw a half-empty water bottle on Harrison's desk and grabbed it for her. She gulped the contents and sighed. "That's better. Giving pushy government types grief is my Prime Directive. You should know that. It's not like *we* started out on great terms."

"Yeah, but you're cute when you're being snippy. That's when I started to fall in love with you."

"Oddly enough, my witty repartee doesn't seem to have had that effect on Thug One and Thug Two." She nodded at Harrison, who was listening in total bemusement to a three-way topological debate about open and closed sets and boundary conditions, and then at Dean.

"Is he the one who hit you?" Lensky asked, looking at Dean. His finger traced the blossoming bruise on her cheekbone.

"No, that would be Tall, Balding, and Ugly over there."

Lensky turned on Harrison, who dodged behind the desk. "Brad, try and remember that I'm your boss!"

"No, you're the man who beat up my wife." He moved towards Harrison, but Thalia hung her full weight on his arm, dragging him down.

"What's your problem," he said, aggrieved, "don't you want me to hit him?"

"I don't want you – to wreck – your career!" Thalia panted, gripping his arm with both hands and leaning backward with her full weight, all ninety-five pounds of her. He tried to pry her loose, but her fingers were so tightly clenched he would have had to hurt her to free himself.

"If it requires my standing by while the Company maltreats my wife, I don't want this career!"

"You don't understand!" Harrison began, holding up his hands placatingly.

"Brad, we *had* to get their cooperation. We don't have any time to waste. And why aren't you helping Patel with Sandru Balan?"

Ingrid abandoned the topologists' debate and joined in this one. "You could have tried asking politely, instead of drugging and kidnapping and threatening," she told Harrison.

"You could even have gone through Lensky," Ben chimed in. "Isn't that what he's in Austin for?"

"We needed him elsewhere," Harrison defended himself, "and—there's no time, dammit, no time! Brad, go ahead and hit me if it'll make you feel better. I won't write you up. Just help me get these maniacs' cooperation and afterwards you can beat me to a pulp."

Lensky relaxed slightly. "I've been known to call them maniacs myself. What exactly do you want, and what's the desperate hurry about? Of course you want to get whoever pulled off this bombing. I'd like that myself. But terrorizing a bunch of ivory-tower academic types isn't going to get us there."

"You don't understand," Harrison repeated.

"Try me." Lensky reached for a chair with his free hand, pulled it towards him and sat. Thalia finally relaxed her death-grip on his right arm. With luck, full circulation would resume any minute now. "What exactly, apart from the fact that it targeted our headquarters in Langley, makes this bombing so different from all other terrorist attacks that we have to throw the rule book out the window?"

"We've managed to keep it out of the media," Harrison said slowly, "but it wasn't just headquarters that was targeted. It was the day-care center."

"The *CIA* has a *day-care center*?" That was Ben.

"For obvious reasons, we prefer not to publicize it. But just like every other large organization," Harrison snapped, "we have employees with young children, and employees with school-age children who need after-school care. Unlike other organizations, though, our people are always at risk. It seemed best to take care of these problems in-house, where we controlled security, rather than expecting our employees to come up with their own patchwork of child-care solutions."

"So… how many children were killed?"

"None. Someone called in the bomb threat in plenty of time for us to get all the kids and their teachers into the safe room. And the bomb itself didn't amount to much. If we're forced to release anything about the day-care to the news media, though, we may say that three children were killed."

"Why?"

"Because…" Harrison looked sick. "Because that's how many are missing."

"*Missing?* You're sure…"

Harrison looked around the room. First at Thalia, standing beside Lensky, and then at the other three topologists. "I'm not sure we ought to continue this discussion in front of people who aren't cleared to hear it. I probably shouldn't have started it. I'm supposed to verify they have special abilities that can help us before sharing any information with them."

"And how has that been working out for you?" Lensky asked, keeping his tone superficially cordial.

"As you see." Harrison bit off the words.

"So maybe we try it the other way around. Get chairs for everybody, get them something to eat and drink, have a civilized discussion."

"If this doesn't work," Dean muttered to Lensky while Harrison was making calls to get all that organized, "your job is toast."

Lensky gave him a cold stare. "If I hadn't gotten here before you escalated to actual torture, you would be toast. You lying, insinuating, sadistic bastard. Don't think I can't guess who egged Harrison on. You've always been too damned fond of hurting people."

Dean laughed. "Hey, dummy, relax. We hadn't even waterboarded your little friends yet!"

This time Thalia wasn't hanging on to him, and it was tremendously satisfying to see Dean go down with a crash.

In the interests of peaceful discussion, Harrison suggested that Dean take himself off to collect the food while the rest of them settled into the ex-prison's best excuse for a meeting room. At least it had a table and nearly enough chairs. A row of empty vending machines took up most of one wall; this must have been an employee break room, back in the day.

Harrison did bring in a third player, a Rob Torres, who evidently represented the skeptical side of the debate. He protested vociferously when Harrison began to outline the situation, and only shut up after a direct order.

As Harrison had said, three children were missing: two boys and a girl. And they probably had not been selected randomly. One was Harrison's son Sam, nine years old, who had been kicking his heels in the day care after his summer science camp until his father could take him home. The other two, a boy of five and a girl of six, were also the children of highly placed CIA officials.

"You think they were targeting your boy?" Lensky asked. If so, that would have limited the hours during which it was useful to strike at the day care center. Unlike the younger children, Sam Harrison was only there for a couple of hours after camp each day. That would explain the late-afternoon timing of the attack.

"Yes. No. I think so, yes." Harrison scrubbed his face with one hand. "Getting hard to think…"

"Mr. Harrison," Thalia spoke up. "Have you slept at all since the bombing?"

"Huh? Yes. Probably. I don't know."

"That might explain some of his poor decisions," she said to Lensky. "Can you guys talk him into taking a break?"

"No! Not when—we don't have *time*." Harrison hunched forward over the meeting room table. "Every hour that passes, every *minute*…"

"Tell us how you think we can help, then."

Harrison stared at her. "Does that mean – you will help?"

"Yes," Ben said. His youngest sister was eight years old.

"Probably," said Thalia.

"I… don't know," Colton said.

Ingrid just looked down her nose. "It all depends. Is my fiancé all right?"

"Who's that?"

"Jimmy DiGrazio. He wasn't in the office when you grabbed me, and neither were Annelise and Meadow."

"Oh, the support staff? We just needed to get them out of the way while we were collecting topologists." Harrison relaxed slightly.

"They're all fine," Lensky reassured his people. "Dr. Verrick has seen them."

Beside him, Thalia stirred.

"What about Mr. M.?"

"Who?" Both Harrison and Torres looked blank.

She gave Lensky a dirty look. "Don't tell me you've been censoring Mr. M. out of your reports."

"I try to limit the number of impossible things I ask my superiors to believe in any one report," Lensky defended himself. "I was going to tell them about Mr. M. Eventually. Just as soon as I didn't have half a dozen other weird things to explain."

"Well, he was around my neck when these goons grabbed me, and he wasn't with me in their van. I just want to know that nobody stepped on him."

Torres was shaking his head well before Thalia finished. "What is she talking about? There wasn't anybody else in the office when we collected her. She was the last one."

"Thalia," Lensky said in an urgent undertone. "Can we put the matter of Mr. M. aside for now? You know as well as I do that he's probably off pursuing some mischief of his own, and I don't think I can calm Steve down enough to give him a full explanation of Mr. M. until he has some sense of progress in this matter."

"I'm worried about him," Thalia said.

"Look, if these idiots pissed him off in the course of kidnapping you, they're the ones who should be worried."

Thalia sputtered. "You have a point there. Fine, fine. Let's get back to finding out what they need and what we can do for them. It won't be my fault if they're attacked by a highly pissed-off, hyper-caffeinated Babylonian turtle mage even as we talk."

"Who's Mr. M.?" Harrison asked.

"We can go into that later. Tell me why you're so desperate to use my people on this case."

"Because there's reason to believe that whoever carried out this attack also had paranormal abilities." Harrison laid out supporting details. The three children had disappeared from an internal "safe room" that was locked down as soon as all the day-care kids were inside. No, they hadn't simply been left outside by accident; one teacher and several other children insisted they'd seen all three missing children inside the safe room after lockdown. There had been no overt attack on the room and there was no evidence of any tampering with the hi-tech locking and security system.

"What do your colleagues think about the paranormal hypothesis?"

Harrison sighed. "The DDO started from the assumption that it wasn't possible and leaned on the teacher, who must have been – in his view – complicit. I managed to get an interview with her, told her *I* believed she was telling the truth, and got a little more information. She said she caught glimpses of a dark-skinned man in white robes, but there was something off about them. The glimpses. She couldn't explain exactly, she just said it was like he was a projection, maybe a holograph, not really there. Something else human-shaped was there but wasn't properly visible; a kind of darkness in the air, with a shimmer like flames. Naturally she hadn't told the DDO any of this, he would just have taken it as more lies."

The food arrived then, brought in by a scowling Dean, and discussion slowed as the four topologists fell on the sandwiches and soft drinks as if they were starving. Which, Lensky thought, they probably were.

"Did all of you teleport back to Austin, or was that just you?" he murmured to Thalia.

"We all did."

He asked Harrison to send out for a couple of boxes of doughnuts. Sandwiches were a good start, but his people were used to inhaling doughnuts for a quick lift after major applications of topology.

"Don't bother," Thalia interrupted after gulping down the last bite of her sandwich. "That was an adequate refill. I'll get the doughnuts, and make your buddy Thug One happy at the same time. If I could have my wallet back?"

She stood up, slid the wallet into her hip pocket and put one hand in her right front pocket, and disappeared. Torres shouted in alarm.

"Give it a few minutes," Lensky suggested. "She'll be back."

"I hope she gets some of those chocolate-covered ones with chocolate cream filling," Ben said.

"You have crude tastes," Ingrid told him. "Chocolate is actually even better paired with other flavors. Raspberry jam filling, for instance."

Ben looked hurt. "I know that. Didn't I invent the chocolate root beer float?"

"I retract 'crude.' A better term would be 'barbaric.'"

"I'd settle for an apple fritter," sighed Colton.

The topologists' matter-of-fact demeanor persuaded the CIA men to sit quietly and wait, though Torres was restive.

A few minutes later there was a widening slit in the air, briefly displaying – well, only a colorless chaos to the CIA officers; Lensky knew that the topologists claimed to see a blackness shot through with points and streaks of colored light. Then Thalia stepped through the slit into the conference room, carrying two pink cardboard boxes, and the opening in the air healed itself. She leaned forward, flipped one of the boxes open and held it out to Harrison. "Care for a doughnut?"

His eyes were very wide.

"How did you do that?"

Thalia set both boxes on the table and smirked. "Not many people could have pulled it off at this hour. But I happen to be familiar with the location of the best twenty-four-hour doughnut shop in Austin." She tapped the nearest box. It was imprinted with the name of the shop and an address on Ben White Blvd.

"You went all the way to Austin for those? But I thought you couldn't…"

"You were misinformed," Thalia cut him off. "We can travel farther than you think. And it was much easier to teleport two hundred miles to Austin than it would have been trying to buy doughnuts after midnight in, what's the nearest town, Brad?"

"Eden," he supplied. "She's right, you know, Steve. Eden probably rolls up the sidewalks after 10 PM. I was surprised you were able to get sandwiches."

"They weren't very good ones," Ingrid said, wrapping up the crusts left over from her second egg salad sandwich.

"Oh, I don't know," Ben argued. "Pre-made, sure, but no worse than the ones the Student Union sells."

"As I said – not very good." Ingrid helped herself to a chocolate-covered doughnut with raspberry filling. "Everything about this so far has been second-rate, except for the music."

"The... music?" Harrison now looked completely lost.

Lensky found it in himself to be sorry for his boss, and not just because of the torment of losing – possibly losing – a child. This was Harrison's first experience of topologists' ability to miss the point and go galloping off into the distance focused on some minor detail. He hoped the man's sanity would survive further contact with his mathematicians.

"Just before the pepper spray they were trying to torture us with obnoxiously loud music," Thalia murmured to him. "But one of their selections just happened to be Wagner."

Lensky felt a smile growing. "Don't tell me. Not—"

"The Ride of the Valkyries," Thalia nodded, and Lensky laughed outright. "Steve, you need to start reading Thalia's informal reports; you're missing all the good details. You're lucky Miss Thorn wasn't inspired to retrieve her favorite new fashion accessory to go with that music."

"Who says I wasn't?" Ingrid put down the doughnut, reached down beside her chair, and pulled something out of nothing. She twirled it around her wrist and Harrison flinched away from a bright circle of sharp-edged steel. "An authentic Viking axe," Ingrid explained. "Well... authentic in style, anyway. I don't think the Vikings had quite such good quality steel." With a startling *thunk*, she buried the axe in the top of the battered table. Harrison edged away from her.

"Where did that *come* from?" Torres demanded.

"It was an engagement present from Jimmy. Oh – you mean literally? I got it from my apartment in Austin. Where else?"

"No, I mean right now. There wasn't anything beside your chair."

Ingrid looked down her nose at him. "It was camouflaged, naturally. I recently worked out how to remove the camouflage open cover from myself while leaving it over objects in my possession. I had intended to demonstrate for you tomorrow… today?" she turned to her colleagues, "before these louts interrupted."

Torres frowned at the table top. The axe looked very real. So did the damage to the table.

"That camouflage thing could be very useful," Harrison said thoughtfully, "if we needed to bring weapons in somewhere unobserved."

"I think a metal detector would still pick them up," Lensky said.

"I can think of some variations on the algorithm that might help with that," said Ben.

"A lot of the places we infiltrate don't have metal detectors," said Torres.

"The original camouflage works like this," Ingrid said, and vanished.

For Lensky, she hadn't so much vanished as become very difficult to see; he'd become used to this topological effect, and so he registered the wavery blur of Ingrid's chair as evidence that she was still sitting in it. Harrison and Torres, though, jumped and started looking around at the door, under the table, even behind the vending machines. Lensky sighed.

"Don't tease them, Ingrid."

She reappeared in her chair, as calm and collected as if she'd never left it. Which, of course, she hadn't. That would have been teleportation, which Thalia had just demonstrated.

Lensky contemplated trying to explain the differing properties of teleportation, camouflage and telekinesis to his colleagues. The thought lent conviction and persuasiveness to his argument that everybody would do better if they took the rest of the night off and reconvened in the morning. There was a decent hotel in Eden….

"I'd rather just go home," Thalia said under her breath.

"I think that'll make them nervous."

"They don't have any more control over us here than they have in Austin."

"I know," he muttered, "but please don't explain that. They'll feel better if we stay right here in Concho County. And if they really understood your abilities and limitations, you'd be handcuffed to the walls and we'd all be much more unhappy."

Thalia glowered and made *sotto voce* remarks about Riemann surfaces and people's pants catching on fire, but she went along with the negotiated decision that the topologists and Lensky would stay at the Paradise Inn for what remained of the night. Harrison, Dean and Torres, of course, already had rooms there.

***

The good thing about Greek hair is that if you keep it just long enough to fall into its natural curls, your hairstyle is virtually indestructible. Even after a twenty-minute hot shower to wash off the last of the pepper spray, all I had to do was rub my head with a towel and run my fingers through the curls a couple of times to look good as new.

Hair-wise, anyway. In other respects, what I saw in the mirror was not totally encouraging. My eyes and nose were still red and the bruise on my cheekbone was darkening. Worse, I looked fragile. Shaken up.

Which I was. For all my insistence that Brad would get us out of there, I hadn't been able to repress the thought that it might be too late when he found us. That he would find us and would free us, you understand, I never had the slightest doubt. The only thing I hadn't been sure of was whether I had the strength to hold out until he came.

If they had broken me – if I had given in, agreed to serve them regardless of what they wanted – I wouldn't have been the same person any more. The person Brad had married. I would have been — oh, something less. Something not worthy of him.

I needed to talk to him, to reason it out logically and unsentimentally. So, of course, when I opened the bathroom door and he held out his arms to me, I threw myself at him and wailed and wept into his shoulder like any idiot sentimental female. And he just held me close and tight and safe and never even suggested that I use the hotel's box of Kleenex instead of turning his shirt into a sodden rag.

"I'm sorry," I said when I was too dehydrated to cry any more.

"No, *I'm* sorry," he said, "for not getting to you sooner." He patted my back gently. "You've never cried on me before, even after Sandru Balan tried to blow you up. What aren't you telling me? Was it very bad?"

"N-no, it wasn't that bad, not yet. I had a feeling they were just getting started, though." I pulled back enough to look at his face. Nobody had ever accused Lensky of being smooth or handsome, although to hear him tell it, his big brother Aleksi had possessed both qualities in spades. Lensky looked just what he was: Solid. Steady. Reliable. The kind of man you wanted when you were prone to being attacked by vengeful mages or kidnapped by bullies with a bent for torture.

"And you came faster than I'd dared hope," I went on. It was easier — a lot easier — to keep my voice steady when I could look into his dark blue eyes and see the love in them. "I thought Dr. Verrick would see my note tomorrow and then I didn't know how long it would take him to get ahold of you and then, well, I was sure you'd find us as soon as you could – not more than a day or two." But I hadn't been equally sure that I would hold out that long.

"Thalia, why didn't you just do what they asked?"

"You don't get it, do you, Brad? They *didn't* ask. They grabbed us, drugged us so we wouldn't be able to apply topology to defend ourselves, and threw us in a windowless van. Put us in separate cells at that place, and started right in with the threats. They could have been anybody."

"But you said in your note that they were CIA. So they must have told you something."

"Your boss, who by the way did not impress me as the sharpest knife in the drawer, let that slip. Accidentally. In between threats and general… unpleasantness."

"Yes, well, now you know why he was acting crazy."

That I did. And being out of his mind with worry about his son was enough to excuse just about any craziness. "Yes. And… well. *Tout comprendre* is not necessarily *tout pardonner*, but I'm willing to overlook the bad start and do what I can anyway. You already know that; I wouldn't have shown off with the doughnuts if I hadn't been willing to cooperate. I would have from the beginning, you know, if they'd just told us what the problem was and asked nicely for help. Your boss's stupid ideas about saving time with a show of force actually cost him half a day. Night. Whatever."

"What about the others?"

"We'll find out in the morning." Which was already way too close. "I'm guessing that Ingrid's Viking axe display means she's on board too. Don't know about Ben and Colton." I didn't entirely have my mind on Steve Harrison's heartbreaking problem any more; Brad was investigating the big hotel-provided terrycloth robe I'd wrapped up in after my shower.

"What did you do, wrap this thing around yourself three times and tie it down with every knot you knew? Both of them?"

"Only the sash part. I'm not a midget."

"Fortunately," he said, wrapping the sash around one hand as he loosened it and slipped it free, "I was the star of my Scout troop at knot-untying."

I faked a yawn. "Don't you mean knot *tying*?"

"That was the official badge. This one was strictly unofficial – and not as rewarding as I'd hoped. Sandra Mae Finney was the model, but she drew the line at being the prize as well."

"I love getting these glimpses into your misspent adolescence. Did you even know what to do with a girl after you unwrapped her?"

"I do now."

And so he did.

5. There are quite a lot of men I'm not married to

"I don't think this was a good idea," Ben muttered at me.

I really didn't need him reinforcing my own fears.

"Don't worry. We just need to stay long enough to mark a couple of locations to teleport to later. Then we'll make some excuse and get out of here."

"That may be your plan. I'm not sure it's their plan."

He gestured at the cluster of grinning young men who had casually drifted between us and the door.

"Don't forget, we can always teleport out of here if we have to."

The house itself, a modest structure in a glum Frankfurt suburb, was extremely unappealing: dark, grimy, with mattresses and bags scattered around as though the occupants thought of it as a train station. There was a pervasive smell of inadequate plumbing, overlaid by the scent of beer; not just the beer they were drinking now, but the beer that had spilled on rugs and furniture, soaked into upholstery, and left white rings everywhere. I could imagine some good German *Hausfrau* incandescent with rage over what her tenants had wrought.

The young man who let us in had pressed a large plastic cup of beer on me while leaving Ben to find his own drink; then he'd draped an arm over my shoulders and tried to steer me away from Ben. I'd ducked out from under his arm – sometimes it's an advantage, being short – and he had grinned and said something that Mr. M. told me translated as "Later."

I thanked him for the translation and resolved to keep one eye on our host at all times, because as far as I was concerned there wasn't going to be any 'later.'

"You're going to be a tremendous help," I told Mr. M. He worked best with copious servings of praise and admiration. "I don't speak any German and I don't think Ben does either."

The turtle head at the end of the silver snake body gave me a sardonic look. "Clearly. That was Pashto."

"Oh." Mr. M. has never explained how his centuries of captivity to a magic-quelling ring resulted in his being fluent in so many languages. I have always supposed it was the result of extreme boredom; without his magic, he probably had nothing better to do than listen to anyone within earshot. Being removed from the site of ancient Babylon to the Turtle Pond on the UT Austin campus must have been a distinct improvement in terms of the number of people he could eavesdrop on and the varieties of languages they spoke. Still, *Pashto*?

Two more young men, so dark that their skin had blue shadows, moved in on either side of Ben and me. I was going to have a hard time referring to American blacks as 'black,' after seeing these guys. They were the real, undiluted thing.

"What are they saying in Pashto, Mr. M.?"

"They are speaking Somali. Cannot you hear the difference?"

"Honestly? No."

"They have plans for you. Do not allow yourself to become separated from Ben."

Good advice, but I wished, fleetingly, that Colton had accompanied us to Germany. He was just the kind of outsize young man I'd have liked to have by my side in this environment. But after the kidnapping – the CIA's kidnapping of us, I mean, not the terrorist kidnapping of Steve Harrison's son and the other two children – Colton had announced that he intended to work on the family farm for the rest of the summer while seriously rethinking his involvement with an agency that treated us like enemy aliens. Ingrid had been slightly less upset – at least on the surface – but had decided to take a leave of absence from the Center while getting through the last six weeks of preparation for her marriage to Jimmy.

"You know what it's like, Thalia!"

I did indeed.

"Now if it were Jimmy they wanted to take overseas, he could have gone traipsing off to Germany or anywhere else and it wouldn't have made any difference. All he has to do is show up in Britfield on the fifteenth of September."

"Rehearsal and rehearsal dinner," I mentioned.

"All right, the fourteenth."

Mrs. Thorn's wedding plans were an order of magnitude more elaborate than my mother had been able to foist upon Lensky and me. Worse, Jimmy's father was aiding and abetting her, throwing his money in with Mama Thorn's fine Swedish lineage and host of relatives to create the shindig of the century in Britfield this fall. In Ingrid's situation, I'd have 'discovered' that the Center absolutely couldn't do without my presence in Germany or wherever else our investigation might take us outside Texas. I had to admit she was tougher than me; I was avoiding a far lesser problem by joining Harrison's crusade, one that Ingrid would probably have taken in her stride.

So it was just Ben and me following up this lead from Sandru Balan to a Frankfurt suburb. Well, Ben, me, Mr. M., Lensky, and Steve Harrison. Mr. M., of course, was not on the payroll, but he might well be the most valuable member of our team. Now that I'd persuaded him not to harm Harrison.

Since Lensky seems to have been leaving Mr. M. out of his reports, I suppose a brief explanation is in order. Originally a Mesopotamian box turtle and a mage, Mr. M. had been placed in a sort of magical stasis when Nebuchadnezzar, fearing his power, tricked him into allowing a magic-inhibiting ring to be fitted around his neck. Fast forward through a couple of millennia, some recent wars, and (we surmised) a vet with an unusual taste in souvenirs, and he'd moved into the Turtle Pond on campus. There a bungling idiot had found him and removed the ring by chopping up his body and beheading him; the moron thought the ring, not Mr. M. himself, was the important part. Mr. M. had had a brief, unhappy bodiless half-life until, with the help of the infinite set of stars he had brought from Babylon and a robotics engineering student, he'd been fitted with a prosthetic body originally designed for a robot snake. Since then he'd been a valued, if sometimes difficult, member of the Center team. We'd been reunited after the kidnapping when he descended upon Steve Harrison with the intention of taking vengeance.

I suspect what annoyed him the most was that Harrison's goons hadn't recognized that he was worth kidnapping.

There. Everything clear now?

Harrison and Lensky weren't at this party. Brad would probably not have approved my checking out the house where the terrorist cell was supposedly centered. Harrison had distracted my husband with a long, long transatlantic conference call to Balan's interrogators before he casually trailed me past the coffee shop where the Afghan students hung out and watched me finagle an invitation to this party. (That had taken all of thirty seconds, and twenty-five of those seconds were taken up by their search for a compatriot who spoke English. I had the feeling they'd been striking out with the local girls.) And tonight, to give me freedom of action, he'd dragged Lensky out for a reunion with some old colleague who'd retired here.

I still didn't like or trust Steve Harrison, and with good reason. It was clear that he'd sacrifice me, Ben, or anyone else if it would get his son back. I couldn't exactly fault that – I'd certainly find Harrison expendable if, for instance, somebody had kidnapped Brad and wanted to trade for him – but it didn't make for a cozy all-colleagues-together relationship. Still, he had his uses; case in point, detaching Brad tonight so that I'd be free to help Ben with the little chore that would enable us to bug the house later.

I had been staring at a rather attractive arch between the living room and the beer alcove while thinking all this out. Now I felt I had it adequately fixed in my memory. It was time to move on and establish another teleportation point. When planning a surreptitious entry to someone's home, I always like to have two or three alternative arrival points to pick from, just in case my first choice isn't available when I'm ready to use it.

"Ben, have you got a good mental picture of the arch? Good, me too. Why don't we see if we can get a tour of the rest of the house?"

"You want see de *Haus*?" one of the Somalis said. "Come *mit*." He wrapped an arm around my waist – he wasn't tall either – and hauled me away from Ben. The other one stepped between Ben and me and started haranguing Ben and tapping on his chest, startling him.

I did not like this turn of events. The two men had moved so smoothly that I felt sure they'd used this maneuver often before. Now I was being strongly urged towards a back room, while the Somali's hold on me prevented me from simply teleporting to safety; wherever I teleported, he would be with me. And now it was just me and Mr. M., with Ben separated from me by far too many people.

I tried to dig my heels into the floor, but the guy who'd wrapped himself around me was so strong that I don't think he even noticed. So I poured my beer on him.

He jumped, let go, shouted something that I did not ask Mr. M. to translate, and hit me in the face with his open hand. Probably in his culture that was just a gentle reproof and I was supposed to be grateful that he hadn't used a fist. But he'd hit hard enough to rock my head back and make me dizzy, and the main force of the blow had landed right on my bruised cheekbone.

I wasn't overwhelmed with gratitude.

Then he grabbed the back of my neck. Somebody else, laughing, handed him a fresh cup of beer and he shoved it up against my lips. "*Trink!*" A painful squeeze on my neck accompanied the command. I started to yell and got beer slopped into my mouth.

It wasn't even good beer. Really, I'd expected better of Germany.

I swallowed more than I wanted to before I managed to spit the cup out, but that wasn't necessarily a bad thing. It was truly disgusting beer – warm, too – and my gag reflex came to the rescue. The Somali released me and reeled back, cursing, as I covered him with recycled beer. Unfortunately, two other men had come up behind us and they grabbed my arms. I could hear Ben shouting somewhere behind me. His shouts were interrupted by a meaty smack and a noise like someone falling into a stack of chairs.

Oh, hell.

Why hadn't he raised a shield before anybody hit him?

I guess we were both kind of distracted. I should have ignited the grabby bastards' pants with Riemann fire instead of reverting to my childhood style and trying to drive an elbow into the pit of one guy's stomach while I kicked backward at the other one's shins.

Yeah. It never worked too well on Steve and Yanni, my brothers, either. Now these guys dragged me through an open door and shoved me down towards a mattress on the floor.

That was their mistake.

They let go of me with that shove, and I never reached the mattress. On the way down I gasped, "*Brouwer,*" and the bleak little room dissolved around me. I hit the sidewalk outside the party house and scrambled to my feet.

"I recommend you teleport again," said Mr. M. "Back to the hotel, for instance."

"Can't leave Ben." I reached down and drew Mr. M.'s long, sinuous prosthetic snake body out of my belt loops. "Besides, don't you want to rout the enemy?"

He curled across my shoulders, quivering with the joy of battle. Brilliant lights popped around the doorway with deafening bangs, while I filled my hands with stars and threw them at the heads of the men in the front room. Ben was staggering to his feet; I went up the steps, leaned in through the open door and grabbed his hand. "Come on, we have to get out of here!" A humming noise told me that Mr. M. had extended his cobra hood to deploy another of his augmentations. Ben reeled slightly as the edge of one of the turtle-mage's focused ultrasonic beams caught him. I pulled, we went down the front steps backwards, and he landed on top of me. By an admirable exercise of will power, I did not vomit again.

By the time we were back on our feet, Mr. M.'s ultrasonic weapons had reduced most of the partiers in the front room to a state like ours – staggering and nauseated. I said, "*Brouwer,*" again and the sedate brown calmness of our hotel room formed around us.

48

Ah, that was "our" room as in mine and Lensky's, of course. Ben may be my best friend, but I really prefer to share a room with my husband.

At the moment, though, what I had was Ben, Mr. M., and a desperate need for a shower and clean clothes.

"Go to your own room." Ben still looked slightly dazed. I gave him a light shove and handed him Mr. M. before making for the bathroom to strip off my soiled clothes.

They didn't go, though. I could hear them talking at cross-purposes on the other side of the door.

"I need more flash-bangs. And grenades!" That was Mr. M., always lobbying for an increase in the military budget.

"If Harrison wanted to meet Somalis, there are plenty in Minneapolis," Ben groused.

"And one of my laser turrets is bent."

"Why did we have to come all the way to Germany?"

"Ben, you know why," I yelled while waiting for the water to warm up. "He isn't looking for Somalis, he's looking for the terrorists who organized the bombing."

"Fine, based on tonight's events I'm betting on that Somali group. What are they called? Al Sha- something?"

"Me too, but I'll go back around dawn and plant some bugs. Then we can find out for sure."

"You're not going back to that house!"

The water had gone from frigid to temperate. That might be the best I was going to get. I jumped in the shower and yelled, "Can't hear you when the water's running!" before shutting the stall door and getting down to the serious business of removing beer and worse substances.

A moment later the hot water came on, full force. I screamed, groped for the faucet, and adjusted the spray just in time to avoid getting scalded. Thereafter I concentrated on using the hotel's generous supplies of shampoo, conditioner, body scrub and lotion. Arguing with Ben could wait; washing that party right out of my hair was serious business.

In some respects Eden's Paradise Inn outclassed this big Frankfurt hotel.

There was plenty of scented stuff to splash on myself, but nothing to wrap up in afterwards except a thin white towel that was, frankly, not as big as it might have been. Even I found it difficult to pull the skimpy towel around myself and tuck in the ends. Oh well, at least this time I would have clean clothes to change into.

When I stepped out of the shower, Ben was gone. In his place was my husband, looking less than thrilled to see me.

"Oh! I didn't think you'd be back so soon."

Lensky sighed. "Thalia. Do you try to phrase things in the way that makes you look most guilty, or do the words just pop out of your mouth like that?"

"Must be Door No. 2," I said cheerfully, "because I certainly don't feel guilty." On the contrary, I felt extremely chipper. That shower had been my Ruby Ridge – no, my Rubicon. If that's what I mean? Neatly dividing my evening. On the pre-shower side there'd been the attempted-rape party, bad beer, and Ben blathering on about Somalis. Post-shower, I'd replaced the refugee party house with a nice clean hotel room and Ben with Lensky. Things were looking up all over, seemed to me.

Lensky sighed again, even more deeply. "Did you set this up just to test my trust in you?"

"Set what up?"

"Come on, you can't be that oblivious to the way it looks!"

A very narrow ray of light began to dawn, and I suspected I was not going to like what it illuminated. "Brad, are you suffering from your thing about me and Ben again? And what set you off this time?"

"Isn't it obvious? I come back to the hotel early, leaving Steve and his old boss to their reunion. When I walk into our hotel room, who should be there but your buddy Ben, looking the worse for wear and smelling of cheap beer."

"Well, that's not my fault. I told him to go back to his own room, but he wanted to stay and argue about Somalis."

"Wait, it gets even worse. After Ben jumps six inches and vanishes, leaving nothing behind but the memory of his shifty expression, I discover that my wife is here too. Only *she* is stark naked."

"You expect me to shower in my clothes?"

"No, but you might think twice about stripping down and jumping in the shower when the only other person in the hotel room is the man you're *not* married to."

"That's imprecise," I pointed out. "There are actually quite a lot of men I'm not married to."

"Stop interrupting, I'm not done yet. When my blushing bride comes out, wearing nothing but an overabundance of floral perfumes and the skimpiest towel ever manufactured – are you sure that thing isn't an oversized washcloth? — her surprise at seeing me instead of Ben is abundantly clear. 'I didn't think you'd be back so soon,'" he quoted through clenched teeth. "Good of you to admit it! Were you planning to entertain Ben in your present costume?"

Okay, now I could see clearly, and I was right: I didn't like the view. Were we doomed to keep having this fight forever? *Damn* the man.

"You sick, paranoid son of a bitch! I wasn't expecting to see anybody in this room, I just wanted to grab some clean clothes. Don't you ever wait to find out what's happening before jumping to conclusions?" For punctuation, I threw my hairbrush at him. It hit a framed picture of the Brandenburg Gate.

"Not when the conclusions might as well be painted on the wall in letters a foot high!"

There was a half-full water glass on the table. This time I had better aim, but the man caught it. At least his shirt got wet. "For a professional collector of information, you suck at interpreting it! If you couldn't trust me any better than that, why did you marry me?"

"I'm beginning to wonder that myself!"

Ohhh! *That* was unforgiveable – and I was running out of things to throw. Even the lamp was bolted to the bedside table. I tried to hit him, but he intercepted my fist without even blinking. And, of course, the towel fell off. I tried to jerk free of his grasp to retrieve it, but he put his free hand on my waist and pulled me to him.

"Let me go, dammit! I've been mauled enough tonight!"

He dropped his hands and stepped back. "So Ben *was* coming on to you."

"He was not. Never has, never will. And you are a damned fool!"

"Not," he said between his teeth, "fool enough to let the best thing in my life slip away without even putting up a fight. I'm the man you *did* marry, remember? Or do I need to refresh your memory?"

"Put it down to youthful folly," I said, my own teeth gritted now. "I'll be only too happy to give you your freedom."

"That's not what I want from you, and you know it. Thalia… doesn't it ever occur to you that Ben might get the wrong idea when you're so casual with him?"

I relaxed slightly. "No. Honestly, Ben's quite harmless."

"I understand he cut quite a swathe through the girls before he settled down with Annelise."

"Yes, but not with me. Ben and I do math together, not silly flirtation games."

Lensky looked as though I'd just slapped his face – which might have been a risk a couple of minutes ago, but not now. "*I* can't do math with you."

Oh, right. Another perennial sore point with no basis in reality. He wasn't a mathematician. That was fine with me, but he was insecure about it.

I moved forward and put my hands on his shoulders. "Oddly enough, mathematics is not anywhere near the top of my list of things I'd like to do with you."

He put his own hands on my waist. "Oh? Well, I *can* think of some alternatives…"

I would like to make it clear, right now, that I do not approve of settling a fight by jumping into bed. Sex should be a matter of mutual consent, mutual respect, and… and… well, anyway. Certain of Brad's qualities commanded respect regardless of how furious I might have been at him to begin with.

Passion, for example. Focus. And let's not forget stamina.

By the time the non-verbal part of the debate was over, I was feeling much too good to stay mad.

"Brad?" I said when my breathing was more or less back to normal.

"Mmm?"

"You didn't really think that Ben and I…?"

"I guess not. It just, just scares me whenever I think that you might trade me in for a mathematician."

"Not going to happen."

He chuckled. "You displayed a very reassuring degree of enthusiasm just now. Especially when you did that thing where you —"

"Yes, well, never mind that now." I could feel the blush rising to my cheeks.

"Mind? It'll be among my most cherished memories of all time. The way you—"

"If you don't shut up," I threatened, "I'll never do it again."

"Bet I can change your mind about that."

"Oh, stop gloating and tell me you're over your thing about Ben!"

Lensky put his hands behind his head and stretched out on the bed. I tried not to drool. All that toned flesh and taut muscle, unwrapped just for me; it was amazing I could keep my head well enough to carry on a conversation. "I suppose so. It's just – look, you do keep appearing in juxtaposition with Ben, water, and inadequate clothing. Happens every few months. And when you say stuff like, 'I didn't expect you back so soon,' what construction do you expect me to put on *that* statement in *those* circumstances?"

"That I didn't expect you back so soon, and that the circumstances have a perfectly innocent explanation which you would have heard already if you hadn't staged that paranoid freak-out."

"So? Explain it to me now."

I didn't get more than halfway through describing the party before Lensky started to get agitated again. He really doesn't like it when I do even slightly risky things without clearing it with him, and I have to admit that this excursion had gone some way past 'slightly risky.' All the same, I hadn't been as helpless as the nice German girls our hosts were probably used to—

"Girls who, unlike you, had better sense than to go to a party in a house full of African and Arab migrants," Lensky interrupted. "Don't you know what's happened to Germany's rape statistics since they opened their borders to the Middle East and Africa?"

"How would I? Unlike you, I don't read Interpol crime statistics for fun. Nobody told me!"

"Well, now you know."

"Yes, and Ben and I got out of the situation unharmed and I won't repeat that mistake."

"So you're not going to teleport in there later to place bugs for Harrison?"

"Well… Ben and I are the only ones who can do that."

"Fine. Let Ben do it. You stay out of it."

I wasn't okay with that proposition, because although Ben is a superb topologist, he does get rattled if things go south. Consider his failure to shield when the party started going bad. I tried to explain that to Lensky and he only got more agitated. I tried to calm him down and we got kind of sidetracked, to the point where I wound up doing that thing he liked so much again. With, all right, a certain amount of enthusiasm.

"Told you I could change your mind about that," he said afterwards.

Hmm. Perhaps he was just slightly more subtle than I'd given him credit for?

6. The Rightly Guided

I bounced and jittered around in my seat as the plane came in to Mogadishu airport, trying to get a better look at the blue vista outside the window. "Is that the *ocean?*"

"Well, *duh*. Mogadishu

is a seaport, you know," Ben said, as though anybody could be expected to know exactly where Mogadishu was.

"So that's the, the… Pacific Ocean?" That sounded wrong, but I couldn't think why. It couldn't possibly be the Atlantic, could it?

"The Indian Ocean," Lensky said. "Somalia is on the east coast of Africa."

I thought that over. "Then how come it's not the African Ocean?"

"It just isn't, okay? Don't you know *any* geography, Thalia?"

"Not much. Mrs. Vasiliu."

"Huh?"

"Sixth grade," I explained. "I am lousy at drawing maps, so every time she started a geography lesson I asked her something about Romania. She got out just before the collapse of the Soviet Union, and she could rant about the abuses of the Ceausescu regime for hours."

Lensky shook his head. "You have the craziest explanations for things. Just quit bouncing around for a few minutes, okay? Once we're safely on the ground I'll show you a map of the region."

We would probably have been more comfortable in a civilian aircraft. The only trouble is, it turns out that getting from Frankfurt to Mogadishu by commercial flights can take 40 to 50 hours, with plane changes at places like Istanbul and Djibouti. (With a menu of options like that, you really can't blame me for being geographically confused.) Harrison had pulled strings to get Ben, Lensky and me on a military flight delivering supplies to the CIA compound in Mogadishu. The only seats were arrangements of metal tubes and webbing that folded out from the walls, and there weren't any complimentary drinks. But it did cut our travel time down to nine hours. Lensky was very happy with the arrangement; it meant he didn't have to negotiate with airline security people about keeping his Glock.

I was reasonably happy too, because Brad had actually managed to persuade Steve Harrison to return to Langley instead of looming over us and jittering all over every move we made. His arguments had been one, that if Steve had been specifically targeted by their taking his kid then he was the last person who should be exposing himself to al-Shabaab in Mogadishu; and two, that Steve needed to be back in Langley to manage the response to ransom demands, in case there were any. I think the second argument had weighed somewhat with Harrison, the first not at all. I was just glad Harrison hadn't thought of the possibility that al-Shabaab would demand he trade himself for Sam. He would have agreed in a heartbeat.

It was a major disappointment to learn that we weren't going to be staying at a hotel on the beach. We weren't even going to get out of the Green Zone.

"I thought the Green Zone was in Baghdad," I grumbled. Not that Baghdad would have been all bad; I was sure Mr. M. would enjoy revisiting his homeland. (Babylon *is* near Baghdad, right? Ben and Lensky are rapidly destroying my faith that I know any geography whatsoever.)

"Well, there's one here too," Lensky said brusquely. "It was named for the one in Baghdad."

Who knew?

"And can we go anywhere we like inside this Green Zone?"

"Sure!"

That sounded a little better. "Ok, so what are the boundaries?"

"The airport."

"Right, I actually did figure out that the airport had to be inside the Green Zone. What else?"

"That's pretty much it."

"The *airport*?"

"Has a fortified perimeter, and you and Ben *will* remain inside it."

"Can't we even go to this CIA compound you were talking about?"

"Oh, sure. That's where we're staying. It's inside the airport perimeter and they've got their own hangars, so we'll land there and go straight to the compound."

Great. This was practically the first ever time I'd had a chance to use my passport – London doesn't count; I was only there one night, and I spent most of that night dodging German bombs. And what did I get to see on this trip? An airport hotel and a rape house in Frankfurt, and a fortified perimeter in Mogadishu. Oh, and one tiny glimpse of the African, excuse me, *Indian* Ocean from the airplane window.

"Stop pouting," Brad told me. "This is not America, or even Germany, and I'm going to keep you safe whether you like it or not. Ten days ago, al-Shabaab blew up a market in the city. Four days ago, they kidnapped a German nurse who made the mistake of working in a hospital outside the Green Zone. Yesterday a car bomb exploded on Maka al Mukarama – that's like the main street of Mogadishu."

"What did they demand?"

"Huh?"

"For the kidnapped nurse?"

"Oh." Brad looked sick. "They... didn't want a ransom. Her body... has been found." His tone suggested that I didn't want to know the details. I decided to quit grumbling about things like having to stay in the nice safe Green Zone.

Er, make that mostly safe. Two hours before our arrival, mortar fire from outside the perimeter had destroyed most of a runway and all of a Turkish Airlines 737 bound for Dubai. Fortunately, most of the passengers hadn't boarded yet.

Just another day in beautiful sunny Mogadishu.

Jerry Ortiz, the very junior field officer who had been sent to escort us to the CIA compound, imparted that bit of information as a way of encouraging us to hurry up and get off the runway. It did not noticeably dampen his cheerful assurances that Mogadishu was much, *much* calmer now than back in the bad old days of, say, three years ago, when al-Shabaab still controlled a significant part of the city. Apparently kidnappings, car bombs, and occasional mortar fire were just nuisance-level problems, like, say, traffic accidents. Besides, an immediate retaliatory air strike had already wiped out that particular mortar position.

And we would have plenty of people to talk to, even stuck inside the Green Zone, because the CIA compound was where American and African instructors ran a counterterrorism training program for Somali intelligence agents. Many of them, Brad informed me, were defectors from al-Shabaab being trained to go back out and fight their erstwhile comrades.

Well, Ben and Brad had plenty of people to talk to. I was told that al-Shabaab fighters were pious Muslims -for some definitions of 'pious,' anyway – and would not respond well to being interrogated by a mere female. So – having made that resolution to quit grumbling about the unfixable – I smiled sweetly and accepted Jerry Ortiz' offer to show me around the compound while the *men* did the *important* work. OK, maybe I did grumble a little, but mostly internally.

It was a sizeable place; had its own walls, with guard towers at each corner, protecting a lot more buildings than I'd expected. One of them sported extra Somali guards at the entrance. Armed, of course. "That's where we keep the detainees," Jerry said casually. "Suspected of being with al-Shabaab. We interrogate them to determine which ones can be turned or at least released back into the community."

"*You* interrogate them?"

A flush colored Jerry's face and made him look even younger; kind of like my kid brother Andy, only with sideburns. Somebody really ought to tell him that the sideburns didn't make him look older, they just made him look like he was trying too hard. Wasn't going to be me. "Well, not me personally, but sometimes I sit in on the interrogations."

"What else do you do here?"

He flushed even harder and began a series of rambling statements that all sounded like variations on 'open the mail,' and 'take lunch orders.'

"Not you personally," I said, "the CIA in general. This office must be pretty active if you need so many buildings. How many operations do you have going on?"

"None," Jerry said with surprising firmness. "We do not conduct operations here; we're strictly here to advise the Somali national security forces."

"*Uh*-huh." And in between offering advice, they probably sold bridges in Brooklyn and oceanfront property in Lampasas. Ten buildings – I'd counted them now – just for advisers and trainers? But it wasn't nice to put Jerry on the spot. I could probably get the real story from Brad, later. For now, I just let Jerry continue his spiel. He told me the best place to get seafood at the beach (Banadir Beach Restaurant, unbombed since 2016 – not that I had much hope Lensky would agree to take me there) and the best time of year to visit Mogadishu (now; it was the cool season – yes, really, this was a lot cooler than December – and the rains were mostly over.) "Just two months ago, Maka al Mukarama was under water!" he exclaimed dramatically.

"What, the main street? Don't they do drainage around here?"

"You recognized the name!" Jerry was flatteringly impressed. I may be somewhat ignorant of a few geographical details, but I'm not stupid. Lensky had just told me about Maka al Mukarama.

"For years Somalia's problem has been drought," Jerry explained, "but this May a typhoon moved in and *sat* over the country for days. Nobody was prepared for that; the Long Rains haven't delivered much rain for a decade. Then it all arrived at once."

Made me feel right at home; Texas has much the same pattern. It really, really doesn't rain until you've all but forgotten that water *can* fall out of the sky; then it really, really rains until you completely lose that urge to run outside screaming, "Free water! Free water!"

We do have working storm drains in Austin, though. Well, mostly working. Well, only a few minor, low-lying places flood on a regular basis, and none of them are anywhere near Congress Avenue, which you could consider our main street. Well, they're not near the part of Congress that's north of the river, anyway.

Maybe I wouldn't be making any snide comments about Mogadishu's infrastructure, or lack thereof.

After graphic descriptions of the havoc caused by the flooding, Jerry seemed to run out of things to say. I seized the chance to ask him one of the questions Ben and Lensky were presumably asking al-Shabaab defectors at this very moment. "Have you ever heard of an al-Shabaab leader called Omar al-Zanji?"

That name had been one of the rewards of bugging the house in Frankfurt. That, and the presumption that if Somalis knew inside details about the bombing the perpetrators must have been al-Shabaab, had brought us to Mogadishu. Oh, and the temporary presumption that Harrison was right in his guess that the perpetrators had paranormal abilities. Most of the CIA investigation was happening in America, for obvious reasons. Normal people, no matter how good their network of terrorist cells, might have had some difficulty reaching out from Somalia to stage an attack in the United States, let alone right inside CIA headquarters. They might have had even more difficulty in smuggling three kidnapped American children out of the country and across the globe to Somalia.

But we had encountered beings – perhaps not technically human – who could have done it without breaking a sweat. Take Shani Chayyaputra, the Master of Ravens, for example. He didn't even suffer from the limitation that handicapped our topologically based teleporting, the need to have visited and assessed a location physically before teleporting to it; we knew that from the events of last January. In response we had hardened the anti-teleportation shields over the Center's offices and employees' homes. But it had never occurred to us to offer such protection to the entire CIA headquarters. Look, after the attack that may seem like gross negligence. All I can say is that a week before this bombing, an offer from us to wander around the Langley offices scribbling topological diagrams on the walls would have been met with hearty laughter. Actually, I don't think the reaction would have been very different even after the bombing.

No, I didn't think the Master of Ravens was behind this. He attacked for financial gain or for revenge, not for political reasons. And his last encounter with us had apparently encouraged him to give up operating in America altogether.

But it seemed entirely possible – probable, even – that there could be other beings, natural or supernatural, with abilities similar to his. We were certainly a lot more open to that possibility than were most of the people at the CIA, and they were the ones funding us.

Naturally I didn't go into all that with Jerry Ortiz. I just tossed the name out and let it float around in his mind for a few minutes.

"Al-Zanji," he repeated, and then slurred the words to something that sounded like 'Azzanzhi.' "That's a strange name for an Arab."

I shrugged. "Not saying he *is* Arab. He's just… a person of interest. Surely al-Shabaab isn't run by Arabs? I thought it was a Somali group."

"An Islamic Somali group," Jerry said, "and most of their leaders take Arab names. Prestigious-sounding Arab names that translate to things like 'Father of Storms,' or 'Death to the Infidel.' Your guy's name just… well, if it means anything, it would mean 'Omar from Zanzibar.'"

"Oh." I didn't want to ask where Zanzibar might be when it was at home; fortunately, Jerry's zeal for imparting information led him to tell me anyway. "It's a large island off the coast of Tanzania – well, technically it's part of Tanzania. Before Independence they were separate countries, Tanganyika and Zanzibar; then they got sort of welded into one, called Tanzania. But Zanzibar's always been a bit different from the mainland. Very isolated, very Islamic, supposedly very haunted."

This all sounded promising.

"If you weren't so sure this guy is al-Shabaab," Jerry went on, "I'd say he sounds more like a member of Jeshi-la-Rashiduni – the Army of the Rightly Guided. They split off from al-Shabaab about six months ago to form their own group, more Africa-oriented, more about restoring the independence of Zanzibar and the Swahili coastal belt."

"Would there be anybody here who knows about Jeshi-la… what you said?" I would have to start writing stuff down. My funny-word stack was overflowing.

"Mmm. Well, there's this one woman who might talk to you; I think her boyfriend was involved. Thing is, Fadiya doesn't speak English. Or Somali. She's from Kenya. The coast. And we don't have a Swahili terp – ah, interpreter – available for you right now."

"I'd like to meet her anyway. Woman to woman, you know… we might understand each other better than you think."

Heaven knows what Jerry thought that nonsense meant, but he gave me a slow nod as though I'd just invoked some deep feminist wisdom. What *I* meant was that if Mr. M. spoke Swahili as well as Pashto, Somali, and everything else, Fadiya and I would be able to communicate just fine. Always assuming she could deal with a talking turtle-headed snake as an interpreter. I figured there was no need to bother Jerry with those details if I could just get him to leave me alone with Fadiya.

I was feeling considerably more dubious about my plan to use Mr. M. by the time we tracked down Fadiya in a courtyard just outside the prison building. She was covered from head to toe in a black nylon sack that must have been hellishly hot in this weather. One small, plump brown hand emerged from a slit in the black draperies to hold a flat basket of rice. Every once in a while she gave the basket a languid shake and something inside the sack jingled musically.

"Jambo, Fadiya," Jerry said slowly.

The black-veiled head inclined. "*Sijambo,* Jeri."

"Ah… Hiki Thalia. Jina lake Thalia." Jerry had found an all-new pronunciation for my name: thah-LEE-a. He shoved me towards her and retreated. "That's all the Swahili I know. You're on your own now."

"Sa-LEE-ah," the woman in black repeated.

What the heck, I've been called a lot worse things. "Saliya," I agreed.

"Jina langu Fadiya." She paused, waiting.

That had to mean, 'My name is Fadiya,' didn't it? OK, I could do this.

"Jina langu Saliya."

"Hujambo, Saliya."

"Hujambo, Fadiya."

The black veil erupted in giggles. "*La! La! Sijambo!*" She added something else that I couldn't relate to anything that had been said so far.

"She asks if the man has left," Mr. M. informed me. "Tell her, '*Ndiyo.*'"

"Undeeo?"

Another burst of laughter, and the veil over Fadiya's nose and mouth dropped, revealing a round, merry face framed in folds of black. "*Unasema Kiswahili kama mzungu, Saliya!*" She took my hand and I saw what had been making the noise; both wrists were covered with brilliantly colored thin glass bangles.

I'll quit describing the multilingual details there, if nobody minds. It wasn't at all straightforward, and I almost got thrown out right at the beginning, when she realized who – or what – was interpreting for us. She shrank away from Mr. M., whispering something about *majini* and *shetani*, and reached for her veil again. He intoned something long and musical that didn't sound anything like Fadiya's language.

"Of course it did not sound like Swahili; it was Arabic," he informed me later. "I quoted from a sura of the Koran."

"There's something in the Koran that tells people not to be afraid of talking turtle-snakes?"

Mr. M. preened and admired his own reflection in his shining scales. "Do not be silly. It would not matter what the verse said, she does not know Arabic anyway."

If you ask me, there's a good reason why Americans don't do foreign languages. The possibilities for confusion and complication seem to be endless.

In any event, after Mr. M. established his Islamic *bona fides* by chanting Koranic wisdom at her, Fadiya became positively chatty—and I discovered that I had struck gold.

It was easy to see why she was so willing to talk; there didn't seem to be a lot of women in the compound. Clearly she was bored, lonely, and ready for any entertainment. Once you've been reduced to shaking the husks out of a few handfuls of rice for employment I suppose anything – even telling your life story to an idiot *mzungu* girl who has to have everything explained in the simplest possible terms – seems like an improvement.

(*Mzungu*, by the way, means 'European,' 'foreigner,' 'not African,' or 'white,' depending on whom you ask. A Kenya-born farmer of English heritage is *mzungu*. The very black American CIA field officer I was to meet later was described as *mzungu*, but only after he opened his mouth to speak Swahili with a strong Brooklyn accent. I was *mzungu*. But a Chinese contract worker who spoke no African languages, he wasn't *mzungu*. All clear now? Sheesh. This kind of thing is why I prefer mathematics to languages. At least our definitions are consistent.)

Fadiya had quite a story to tell, once she got started. To me it was a heartbreaking story, but she recounted it with smiles and laughter. Except the part where – well, I'll get to that.

She herself was from Mombasa, which I can now tell you is *not* the same as Mogadishu; it's another seaport, some way south of Mogadishu, on the coast of Kenya. She had married a man from Zanzibar last year, when she was fourteen. No, she wasn't forced to marry him, she had loved him from the moment her parents introduced them. He was from a good Arab family in Zanzibar and was considered quite the catch for a girl from a poor neighborhood in Mombasa. Also, he was extremely good-looking. He was very religious; he never missed Friday prayers and always gave alms to the street beggars afterwards. And he was very generous to Fadiya. Here she showed me her bracelets. There were thin gold bangles here and there among the jingling glass ones. That was a *lot* of gold to give to a wife who hadn't even borne a son yet, she told me.

According to Fadiya, all was peace and harmony until her new spouse met those men from al-Shabaab. He took to bringing them home with him on Fridays; she set out the meal for them and retired modestly into a back room, but she could hear their arguments. They said that a young, healthy man like her Omar—"

I startled and Fadiya lost the thread for a moment, inquiring if something had bit me. I apologized and assured her that I was fascinated by her story. The truth, that.

Well, Omar's new friends had told him he had a duty to join their jihad against the infidel. He hadn't exactly disagreed, but he'd said that there were plenty of opportunities for jihad right there on the coast, freeing the Swahili people from colonial oppression.

(I asked Brad about that later. Hadn't Kenya been independent for, like, over fifty years? How much colonial oppression could still be happening? He explained that to the Moslem Swahili, the tribes that had taken over Kenya after Indepenence were as foreign as the British. Jomo Kenyatta's tribe, the Kikuyu, had monopolized the government of the new country for many years, and even now power moved uncomfortably between Kikuyu, Luo and other inland tribes which the Swahili considered practically pagan. The current president, Uhuru Kenyatta, was Jomo Kenyatta's son.)

Over the weeks, Omar's friends began winning the arguments. Still, it was a shock to Fadiya when Omar announced one day that they were going to Somalia to join the jihad with al-Shabaab. A foreign land, far from her family, where they didn't even speak Swahili!

"Was that when things started going wrong?"

Fadiya shook her head decisively. No, it was a woman's duty to obey her husband. Naturally she had come with him to this strange land, and had continued cooking his meals and warming his bed in between the unexplained absences that began after they came north. She assumed he was going out with his friends from al-Shabaab to strike at the imperialist *wazungu*, but of course it wasn't a woman's place to ask about such matters.

I began to understand why Brad and Ben had been okay about only talking to men.

The real trouble, Fadiya said, had begun after he was detained here in the CIA's unofficial prison on suspicion of working with al-Shabaab. They'd questioned him for a month, and when he finally got out he was different: harder, angrier. Hating America even more than he hated the people who'd actually controlled the Swahili coast, from English to Kikuyu. And particularly hating the CIA, whom he accused of insulting and humiliating him.

Shortly after that, he disappeared again. This absence lasted for nearly two weeks, and his Somali 'friends' had started hanging around and bothering her. She'd threatened that if they didn't treat her with respect, Omar would kill them on his return. And she'd been ecstatic to see him again – but it hadn't been what she expected.

"He had been back to Zanzibar," she said, "and he had taken another wife!"

"Ah – that's permitted, isn't it? In Islam?"

"Yes, but I told him I would not share a house with that fiend he married – and he divorced me! And then his friends wanted to share *me*, and I ran away to a house I knew of in the city. But they did not want anybody to think it was possible to leave al-Shabaab, so they sent someone to the house to kill me. That is how I got this," she said, pushing back the black folds around her face to reveal an ugly scar on her cheek. "But that was good luck, because they failed and I was taken to the Red Cross hospital, and when I told them what happened an *mzungu* took me to this place and said I would be safe here. And so I am, but there is no one to talk to and nothing to do and I want my mother!" She burst into tears and I patted her shoulder, feeling extremely awkward. It did seem to me that going home to Mother would be the best thing for the kid, but after that short burst of weeping she told me that it was absolutely not possible. She had dishonored the family by running away from her husband and they would have to kill her if she came home and everybody knew what had happened.

I couldn't believe that. "What, running away from a jerk who had divorced you anyway is worse than sticking around to be abused by his slimy buddies?"

It took Mr. M. a while to translate that, but when he did get it across, Fadiya nodded and sniffed dolefully and started to repeat herself. It took me a while to understand that in her culture, what actually happened wasn't nearly as important as what was known. She felt absolutely sure that no amount of explanation would erase the scandal of her returning to Mombasa alone, without her husband.

I still wasn't quite so sure, but when she said, "You don't know my father," I found myself nodding reluctantly. I'd said the same thing to various friends who didn't grasp how crazy *my* father was.

I'd never been afraid that he'd kill me, though.

Lucky me.

"So… is Omar still in Mogadishu?"

"Oh, no. He left soon after he divorced me. He had always been unhappy that his comrades in al-Shabaab did not care about freedom for us Swahili, and that *fiend* he married in Zanzibar persuaded him to leave and start his own group. They call themselves Jeshi-la-Rashiduni."

Jerry had mentioned that name, or something very like it.

"And so he went back to Zanzibar?"

"No. It is too hard to travel from there, to organize and make attacks. He is in Mombasa now. And he said that if I troubled him, he would tell everyone he had divorced me for being with another man. So you see, I cannot possibly go back there."

But Brad and I could go there, couldn't we?

I was so excited about what I'd learned that I actually ignored the single most important word Fadiya had used.

Twice.

7. A pessimistic culture

It took us nearly as long to get from Mogadishu to Mombasa as it had to fly from Frankfurt to Mogadishu, which makes absolutely no sense when you look at a map. The world map in the back of the airplane magazine, for instance, made Mogadishu and Mombasa look like two little dots barely a finger's width apart. That just shows you how useless map drawing skills are; good thing I never wasted my time acquiring any. In real life what matters is how you get there, and this time we were stuck with commercial flights. Lensky explained that there is barely any CIA presence in Mombasa; they think it's a backwater, an occasional target for terrorist attacks but not a source of them. They may have been correct before the formation of Jeshi-la-Rashiduni. So there wasn't any convenient military aircraft for us this time, nor did we have a whole lot of support from the CIA in Mogadishu; they thought we were going on a wild-goose chase.

Their main reason for doubting my lead, it seemed to me, was that I was a *girl* and I'd gotten my information from another *girl* and so all my data was covered with icky *girl* cooties. Leads were supposed to be developed by strong, silent men sweating them out of other strong men in basement cells lit by a single naked bulb... oh, all right, all right, Brad says I'm over-dramatizing and he may just possibly be right. The fact that I wasn't CIA-trained may have been the real problem. In any case, he and Ben didn't question the value of my lead on the kidnappers, and that was all that really mattered.

It was a drag, though, having to take a commercial flight from Mogadishu to Nairobi, then waiting half a day to catch a flight from Nairobi to Mombasa. Brad was forced to deal with more security officials for permission to keep his weapon, and he was not happy about that. He gets all the more credit for not questioning what I'd learned from Fadiya, not all of which bore directly on Omar the Zanzibari. It would have been rude to rush off the minute I'd learned what I wanted to know, and besides, I hadn't expected to see the guys again for some hours. So I'd stayed there, chit-chatting and picking up Swahili phrases – and, okay, racking my brains to think of some way to help Fadiya. I drew a total blank there.

"Don't beat up on yourself," Brad said when I got to that part. "It's a very tricky business, fixing the problems of somebody from such a different culture. Easy to do more harm than good, especially when you don't know how the society works."

I made a few rude comments about a 'culture' that punished little girls for having been abused by the men their parents sold them to.

Brad made soothing comments back at me.

"Okay," I said finally, "but after we finish this job, I want to do *something* for Fadiya."

Brad sighed. "Let's talk it over with the Mombasa field office. They probably understand the situation better. What else did you learn from Fadiya?"

"Nothing directly relevant to finding the kids, I don't think. She did teach me a handful of Swahili phrases. It seems to be a very pessimistic culture."

"What makes you say that?"

"You know how you say hello in Swahili?"

"Sure. *Jambo*. It's in all the movies."

"That," I said sweetly, "is the cut-down, simplified, vastly inferior version of Swahili used inland – I mean, up-country. In Mombasa you say *Hujambo*. That means, 'You don't have any news, do you?' And the answer is supposed to be *Sijambo*. 'No, I don't have any news.'" I'm no more talented with languages than any other normal American; I quite enjoyed this first chance to explain the finer points of a foreign language to somebody else.

"Considering the nature of recent headlines," Brad commented, "I'm not sure whether I would call that pessimistic or merely realistic."

Once we landed, he insisted that we not take the first taxi assigned to us. He stepped aside and motioned a pair of Japanese tourists forward, then a group of American students who wanted to be taken straight to Diani Beach. The third taxi, driven by a turbaned Sikh with a chin net confining his full beard, met with his approval. "Royal Court Hotel!" Lensky shouted over the noise of airport traffic and announcements. The driver took off with a squeal of rubber, cutting around the taxi in front of us where the American students were still getting themselves and their luggage sorted out.

I had planned to take in every minute of the taxi ride; based on recent experience, this might be the only time Lensky allowed me a view of the streets. But after the episode with the overloaded truck (men hanging off each side; good thing they weren't very fat) and the subsequent plunge through an entire rank of funny little three-wheelers painted in bright colors, my nerve failed me.

"You're missing the elephant tusks!" Ben shouted at me.

I opened my eyes and peered up at the enormous arch, made up of two white tusk-shaped things with crossed points, that rose across our side of the road. A matching arch stood over the other side. "Nuh-uh. Those things are way too big to have come off of any elephant."

"Of course not," Lensky said. "I think they're aluminum, actually. If they were made of ivory, they'd have been cut to pieces and stolen by now."

A black Mercedes flanked by armed motorcycle riders cut us off with easily half an inch to spare.

"Politician," Lensky commented.

I closed my eyes again.

"Don't you want to *see?*" Ben was clearly disappointed in me.

"No. If I'm fated to die on the streets of Mombasa, I don't want to see it coming. I'll just go gently into that good night." Anyway, I could hear more than enough. Brakes screeching, some kind of sonorous horn (I learned later it was someone at the Hindu Temple blowing a conch shell), pedestrians shouting, an echoing chant (the call to prayer, from roughly fifty-seven different mosques with fifty-seven overloaded loudspeakers), beggars whining… I could get overwhelmed without ever opening my eyes.

The Royal Court Hotel was large, and red, and air-conditioned. I approved.

"You missed a lot by not looking." Ben wouldn't stop harping on that. "It was like *Casablanca*, only in color. There were guys in white dresses, and a bunch of fruit and vegetable stands right out on the street, and a whole row of shops with nothing but burlap sacks full of some kind of different colored powders, and these dinky mini-buses with people hanging off the sides, and some real dark guys wearing nothing but some kind of towel wrapped around their hips, and a bunch of women who looked like somebody threw black bags over their heads…

"That's a *bui-bui*," I told him, "Fadiya wore one. She showed me how to tie it on and drape it, too." A tardy thought occurred to me. "How come you weren't scared to look?"

"It's a different philosophy," Ben told me. "I wanted to see whatever was about to kill me."

Lensky regarded us with the tolerant smile of an adult listening to the children's bickering.

We had time to wash and change clothes before meeting the local CIA contact for dinner – right there in the hotel. "Isn't that kind of, um, public?" I asked. While I was shaking out my respectable dress, Lensky had explained to me that the funny business with the taxis wasn't anything that unusual; just good tradecraft, he said, never taking the first option anybody offers you.

"Or good paranoia."

"Often a basic part of tradecraft," he allowed.

Sitting down to dinner with the head of the Mombasa field office, right there in the hotel restaurant, didn't seem terribly consistent with that level of paranoia. I had the feeling Lensky wasn't totally happy with it either, but the message had been waiting when we checked in and he didn't want to start off on the wrong foot with this guy.

He looked a lot happier when we walked into the restaurant and a tall, dark-haired man rose to greet us. "Finch! What are you doing here? I thought the local office was run by someone named Taylor."

The dark man grimaced. "My titular boss. He's out of the picture for a few days; some kind of fever, or so he says. Not that it makes a lot of difference; I do most of the day-to-day work anyway."

"Well, it'll make a difference to me," Lensky said heartily. "I couldn't have asked for better luck! Thalia, Ben, this desperate character is Nelson Finch. We went through our training at the Farm together, so you can believe me when I tell you not to trust him farther than you can throw him! Nelson, my wife Thalia, and her, ah, colleague Ben Sutherland."

Over dinner Lensky and Finch reminisced about good times at the CIA training facility known as the Farm. Nothing seemed to make them happier than remembering the time they got themselves first tangled up in blackberry bushes, then lost in a swamp, and finally almost drowned on a training exercise to exfiltrate a compromised agent. I wondered if they'd actually enjoyed it as much at the time.

Then they moved on to discuss the variety of weapons they'd learned to fieldstrip and clean, blindfolded, and the conversation got *really* boring. Ben kept trying to interject knowing comments, which was difficult because he doesn't know any more about guns than I do. I suppose it was the Testosterone Imperative: Real Men Like Guns. Me, I kept my head down and concentrated on my excellent beer and the beyond-excellent Lobster Thermidor recommended by Nelson Finch. I wasn't sure why the mix of lobster, cream and cognac stuffed into a lobster shell was named for a month in the short-lived French Republican calendar, but whoever was responsible for the recipe could call it anything he liked as far as I was concerned. I just wanted to remember the name for future reference.

"Remember the time we totally demolished that school bus with twenty pounds of C-4?"

I looked up, shocked, and Brad patted my hand. "It was empty, Thalia."

"Oh, good."

They went on into stuff like improvising pressure bombs with a condom and aluminum foil, using graphite to smuggle a pistol past a metal detector, and the best way to mix fertilizer and fuel oil for a really satisfactory explosion. By now Ben was hanging on every word. What *is* it about men and explosives, anyway? First Colton got into the building demolition business, and now Ben was storing up everything these two said for future reference. I remembered Ingrid saying that she hoped Ben's interest in applying topology at the molecular level never led him to thinking about bombs. I had a feeling that ship had just sailed.

We retired to our hotel room for after-dinner coffee and serious discussion.

"Oh, don't worry, Lensky, the room's not bugged!" Finch brushed aside my husband's suggestion that perhaps they should find a more secure locale.

"And you know this how?"

Finch shook his head and treated us to his slow, charming smile. "Trust me, I know my territory. Now what's brought you pell-mell to the most boring field office in Africa, Lensky? Trying to get the Company to pick up the tab on a honeymoon tour for you and your lovely wife?" He turned the smile on me, full wattage, and I batted my eyelashes at him. I do not care for men who try to charm me as a way of annoying or distracting Lensky.

A brief description of the crisis that had brought us here, including my role in developing this lead, had Finch's smile looking more like that of a man who was politely trying not to laugh in our faces. "You've been out of the field for a long time, haven't you, Lensky?"

"Fifteen months," he said tightly.

"How odd, I thought it was longer since you got run out of Romania."

"I did not go directly Stateside from Romania," Lensky said.

That was news to me; in Brad's all-too-brief mentions of his CIA career before being posted at the Center for Applied Topology, he'd always segued from Romania to his current posting as though there'd been nothing to mention in between.

"Oh? Where *did* you go?"

"Need-to-know," Lensky said dismissively.

"Oh, but you can tell me. Or is it simply too boring to discuss?"

"You could say that."

I knew when Brad was being evasive, and it usually wasn't because the subject was boring. Evidently his dear old friend Nelson Finch didn't know him quite that well, though, because he accepted the evasion at face value. I would have to conduct my own interrogation later.

"Well, it can hardly have been as boring as Mombasa. Nothing ever happens here, bar an occasional al-Shabaab attack, and those guys come from the north and zip right back into Somalia before the Kenya cops get around to investigating anything. Believe me, this is the last place to look for any kind of terrorist activity. I'm sure your lovely wife is eager to make her contribution, but we really cannot run this office on the basis of gossip among the ladies." He treated me to another smile with oodles of charm.

A dismissive insult all wrapped up in fake flattery and that I'm-so-cute smile. I was rapidly developing a strong distaste for Brad's old friend. He was being pretty damned dismissive of Brad, too.

"If there's so little going on," Brad said now, "I'm surprised the Company keeps two of you here."

"We-el, for all practical purposes it's just me," said Finch, oozing self-satisfaction. "LeShawn Taylor doesn't do much. Typical Affirmative Action hire, you know?"

"I do not," Lensky said with a snap. "The Company is not given to hiring people who can't do the job, whatever their color."

Finch shrugged. "If you stay here long enough, you'll probably meet him. But I suppose you'll be heading right back to Mogadishu, where the real action is."

"Oh, I think we'll stay and look around for a while," Lensky told him. "As you said, it's a much better spot for tourism than Mogadishu. Take my wife to the beach, take her shopping, that sort of thing."

Finch laughed. "If you can get the Company to spring for your honeymoon trip, far be it from me to interfere."

"We'll need some place less conspicuous to stay."

A shrug. "Why? This is one of the best hotels in Mombasa, and they have a courtesy van to the beach. You'll be quite comfortable here – and it's not as if you'll have to pick up the tab."

"Not good tradecraft," Lensky said.

"Oh, well, come by the office tomorrow and we'll work something out."

Finch dropped a card on the table and stood up to leave.

I picked up the card while he and Lensky were saying good-bye. "Columbia Import Association?"

Lensky closed the door behind Finch. "What, you thought it would say CIA?"

"Might as well, don't you think?" If the Company wanted to play silly initial games it was not my problem. Something else was bothering me, but I waited to raise it until Ben had left.

"Brad," I said once we were alone, "how well do you really know Nelson Finch?"

Lensky looked at me, eyebrows raised. "How well? Weren't you listening at dinner? We went through everything together at the Farm. The man's like a brother to me."

Given that Lensky's only brother had been a compulsive gambler who came to a nasty end at the hands of a New Jersey gang, this did not impress me as a great recommendation. "Well, he doesn't seem to have much respect for your judgement."

"Ah, that's just how Foreign Ops people feel about Domestic Operations. Intra-agency competition, you know? Give him a few days, he'll realize I haven't lost any of my edge just from kicking my heels Stateside for a little over a year."

I thought back over the last fifteen months. "If 'kicking your heels' is how you describe being shot at, nearly blown up, and kidnapped into the middle of a war in another century, I hate to think what you'd consider a stimulating work environment."

"Ah, you forgot to mention the most important event of all. Getting married to a crazy topologist." He wrapped one arm around me and drew me close for a long kiss. "I wouldn't trade the past fifteen months for anything; they brought me you."

Fifteen months, that was one thing. But how, I wondered, did he feel about the prospect of spending the next fifteen or more years kicking his heels in Domestic Operations?

8. A lovely place to set up a perimeter with trip wires

The next day, Lensky went off on his own to the address Finch had given him, suggesting that Ben and I do some sightseeing and try to act like ignorant tourists. ("You're certainly ignorant enough," he muttered. I pretended not to hear him. His leaving Ben and me at loose ends was a gigantic gesture of trust after our fight in Germany, and I didn't want to spoil it by unnecessary bickering.)

Growing up in Texas turned out to have been excellent training for Mombasa. Oh, the hotel was air-conditioned, but the minute you stepped out onto the street the hot, humid air closed down like a stifling blanket. All around us I could see English and German tourists wilting before retreating to their air-conditioned hideouts for another cold drink. Ben and I weren't quite so fragile.

Ben thought this would be an excellent time to go to the beach. So did I, actually, but I felt guilty about getting Lensky here and then leaving him to do all the work. It seemed like the least we could do was roam around the city and try to find out something about Jeshi-la-Rashiduni.

Given Fadiya's first reaction to Mr. M., I felt it would be tactful to leave him napping at the hotel while we made our first approaches. This was an international port, after all; there must be a lot of people who spoke English.

Maybe there were, but all I learned in that first morning's work was that English-speaking locals did not want to talk about Jeshi-la-Rashiduni. In fact, once you mentioned that group, whoever you were talking to not only never heard of them, he also didn't know anybody named Omar, never went to mosque except during Ramadan, and was about to leave town to visit his daughter who married an up-country (inland) civil servant. When we trailed back to the cool darkness of the Royal Court Hotel at noon I was the proud possessor of four such evasive runarounds and one native carving, a primitive mask almost as tall as I was.

"Why you had to buy that thing escapes me," Ben groused. "It won't even fit in your suitcase."

"Shut up. I'll figure out some way to get it home." My own piece of authentic African art! Okay, it wasn't easy to figure out exactly where it would fit in the condo, but I'd work it out. There was no way I was going to come back from this trip with nothing to show for it.

The bartender at the Royal Court introduced us to two local customs: the shandy, and staying indoors between noon and sunset. Both seemed admirable to me.

"A sandie- shansy – whatever – is a way to drink all the beer you want without getting drunk," I explained to Lensky when he found us in the bar late that afternoon.

He eyed me dubiously. "I'm not sure it works quite like that."

"Sure it does! See, you mix the beer half and half with this English invention called ginger-beer, which is totally non-alcoholic, and then you can chug a tall glass of the stuff while only drinking half as much beer."

"*Uh*-huh. And how many tall glasses have you inhaled?" He gave a pointed look at the empty glasses littering the tabletop.

"Well, that was over a period of…" I started counting on my fingers but gave up. "What time is it now?"

"After five."

I considered the arithmetic. Five minus twelve… negative number. Something was wrong here. "So, that's… how many hours since noon?"

Lensky laughed and pulled me up out of my seat. "Too many, and why didn't you stop her, Ben?"

"You married her," Ben said, "you stop her. I couldn't even keep her from buying this thing." He reached under the table and brought out my prized African mask. Lensky staggered slightly at the sight.

"That's... impressive, Thalia. Why don't you come upstairs with me now and let's discuss what you're planning to do with it?"

"I want dinner. More lobster Thermidor!" I considered that statement briefly. "Well... maybe not lobster. I think it upset my stomach."

"Yeah, I bet *something* upset your stomach," Lensky said. "Perhaps you'd better skip dinner in favor of water and Alka-Seltzer."

I would prefer to pass over the rest of the evening without going into the unpleasant details. Something – I blame the African sun – had given me a hellish headache, and my digestion was jittering around and complaining bitterly about something or other. Probably last night's lobster.

On the next day Lensky thanked me for my investigative efforts, bought a giant economy-size bottle of sunscreen, and put Ben and me in the hotel's courtesy van bound for Nyali Beach.

"I don't even have a swimsuit!"

"Finch assures me there are plenty of shops for tourists. You and Ben can both buy swimsuits, towels, whatever you want. Just, please, no more native art."

Nyali Beach wasn't what I'd call close, but it was beautiful enough to be worth the long ride. And it wasn't like we'd have to do it again; now that Ben and I had seen the place, we could just teleport there whenever we felt like it. I made a note of a couple of places where shops came together at an angle that would conceal somebody stepping out of an opening in the air.

After some intensive shopping, and a few tense moments in a totally inadequate store dressing room while I slipped into my new swimsuit and Ben kept watch, I fell in love with the white sands and rolling blue water.

"This," I said happily while anointing myself with sunscreen, "is what international travel should always be like."

Ben was not quite so sanguine. "We could have gone to Port Aransas and had the same experience."

"Oh, come on. The ocean at Port Aransas is *brown*."

I could have been happy all day alternating sunscreen application, tanning, and splashing in the friendly blue waves that rolled gently to shore, but Ben thought we should go back at mid-day before we were both fried to a crisp.

"I thought you liked beaches. Wasn't that the whole point of your first major?"

Ben had once confided in me that before the discovery of how we could apply topology, his life plan had been to major in marine biology, get a fellowship to graduate school in the same subject, and write his dissertation on some obscure marine invertebrate that flourished only in the Mediterranean. Dr. Verrick's Honors Topology course had been the first crack in that plan; the discovery that he could apply topology to move tiny objects without touching them had been its doom.

"And here you are, on a tropical beach, for *work*, on somebody else's dime," I pointed out. "Want me to get you some jars so you can collect marine life?"

"Like they say, life is what happens while you're making other plans... What about your plans?"

"Working on a world-class tan?"

"Back home." Ben gave me a censorious look. "Thalia, this is a beautiful fantasy, but your real life is in Austin. Have you given any thought to Dr. Verrick's suggestion?"

I had been avoiding thinking about it, actually. Dr. Verrick's strong suggestions were a major force of nature. My main defense against his psychological warfare was not letting his idea into my head in the first place. There was no way I could do what he wanted, anyway. I pointed this out to Ben. "You know that I'm not a leader. I piss people off."

"You also," he said, "naturally take the lead whenever we're floundering. Who organized the resistance to Steve Harrison's CIA goons?"

I was a bit surprised by his attitude. "You, ah, think Dr. Verrick's right? I thought you'd have felt unhappy about it. Passed over."

"I," said Ben, "am really not a leader. I'm a pure researcher through and through."

I pretended to throw sand at him. "Don't malign my purity!"

"Speaking of sex," he mused.

"Were we?"

"Obliquely… How long do you think we'll be here?"

"As long as the job takes. Why?"

"Annelise was thinking of flying into Nairobi for a quick visit."

I don't know a lot of people who could afford to fly to East Africa for an impromptu visit, but Annelise's father was apparently in that income bracket. After he'd provided a private jet to fly her and Ben back from India – long story – I'd stopped asking whether anything Annelise wanted was affordable in any normal sense of the term.

"That would be nice for you."

"If she does come, I thought I could maybe take this weekend off and go up to see her."

"As long as nothing's happening here, I don't see why not." It might be a good idea all round. Lensky would have to be less paranoid about him if Ben went off for a weekend with his girlfriend, wouldn't he?

Despite having a way to teleport back and forth now, we still had to take the van back into the city this once. The hotel driver kept a list of everybody he'd driven to the beach and he'd warned us that the hotel had a totally Nazi attitude about getting back exactly the same people they'd taken out. We didn't want to make trouble for him, and we certainly didn't need anybody asking how we'd returned without taking the van.

Although not as fair as Ingrid, Ben is kind of a pallid Nordic type – light skin, light brown hair – and on top of that, he spends most of his life indoors. On the way back, it became clear that we had already stayed out too long for him. His forehead and nose were red and shiny, and he said his shoulders felt as though they were undergoing the same transformation. I was somewhat better off, having inherited Mom's Greek skin as well as her hair. My olive complexion constitutes a first line of defense against sunburn, and copious applications of sunscreen over that seemed to have prevented any actual burns. I did feel dizzy and flushed, though. Should have bought a hat as well as a bikini.

"I suppose you'll want to spend the afternoon in the bar drinking shandies again?"

My stomach gave one last flop. "Actually, I thought I'd stick to ginger-beer today. Or better, I'll go back to the classics. Diet Cokes."

Brad was much happier when he came back to the hotel this evening, and so – thanks to my prudence – was I.

It transpired that despite spending two days being given the Gospel of Mombasa According to Nelson Finch, his only real progress had been made through back channels.

"Finch doesn't seem to understand our need for a safe house – well, of course, he doesn't think there's anything for us to discover here, so he wouldn't, would he?" Brad excused him. "So I've reached out to other sources and arranged for an American researcher here to rent a place big enough for all of us. He was quite cooperative once I made it clear that he could stay there too and that the agency would pick up the rent and other expenses."

"How do you know an American researcher in Mombasa?" Ben asked.

"I don't. I got his name through an anthropologist at the University of Chicago."

"Whom you know because…?"

"Actually, I don't. Your Dr. Verrick was good enough to put me in touch with him."

Dr. Verrick knew somebody at the University of Chicago? Somebody who wasn't even a mathematician? "There are more things in heaven and earth, Thalia, than are dreamt of in your philosophy," Brad said. He reads a lot.

We didn't check out of the hotel. Oh, well, if the CIA wanted to pay for two hotel rooms *and* a rented house, wasn't my problem. The only difficulty was that we had to leave some of our stuff there so as not to look as if we were running out on them, and we didn't have that much stuff to begin with. We all wore two layers of clothes the next morning, and I carried a huge flowery basket that Lensky had found in the hotel gift shop and that was big enough to hold all the toiletries and other small stuff we wanted to take to the safe house. On the way out, Lensky held us up while he had a long consultation with the concierge about getting my African mask packed to take home. Then he very earnestly asked the concierge to take a message if anybody called, because he'd asked several travel agencies about arranging a safari for himself and his wife.

"I suppose that was all tradecraft?" I asked after the three of us had squeezed into a tuk-tuk – one of the funny little three-wheeled vehicles I'd glimpsed on the first day.

Lensky grinned. "Disinformation."

Too bad. I'd kind of liked the idea of a trip out of the city to look at zebras and giraffes – even after Lensky pointed out that it would have to be a very long trip, because Mombasa wasn't anywhere near the rolling savannahs and game parks that most people associate with Kenya.

"And more tradecraft coming up. Just follow my lead."

He stopped the tuk-tuk and paid off the driver in the middle of a busy block lined with glass-fronted stores, then grabbed my wrist as soon as the driver was out of sight. "We're crossing here!"

"Wait!" I squeaked to no avail as he swung me out of the way of an oncoming mini-bus. I think it shaved the back pocket off Ben's jeans as it passed. A few near-death experiences later, we arrived on the far side of the street. The shops here were less fancy and more interesting. Half of them were open to the street, and they displayed things like a pyramid of yellow cooking oil cans, a bin full of red peppers, those sacks of colored powder Ben had described. I tried to slow down to get a better look at the mechandise, but Lensky hauled me along mercilessly, and Ben followed so closely that he was practically treading on the backs of my sandals.

We went around a corner, cut through an alley, and emerged in front of a hardware store on a similarly busy street. A young man in a battered sedan pulled up, nodded at Lensky and invited us into the car with a sweeping gesture. We all three piled into the back seat and the driver rejoined the stream of traffic.

"Thanks, Victor," Brad said.

"The place is about half a mile from here."

"You can go straight there. I'm pretty sure we weren't followed." Brad turned to Ben and me and explained. "Diving through traffic wouldn't work against any sophisticated operation, but it's a pretty good way to cut out any amateurs trying to follow on foot. And you may not have noticed, but the place where Victor picked us up was on a curve that couldn't be observed from either corner." He was grinning, clearly exhilarated by the chance to use his training. I decided to be very, very nice and not even mention that Ben or I could have frustrated any attempts at following us with a simple topological camouflage.

Victor turned down a narrow street whose pavement had seen better days – possibly during the British colonial period – and parked by a shabby little general store. He led us up a flight of steps at the side of the store. "The second floor is all ours," he said, unlocking an iron grille and then a solid wooden door at the top. "I thought I'd take the room at the front – watching people interact in the street, it's all grist for my thesis – and then here's the kitchen and bathroom, and there's a general living area and two more bedrooms." He glanced at the three of us uncertainly. "Ah, will two bedrooms be enough?"

Brad put his arm around me. "Thalia and I are married."

"Oh, is that going to be your cover? A honeymoon vacation, maybe? You'd better have the back room then, it's bigger." He scrutinized Ben. "You'd better be a friend of mine, visiting from Chicago."

"I don't know much about Chicago."

"That's all right, neither does anybody else in Old Town. You wouldn't believe the number of times I've had to explain that no, I wouldn't know somebody's second cousin who moved to Los Angeles twenty years ago."

"What pretty window decorations!" I said when Victor opened the last door with a flourish. One entire wall of the room had windows from the ceiling halfway down to the floor, and the windows were covered by an elaborate curling grille of iron scrolls and arabesques that looked like beautiful black lace against the light.

"Er— yes," Brad said. He and Victor seemed quietly amused about something. Oh well, I'd find out what it was later.

I peeked out through the grillwork and saw a small rooftop terrace. "That'll be a lovely place to sit outside in the evenings."

"It'll be a lovely place to set up a perimeter with trip wires," Brad muttered, with a disapproving glare at the tree that leaned overhead and shaded most of the terrace.

"*And*," said Victor with the flourish of someone who's saved the best for last, "there's a back staircase at the end of the hall here, that opens right into Msikiti Mkuu – that's Grand Mosque Road," he explained for our benefit. "Prajapati's store, downstairs, is on the edge of Old Town, but Msikiti Mkuu is right inside it. If you want to leave anonymously, you can just put on a bui-bui and stroll right out." He gave our footwear a dubious glance. "Brad, you and your friend might want to invest in some plain sandals. There are plenty of Swahili women with big feet, but none of them wear black loafers."

"Bui-bui?" Ben repeated.

"Those black bags the women wear," I reminded him. "They're a bit more complicated than that, but Fadiya showed me how to tie the head strings and tuck up the skirt and hold the veil, and I'll be happy to teach you guys."

Brad seemed to have come to a decision while I spoke. "Right, then. Victor, could you pick up three bui-buis for us? Will you need our measurements?"

"No, they're one-size-fits-all. The only variable is length." Victor measured us with his eyes. "One medium-short, one standard, one extra-tall. I'll get those tomorrow. I can say they're presents for my girlfriends back in America."

"I don't want to complicate your life," I started to apologize.

"On the contrary. It should raise my prestige tremendously if they think I have three girlfriends back home. It might also discourage Mama Aesha – one of my informants, a formidable old lady - from trotting out nice Swahili girls for me to marry. Really, I should have invented some girlfriends long ago," Victor assured me ebulliently. "But right now, I need to buy some tins from Prajapati."

"Tins?"

"Food tins. You can get take-out here, but they like you to provide your own dish."

"What, no Styrofoam?"

"It's making inroads. Prajapati has a closet full of used packing material in the back. But the good curry places still make you bring your own food tin. Chicken curry all right with everybody?"

The chicken curry was more than all right, and Mombasa went up yet another notch in my estimation. Lobster, shandies, curry, white sand beaches, authentic African art; this was more like what I'd expected when I applied for a passport in the momentary euphoria of actually graduating with honors. I made a mental note to be sure Lensky didn't 'forget' to get that mask shipped home from the Royal Court Hotel.

After we'd eaten Victor capped the evening by producing three bui-buis in varying lengths.

"Turns out Prajapati keeps some bui-buis in boxes at the back of his store," he explained. "It's amazing what the old guy can find in that stockroom. I wouldn't be surprised to find he's been holding the Twelfth Imam and the wreckage of MH370 until called for."

I stepped into the shortest bui-bui, tucked the front vee into the waistband of my jeans, tied the head strap under my chin and tucked the loose fabric of the top part over my forehead and under the strap at my temples. A couple of flips brought the remaining fabric forward to frame my face. I caught the last loose end of black nylon between two fingers, brought it up across my nose and mouth and gave the guys a triumphant look. Ben was still trying to get his Size Elevens through the tubular bottom half of the thing, and Lensky was just listening to Victor's instructions with a bemused look.

"I thought you just draped it over your head," he grumbled.

"Well… actually, I'm not totally sure how it goes," Victor confessed. "Never having worn one myself… You probably ought to get Thalia to show you. She seems to be quite the expert."

"A friend in Mogadishu showed me how to wear it," I explained.

It's not often I catch on to something physical faster than my colleagues, let alone more gracefully. I enjoyed a brief glow of satisfaction; then I tucked the loose end of the face veil out of the way and helped Ben and Lensky adjust their costumes. When we were done, Victor looked us all over carefully.

"Apart from the jeans peeking out under the hem, Thalia looks exactly like every other veiled woman in Mombasa. You probably want to wear something lighter weight under the bui-bui anyway, Thalia, that black nylon is a heat trap."

He turned his attention to the guys, and eventually pronounced that Ben *might* be able to pass for an exceptionally tall and light-skinned Swahili woman once he lost the glasses and replaced his loafers with sandals.

"I'll need sandals too," said Lensky, pushing folds of black nylon away from his face.

Victor's lips twitched. "Don't bother."

"I'm not going barefoot in this cesspool of tropical diseases!"

"That's not what I meant… Thalia, Ben. What do *you* see when you look at Lensky?"

The theory that bui-buis were one-size-fits-all came to grief over Lensky's broad shoulders; they strained the upper part of the loose tube to seam-ripping point. The supposed-to-be-loose tube, I mean.

The bits of the headdress that were supposed to be tucked into neat forehead and cheek folds stuck out from Lensky's head at crazy angles. As for the loose end that was supposed to be held over your nose and mouth by one corner, he'd crumpled it in one fist without even trying to pull it up over his face.

I did not laugh at my husband, but it was a very close thing.

"I'm sorry," Victor said. "Thalia looks natural enough, and you look passable, Ben, but *you*, Lensky, look like – like –"

"A very unhappy, very blond American case officer," I finished for him.

There was a ripping sound as Lensky extracted himself from the black nylon sack.

"I can't return that if you tear it!" Victor sounded alarmed.

"I will happily pay for the pleasure of ripping the thing," Lensky informed him. "I don't need the disguise anyway. I am a highly trained field officer; my tradecraft is quite adequate when I wish to evade surveillance."

And if he needed help, he could call on us to create a topological camouflage. But somehow I suspected it would not be tactful to mention our paranormal abilities right that minute.

"I'm sure you will manage just fine," Victor said, backing away. "And I, I expect you'd like some privacy now." He went on through the kitchen and shut the door to his bedroom in the front.

"Now," said Lensky, "let's see about adding some verisimilitude to this story that we're a honeymooning couple." And he took me, bui-bui and all, back to the gracious bedroom overlooking the terrace.

I hoped that Ben had brought something to read.

9. A smokeless flame

Less than a mile from the apartment over Prajapati General Merchandise was a small house that had originally been a guest apartment in Sheikh Mohamad Aboud's compound. After the assassination of the sheikh by al-Shabaab the entire compound had become unpopular with the locals; it was said to have been occupied by a group of *shetani* who resented a human presence.

Omar al-Zanji had explained to his people that there was no need to fear the *shetani* in the compound, because he possessed a *jini* who was, just like humans, a creation of Allah, and who could command the *shetani*. The men who'd followed him south, and the younger ones who'd joined him here in Mombasa, agreed in theory – but their eyes rolled when they had to enter the guest-house where Omar kept his *jini*. It wasn't that they saw anything, exactly; the djinn manifested herself to them only as a pervasive sense of cold, as a deeper shadow among shadows, as a shimmer of the smokeless flame from which Allah had created her. Only when Omar was alone, as now, did she take her preferred form as an almost-human woman of dazzling beauty.

"I have brought you gifts," he announced, laying out his new offerings on the cushions. A stack of glass bangles sparkled beside sticks of incense, a rosewood chest, two small vials of perfume.

The djinn drifted across the cushions, inspecting the items. The serpent's tail below her veils flicked the perfumes to the floor, shattering the fragile glass vials, and Omar winced.

"I do not love the scents of flowers," she told him. "If you would please me, bring me stronger perfumes. Cannot the perfumers of this city blend musk or civet into their goods?"

"Those are costly."

"You were able to afford them when you entrapped me *here*." The tail knocked over a tall blue glass bottle. This did not break.

"Serve me well, and you shall have them again."

The almost-human face frowned. "Have I not done enough for you already? Not contented with my embraces, with delights unknown to mortal man, you have sent me across the seas to bring lightning upon your enemies, yes, and to bring their children as tribute to your power! The men of the Suahil bow down before you."

"Not enough of them, not yet," said Omar, "and there are in this land other men who know not the proper fear of *majini*. Three such have come into the city, *wazungu* who dare to ask about the Rightly Guided. I must go to my island. After you transport me to Usirudi I wish you to return here. You will watch these newcomers, tell me of their doings, and affright them so that they will flee my wrath."

The *jini* reclined languorously upon cushions and stretched, displaying the seductive curves of her chosen form. "There are many men in this land. If I frighten these, will not more come to replace them? Have a care, little one, lest you draw on my power beyond your ability to repay."

"By the blue glass wherein I trapped you first, I will have it so!" Omar picked up the tall blue bottle and made as if to strike her with it. She winced away from the gesture, looking almost human, almost vulnerable.

"So long as the power of the glass remains, so must I serve you," she said with a very human-looking pout. "But why must you always demand such harsh tasks? *Once* I served you in your bed, and you swore that you would never ask more than the delights I brought there."

"If I did, I was drunk upon pleasure."

"Sweet, sweet intoxication!" She flung a pale, rounded arm around his neck. "We could know that again…"

"After you have made me a great man, as you promised." Omar lifted the tempting arm, kissed the *jini*'s fingertips, then threw her hand away from him. "And after you learn not to come to my bed in *that* form." He pointed with disgust at the scaly tail twitching below her veils. "Your serpent's tail disgusts me!"

The *jini* wept and vanished, leaving only the shadow of smokeless flames in the air.

***

"Did you just feel a cold breeze?" I pulled up the sheet that we had somehow kicked to the bottom of the bed and wrapped it over my shoulders.

"No such luck." Lensky stretched out his arm and pulled me close. "You must be acclimatizing. Only Mombasa lifers could call this cold – aiee!" He shivered. "Does this place have air conditioning? And did Victor just turn it on?"

I didn't think the apartment came with air conditioning. The windows onto the terrace had no glass; only that elaborate ironwork stood between us and the night air. "See, you felt it too."

"Only for a minute. And it could have been you trying to warm your feet on me again. You have the *coldest* feet."

***

In the morning we heard screams and weeping from the store below the apartment. Mr. Prajapati told us that his wife was distraught; some creature had crept into the store during the night and had killed her cat. Worse, she had heard the cat's anguished cries and had run into the store in time to see the killer – or rather, the shadow where the killer was not.

"She is very certain that it was a *shetani,*" he said. "You understand, my wife was born here. She is a good Hindu, but she grew up on the stories of these Arabs who believe in djinn and devils and all manner of evil spirits. I will have to send for a sheikh to heal her, and those bastards – I mean, those good men charge three times the usual price to come to a Hindu!"

Lensky inquired about the price. It didn't seem to be exorbitant – about four thousand Kenya shillings, or forty American dollars. He offered to pay for the exorcism, saying that although we had intended no harm, it was always possible that the spirits had been disturbed by *wazungu* moving into this quarter of the city.

"I just hope Prajapati doesn't make a habit of asking you to pay for exorcisms," Victor said, shaking his head over this generosity.

"Oh, I don't think he will," Lensky said gravely. "Mrs. Prajapati doesn't have any more cats."

***

"I send you against these *wazungu*, and all you do is kill a cat!" Omar grumbled.

The *jini* swished her tail irritably. "You did not warn me that the *wazungu* have a serpent-spirit of their very own. I was lucky to escape with my tail intact!"

"Nonsense! *Wazungu* do not even believe in the spirit world. They could not possibly have a *jini*."

"I did not say it was a *jini*. It was of a form unfamiliar to me. The body glittered like metal, and the head was horribly deformed, all beak and eyes. But it could see me, and if I had not made my escape it would have struck and fastened that beak in my beautiful tail." The *jini* flicked her tail forward and stroked the scales lovingly.

***

"What, could you not see the djinn?" Mr. M. demanded.

"No, I could not see the djinn. Tell me about it."

"She had the face of a woman and the tail of a serpent."

"What about the rest of it?"

"Of her," Mr. M. corrected me. "She was slinky and seductive, for those vulnerable to that sort of thing." Since his acquisition of a robot snake body, Mr. M.'s only sensual temptations involved coffee and sugar. "Richly decorated with jewels and henna patterns and floating silks of brilliant color. A pity you could not see it for yourself. It is the way of the Djnoun—"

"Dudge-noon?"

"*Djnoun*," Mr. M. snapped. "The Arabic plural. It is their way to veil themselves from mortal sight, but you will know of their presence because it becomes cold wherever they pass. When she realized that *I* could see her, she fled."

I remembered the sudden chill last night, and shivered – but not from cold this time. It seemed we had been very, very lucky that Mr. M. had chosen to spend last night with us, in the bedroom overlooking the terrace.

"Can a djinn hurt, ah, real people?"

"Some of the Djnoun are very powerful indeed," Mr. M. informed me. "Did not Solomon use his Seal to compel the Djnoun to build his palaces? Did not the Prophet warn his followers to cover their utensils at night, to close their doors and windows against the Djnoun and keep their children with them? No doubt," he added reflectively, "the Prophet would also have told them to keep their cats close by, were it not that neither god nor djinn nor man can rule a cat."

Lensky had joined us in time to heard that last statement, and he gave a sharp crack of laughter. "Doubtless he would have said the same of topologists!"

I found that I did not like our lovely windows onto the terrace quite as well as I had at first. But Mr. M. promised me that he would spend every night in our room and would be constantly vigilant against the djinn.

Shortly afterwards Lensky received a call from Nelson Finch that wiped the laughter from his face. "I have to go, Thalia. We'll talk tonight."

"What happened?"

"There's been a… communication."

He was tight-lipped, unwilling to tell me anything more than that a video had appeared on the Internet, purporting to be a communication from Jeshi-la-Rashiduni.

"The ransom demand?"

"Finch didn't say. He just said I'd want to see it for myself." He kissed me and was gone before I could offer to save him the trouble of a cross-city journey evading possible surveillance. Dammit! I could have raised camouflage around both of us and teleported him to… no, I couldn't, not without his help. I had never been to the CIA office. For the first time I wondered if Finch had some sinister reason for trying to keep me out of the loop. No, that made no sense. He'd made it abundantly clear that he had no respect for me as an investigator or as anything else. It was probably nothing more than that he wanted to play Spy vs. Spy with his old buddy Brad and didn't want to be bothered with Brad's young wife hanging around. It *couldn't* be anything more than that.

Could it?

Victor was extremely unhelpful when I asked him about tracking down this video that had Finch and Lensky so upset.

"What is it?" I demanded after I got fed up with his vague evasions. "Did Brad tell you not to let the little woman in on anything?"

"No, no, nothing like that!" Victor protested. "The thing is… Look, Thalia, when Dr. Salinas got in touch with me about doing a favor for some friends of his friend in Texas, he didn't tell me you were going after Jeshi-la-Rashiduni."

"What do you know about them?"

Victor backed away from me, hands up. "Nothing! Nothing at all… and I'd like to keep it that way. Look, you people blow in to town, you blow out, you don't care what kind of a mess you leave behind. Me, I've invested nine months in cultivating relationships, finding informants, getting into this community. And I have another six months of work to do, *minimum*, before I have enough data to make the dissertation committee happy. Plus, the director of the Fort Jesus Museum just invited me to co-author a monograph on the Swahili artifacts found at the dig on Shanga. I'm not going to blow all that, get run out of town, probably even have to leave the coast, just because you want to poke sticks into the Rashiduni anthill. It's not healthy to ask questions about those people."

I sat down, slowly, concentrating on looking as small and unthreatening as possible. Very few people actually do perceive me as a threat, but Victor seemed to be well and truly spooked. "Okay. I understand your point of view, and I won't ask you to betray any confidences or put yourself at risk. Only, as a personal favor, could you share with me what you do know about the Rashiduni? I understood they were a very new group. How could they have got everyone in Mombasa so scared, so fast?"

"I don't know about everyone in Mombasa," Victor hedged. But he sat down opposite me.

"Well, I asked around about them on our first day here, and four separate people reacted just like you're doing now. They don't know about any Rashiduni, they don't know anybody named Omar, they hardly even go to the mosque never mind listening to inflammatory preachers, and they were just about to leave town for a long vacation up-country."

"I don't want to leave town for a long vacation up-country. I need to stay here and keep doing my research."

"And the sooner we're out of your hair, the easier that will be. I get that. But Victor, we're not going to go away just because you're uncomfortable with us. There are children involved here. Steve Harrison – Lensky's boss? His son was kidnapped by the Rashiduni, and they took two other little kids at the same time. *American* kids," I emphasized.

"They brought them *here?* How did they pull that off?"

"We're still working it out. But do you really think we're going to abandon those children?"

Victor heaved a weary sigh. "No. I get that. I just – wish you'd left me out of it."

"You've been a tremendous help already," I said, and he winced. Oops – praise wasn't going to work in this situation, was it? Once again, I wished we had developed a practical algorithm for telepathy. I would have *loved* to reach into Victor's brain and extract everything he knew about Jeshi-la-Rashiduni.

Oops again. Maybe it was just as well we didn't have those powers. I was starting to sound like Steve Harrison, wasn't I?

I still wanted to see this rumored video, but that could wait. There was bound to be a wi-fi hot spot in town where I could take out my phone and do a search. For now, I needed to concentrate on, well, finding out everything Victor knew about the Rashiduni.

Politely. Gently. Without force or telepathy – neither of which were available to me anyway. Wasn't that great? Society was still safe from me.

And the Jeshi-la-Rashiduni were safe from Victor, who claimed to know nothing but the most common gossip. They were a new group, supposedly Mombasa-based, but they had consolidated power on some of the offshore islands as well. And he knew absolutely nothing about any children being taken by the group.

He said this so firmly that I couldn't help but suspect he'd heard something even before I mentioned the kidnapping. But I didn't know what, much less how to get it out of him. Lensky was the professional; we could have used his interrogation skills here. But Victor had shut himself up in the front bedroom "to transcribe informant interviews" long before Brad returned to the apartment.

Brad's arrival did eventually tempt Victor out of his room, but by that time we had other things to talk about. Victor hovered, as curious as I was about what the CIA guys had learned today.

"Tell me about the video," I asked. "Was it a ransom demand?"

Lensky sighed dramatically, the way he usually did when he wanted me to feel like an unnecessarily troublesome female. "It was not a ransom demand, but it did suggest that the Rashiduni have Sam Harrison and the other two children. It was nothing but threats. The best that we *wazungu* could hope for was never to see the children again. If we left East Africa immediately, we could enjoy that outcome. If not... we might see their bodies."

I swallowed, hard. How did you deal with people who used the bodies of innocent children as weapons of war?

"So... are we leaving?"

"Thalia, we can't comply with their demands. Even if it weren't against all American policy... who exactly did they mean, when they said the *wazungu* must leave? You and me and Ben? Finch and Taylor? Every foreigner in Mombasa?" He shook his head. "If the three of us leave, we lose our best chance of finding those kids, and yet they'll still be able to claim their demands haven't been met. Where's Ben?"

"Taking a nap, why?" There wasn't much else to do during the hottest part of the day here. Ben and I had both been too curious about that video to take off for the beach again.

"I want him to come back to the office with me to analyze the video.

95

Maybe he can think of some way that your special skills can help us identify the speaker and location."

"Good idea, I'll come too."

"You will *not.*"

"Brad, what did you bring me for, if you weren't going to let me do anything to help?"

"What, specifically, are you offering to do?"

"Well, I can think about topological applications as well as Ben."

"I don't need the two of you on the same task."

"What, you have something else for me to do?"

Victor intervened at that point. "If you like, Thalia, I could introduce you to Mama Aesha's household this evening. She and her family have been some of my most helpful informants. You might learn something from listening to them, if only understanding the culture better. You'll have to leave that snake thing here, though," he cautioned. "They're sure to think it's a djinn." I'm not sure what Victor himself thought Mr. M. was; we hadn't exactly explained much. He mostly coped by looking away and pretending he hadn't noticed the silver talking snake with the turtle head.

Lensky brightened. "The very thing! It would be *extremely* helpful, Thalia, if you could start making contacts in the local community. Just as you did in Mogadishu. We'd never have got this far if you hadn't befriended Fatima."

"Fadiya."

"Whoever."

He went on lavishing praise on me for that bit of luck until even the vainest of women would have had to realize he was overdoing it madly. Easy enough to read between *these* lines. Brad was the founder and president of the "Keep Thalia out of trouble" club, and Victor and Ben had signed on as charter members.

I couldn't force him to let me in on the CIA's plans, though. So I pretended to swallow all the overblown compliments at face value and played like I was perfectly happy to spend an evening getting to know Victor's informants while Brad and Ben went off to do the heavy lifting. I'd just have to find some way to insert myself back into the loop tomorrow.

Besides, I wanted to ask Mr. M. something, preferably out of Lensky's hearing. I'd been thinking over Fadiya's story and thought I'd finally recognized the most important thing she'd told us.

Twice.

In the back bedroom, while I was supposed to be getting myself up in the bui-bui for a visit in Old Town, I asked Mr. M. about his translations.

"You told me that Fadiya referred to 'that fiend' Omar married. What was the actual word she used?"

"*Jini*, of course."

"She wasn't just being rude about her husband's second wife?"

"No. It was an entirely accurate description."

"Omar the Zanzibari married a djinn? Can people do that?"

"Even though they were created of smokeless fire rather than of earth, the Djnoun are also creatures of Allah," Mr. M. reminded me. "They can have faith or reject it, follow the Prophet or not, as their free will dictates. Certainly they marry among themselves, and I know of no reason why one could not wed a human being."

"And – was that the djinn who visited us last night? Omar's second wife?"

"Occam's razor would suggest an affirmative answer."

Mr. M's description of the djnoun suggested another question. "Do they have names? I mean, does this one have a name?"

Mr. M. considered the question. "Not exactly. She is a *sila*, a rare type of djinn who specializes in the seduction of humans, and she thinks of herself simply as TheSila."

"The sila," I repeated.

"No. TheSila. Capital letters, no spaces."

"And you know her preferred punctuation how?"

Mr. M. sniffed. "It is obvious to the meanest intelligence."

Victor banged on the door and asked just how long it was going to take me to put on the bui-bui.

10. A friend and a djinn

Since Victor hadn't been trained in counter-surveillance, I expected that our walk to his informant's house would be straightforward and that I'd have no trouble finding my way back to the apartment.

Anybody who's familiar with Mombasa's Old Town – you can stop laughing now, okay?

Part of the problem was that the bui-bui interfered with rubbernecking. As Victor led me down one twisting alley after another, I tried to take in all the exotic details illuminated by the fading sunlight. There was plenty to look at: the windows covered with ornamental iron grilles like the one in our bedroom, the whitewashed arches opening onto private gardens, the second-story balconies built out over the street, the shops advertising everything from authentic tribal drums to African costumes. I quickly learned that Fadiya's lesson in how to wear the bui-bui had not covered such fine points as how not to trip over the hem while gawking at the carved balcony overhead or how not to drop the veil while raising my skirts above the unidentifiable glop in the gutter at my feet. Victor wouldn't even let me window-shop; he took a firm hold of my elbow through the bui-bui and yanked me away from the infinitely promising Mvita Boutique.

"Only tourists shop there," he told me.

"I am a tourist."

"Fine, you can go back there when you're dressed like a tourist. Right now, you're impersonating a modest Swahili girl. Do you want to ruin my standing with Mama Aesha?"

I gazed wistfully at three women on the other side of the narrow street. Their bui-buis floated freely from the face ties and the skirts were tucked into their belts, displaying their colorful dresses and giving them plenty of freedom to laugh, gesture, and call greetings up to their friends on the balconies.

It did just flit across my mind that I was not personally invested in Victor's good standing with this Aesha woman. But I refrained from picking a fight with him in the street. As he'd said, I could always come back later without the bui-bui.

If I could find the place again. Just as it began to sink in how far from the apartment we'd come and how short on street signs this place was, Victor halted in front of one of those white arches in the wall. It was partially closed off by a huge wooden door standing slightly ajar.

With spikes on.

No, really. Most of the doors along this street were ornamented with patterns of nasty-looking spikes protruding anywhere from three to nine inches out into the street, and this was one of the most impressive doors we'd come across.

"*Hodi*," he called through the opening. "Mama Aesha?"

"*Vikitori! Karibu, mwanangu mzungu!*" An enormous woman draped in black pushed the door out of the way and surged forward, all but enveloping Victor in a motherly embrace. I was impressed. My own mother does quite a majestic surge-and-billow move, but Mama Aesha must have been three times her size. Now *there* was a bui-bui that could have accommodated even Brad's shoulders; clearly Victor had been wrong when he told us they were all the same size.

Like the cheerful women I'd seen on the street, Mama Aesha wore her bui-bui so open that it was only a token cover-up. Underneath it she was wearing a few miles of bright yellow cotton fabric printed with large blue and purple flowers. As Victor struggled out of her embrace, he waved one hand towards me and said something that I assumed was an introduction. Mama Aesha grabbed me with one plump hand and urged me forward into the courtyard. I stepped on my hem and would have gone flat on my face if Victor hadn't caught me; Mama Aesha had taken the hand I was using to keep my skirts out of the street.

More rapid-fire Swahili followed, seasoned with plenty of laughter, as the other women sitting in the courtyard took in my appearance. A couple of the younger women made a sort of half-hearted gesture towards twitching their veils in front of their faces as Victor came in; the old ladies didn't even bother with that much.

"Don't worry," Victor murmured. "They think you're cute."

Many people who didn't know me suffered from the same misapprehension.

"And you made a big hit by wearing the bui-bui," he went on. "Shows you respect their customs."

I really wished I'd ignored Victor's advice and tucked Mr. M. under the bui-bui. How was I going to find out anything useful when I couldn't understand a word they said?

This melancholy reflection was interrupted by a round of "*Hujambo*" and "*Sijambo*" with the women sitting around the courtyard. Okay, so I could understand two words. That didn't get me much farther.

It did get me some smiles of approval, though. Using the correct coastal forms for greetings, rather than the simplified up-country version, might even have bought me more points than the bui-bui. Too bad that was all the Swahili I knew.

Victor's promise to translate for me was worth almost as much as my promise to Lensky that I'd stay out of the CIA's investigation until called for. He did try at the beginning, but there were too many women and children giggling and talking and expecting him to respond. Then an older man wearing a white coat and an embroidered fez-type hat came outside and said something to him, gesturing towards the shadowy interior of the house.

"I'm invited to have coffee with Sheikh Abdallah and the other men before dinner," Victor said. "You'll be all right here. The women will probably talk more freely without a man's presence anyway."

And a lot of good *that* was going to do me.

I'd thought the ladies in Mama Aesha's extended family looked pretty comfortable already, but on Victor's departure they relaxed visibly and the younger women let their veils float free again. There was an extremely old lady squatting on the ground, beneath a huge tree that shaded the whole courtyard. She picked up a flat basket piled with rice and began shaking it, just as Fadiya had done in Mogadishu. Two of the children started peeling some kind of bright fruit, and the woman beside Mama Aesha knelt on the ground to chop up something on a broad, scarred wooden board. Another old lady hobbled up to hand me two coconut halves and an iron thing about thirty inches tall. It had a crossbar at the bottom and something that looked like the silhouette of a pineapple or an outsize grenade at the top. That top bit had ugly-looking sharp edges. I thanked her and looked blankly at the coconut halves. The iron thing was a total mystery to me. I knew what the coconut halves were, but what was I supposed to do with them?

There followed a lively session of laughter – lots of laughter – and demonstrations from Old Lady Two, one of the young women, and a girl who couldn't have been more than seven. Evidently you were supposed to put your feet on the crossbar, clamp your knees around the upright, drop half a coconut over the sharp-edged bit at the top, and move the coconut around over the sharp edges to cut off the meat. Which, when anybody else demonstrated the thing, dropped compliantly into the shallow dish at their feet. When I tried it, I got a few mini-shreds of coconut, most of which flew off to mix with the dirt of the courtyard.

They assured me with gestures that I'd get the hang of it if I kept practicing – and apparently they intended to keep me at it until I got it right. I'd had a softball coach like that once. In fourth grade, where softball was not optional. She gave up on me after three weeks of extra practices.

The young woman who'd given the best demonstration dropped down on the bench beside me. "Don't let them bother you," she said. "They actually love it that you're willing to try."

I wouldn't have described myself as "willing" so much as "bullied into complaisance," but by now I was only too happy to get any positive feedback, however undeserved.

"You speak English!" I said. Being, you know, a highly trained observer and almost an official CIA operative, I pick up on these little details.

"I went to college in America for two years," the girl said. She started to offer me her hand, then realized that both my hands were fully occupied with fighting the coconut half. "My name is Zawadi. Mama Aesha is my great-grandmother."

I blinked in surprise. Sea air must be extremely good for the complexion, if the vital woman who'd hugged Victor was a great-grandmother. Then, remembering Fadiya, I reminded myself that they started early here.

"My name is Thalia," I started, and then remembered that didn't work in Swahili. "Except most people here call me Saliya." I wanted to ask Zawadi a lot of things, but most of them seemed too rude to blurt out on first acquaintance. Things like, "Why on earth did you come back from America?" and "You're not going to *marry* someone here, are you? Because based on Fadiya's experience, I don't recommend it."

For all I knew, she could be a married mother of three already. I settled for an anodyne, "It's nice to meet someone who speaks English. After Victor went inside I was afraid I wouldn't understand anything anybody said."

"Ah, Vikitori." Even Zawadi, who was quite well able to handle the consonant clusters in words like 'great-grandmother,' took a firm line with proper names and forced them into a Swahili format. "Yes, he speaks quite good Swahili... for an *mzungu*. He is your husband?"

"Good Lord, no!" I sawed at the coconut half for a moment, trying to think of a culture-appropriate way to describe our relationship. "Paid agent," probably wasn't a concept that had a large following in these parts. "He is, ah, a friend of my husband's," I managed eventually. "My husband had to work tonight, so he asked Victor to introduce me to some of his Swahili friends." I hoped that sounded adequately respectable.

"Ah, you are married! Lucky you!" exclaimed Zawadi, following that up with, "Married women have *so* much more freedom."

"Not always." I thought of a way to edge round to the topic I most wanted to discuss. "I knew a girl in Mogadishu, her husband married her here and made her move to Somalia with him and then he went back to Zanzibar and married again and then he divorced her and abandoned her in Mogadishu."

"You must not judge all Swahili by one bad man," Zawadi said.

"I suppose you're right. I'd like to find her husband, though, maybe try and shame him into at least paying her way home. She said he'd settled in Mombasa with his new wife. Do any of your family happen to know him, I wonder? Omar al-Zanji?"

Zawadi's whole body tensed, and Mama Aesha spoke to her sharply. She lowered her head and answered humbly, fingers spread in a deprecating gesture. I thought I heard "Omar" and "Unguja," in her brief answer.

"Unguja" was the Swahili name for Zanzibar, I knew that much.

Mama Aesha's long reply ended with her slicing one hand downwards in an emphatic "cut it out" gesture.

Before she got to that, though, she made copious use of another word that I happened to know.

Jini.

11. The Army of Peace

Lensky and Ben still weren't back by the time Victor and I returned from a late dinner at Mama Aesha's compound. We didn't compare notes until the next morning, over coffee and some kind of pastries from the store downstairs.

"These are great!" I told Victor, snagging the last triangular coconut-flavored thingie off the communal plate. Apart from not having a hole in the middle and not being glazed, it was almost like a doughnut.

"*Mahamri*," Victor contributed, beaming. "And the little round things with them are gungo peas cooked in coconut milk."

"Gungo?"

"I don't know another name for them."

"Doesn't matter. They're delicious."

I began to understand my new friends' emphasis on coconut processing. The people of this city could do wonderful things with coconuts.

"And the spicy pastries are *kachori*. They're more of an Indian thing; Mrs. Prajapati makes them herself. The others come from a nearby bakery."

"Well, let's keep them coming by all means."

Victor watched as I licked my fingers. "Too many of those *mahamri*, and you'll start to look like Mama Aesha," he warned.

"Piffle." I chased down a crumbly bit of *kachori* that had somehow been overlooked. "I hardly got anything to eat last night."

Not that the dinner had been inadequate – everything had looked, and smelled, wonderful, and there'd been plenty of it – but I wasn't up to speed on the local table manners. A huge tray of white rice had been the centerpiece of the meal. You were supposed to dip the first two fingers of your right hand into the rice, come out with a perfectly cohesive ball of sticky rice, dip this into one of the delicious-smelling dishes of anonymous glop, and pop the whole thing into your mouth without dropping anything. I didn't have anything like the fine motor coordination required to pull this off. As a result, I'd eaten hardly anything until, way too late in the meal, it occurred to me that this was an excellent situation for small object manipulation. Applying the appropriate topology got me at least a taste of goat curry, spiced chickpeas, and other delightful things. Unfortunately, by then it was too late to make the most of my suddenly developed "skill."

Victor, of course, had eaten with the men of the house. Indoors. First. So he hadn't actually observed my struggles with the rice platter.

"Anyway," I added when the plates on the table were completely bare, "I burn a lot of energy." Applying topology, especially for major jobs like teleportation, is extremely calorie-intensive; one of the primary responsibilities of Ben's girlfriend, the receptionist at the Center, is keeping a supply of doughnuts available for topologists who've overdone it and need a quick blood-sugar fix. But Ben and I hadn't exactly discussed that part of our skill set with Victor, and Lensky would probably disapprove if I tried to explain.

I leaned back with my third cup of coffee. (They were very small cups.) "So, Brad. Did you and Ben get anything new out of that video last night?"

"Well, it wasn't made here in Mombasa," Lensky said. "At least, we don't think so."

That got my attention. "Wait a minute. Fadiya said Omar had come back to Mombasa, and the reaction at Mama Aesha's supported that."

"What reaction?" Victor demanded. "Did you spook my informants? How – dammit, you don't even speak Swahili!"

Shed a different light on his generous offer to let me sit in the courtyard all evening, didn't it? He'd expected I would be totally unable to communicate.

I waved a placatory hand at him. "*I* didn't spook anybody. Mama Aesha took exception to something Zawadi said, that's all." True, she'd said it in response to my questioning, but there was no need to bother our touchy anthropologist with that minor detail.

"Zawadi… oh, yes. One of the younger women, isn't she? How do *you* know what she said, anyway?"

I took great pleasure in informing him that Zawadi had studied in America for two years and spoke fluent English. From the look on Victor's face, it was clear this was news to him. Hmm. Even if Swahili social customs prevented him from spending much time with the women of the household, I'd have thought a competent anthropologist would at least have compiled a list of family members and some basic biographical data.

I told Lensky and Ben what I'd gleaned from the evening out, and in return they told me what they'd learned about the Rashiduni.

"They may organize and recruit here in Mombasa," Brad summarized, "but their real power base is on the offshore islands between here and Zanzibar. The fact that jurisdiction over those islands is split three ways doubtless helps; some of them are under Kenyan control, some are governed from mainland Tanzania, and others are so close to Zanzibar that they're treated as part of the big island for official purposes. While the Rashiduni have been keeping a low profile here, they've consolidated control over a whole set of those little islands in just the past few months. That's one reason we think the video wasn't made here."

Several months ago, when Omar al-Zanji split off from al-Shabaab, he'd taken a crack fighting unit made up of Kenyan and Tanzanian recruits with him. Now they were part of the Jeshi-la-Rashiduni, but just to make things more confusing they frequently used their old title, Jeshi-la-Amani.

"The Army of Peace," Victor interpolated.

As the elite fighting arm of the Rashiduni, the Army of Peace had launched simultaneous attacks on police stations, schools and government buildings all across the southern islands. Those attacks had won huge prestige for the Rashiduni in Mombasa and Dar-es-Salaam. They had also essentially paralyzed the underpaid, poorly supported government services of the little islands sprinkled between here and Zanzibar. Most of the schools were completely closed; the surviving teachers had this strange reluctance to work in places where their colleagues had been beheaded.

An elder on one of the islands was quoted as saying that the Jeshi-la-Amani had told them the children should not go to government schools where they were taught only lies. The Rashiduni would start their own classes in Islamic education and other matters that true men of the Swahili ought to master.

There didn't seem to be any concern about educating true *women* of the Swahili. Why was I not surprised?

"Why hasn't the government gone after them?"

Victor shook his head knowingly. "Do you have any idea how difficult it is to get the governments of Kenya and Tanzania to cooperate? Not to mention the Revolutionary Government of Zanzibar, which routinely opposes the mainland Tanzanian government on principle. They can't even get on the same page for a basic anti-piracy policy, and that's a lot less of a political hot potato than putting down an insurgency. It could take *years* for them to organize a joint military action on the islands. And in the meantime—" He spread his hands and shrugged.

"If Kenya makes a show of force, they can flee to the Tanzanian islands. If Tanzania strikes at them, they can reverse direction. And since neither government is eager to get into another guerrilla war on the Swahili coast, the easiest thing is to ignore the whole problem," Lensky summarized.

"Wait, *another* guerrilla war?"

"Mozambique – ah, that's the next country south of Tanzania, and their coast is also Swahili-dominated – had a remarkably nasty guerrilla war against the Portuguese in the sixties and seventies. After they got independence in '75, that turned into a civil war that lasted all the way into the nineties. And as if that weren't enough, a new insurgency flared up about five years ago over contested elections. The country is a basket case, and you'd better believe Nairobi and Dar-es-Salaam have made note of the trouble a war with the coastal families can cause."

All these wars and rumors of war made my head hurt. I desperately wanted to bury myself in something nice and straightforward like *Introduction to Homotopic Topology*, where definitions were consistent and theorems followed naturally from axioms. I mentally chalked up yet another way in which pure mathematics was vastly superior to all other callings: nobody in the history of mathematics had ever tried to settle a dispute with a Korean-made AK-47.

Yes, the guys had gone straight from civil war stories to an animated discussion of what arms the Rashiduni were most likely using. I think the jumping-off point had been Brad's assertion that he'd recognized the weapon hoisted by a guard in the background of the video as the North Korean version of an AK-47, but both Ben and Victor had plunged into the discussion as though they actually knew what they were talking about. Well, possibly Victor did. But I *knew* Ben was winging it; he'd once asked me, of all people, to explain the difference between a shotgun and a rifle.

I decided to go downstairs and see if Mr. Prajapati happened to have notepads and pens among his stock. I prefer a yellow legal pad and black ink for thinking about topology, but in emergency I could settle for a lined composition book and anything that would make marks.

I never made it past the front door of the apartment, though, because a girl swathed in black nylon was scampering up the stairs, about ten times more gracefully than I ever expected to manage under the handicap of all those layers of fabric.

"*Hodi*, Saliya! *Hujambo?*" It was Zawadi. She'd come to invite me on a shopping expedition. I felt just slightly guilty about abandoning the guys at this impasse. But what the heck – from all appearances, they were going to be doing Gun Talk for the rest of the morning. Going to the sandal shop with Zawadi could hardly be less productive than that.

And it turned out to be a lot more fun. Zawadi wasn't actually in the market for sandals for herself; she just thought I needed something to give me a little flash under the bui-bui, maybe some sandals with gold straps or some pretty beads for my ankles.

Walking with Zawadi was a lot more pleasant than being towed through Old Town by Victor, because most of the time she was as relaxed about our bui-buis as the women I'd seen on the street yesterday. With the waist vee of the bui-bui hitched up into the belt of my one respectable dress and the top half of the thing floating freely from the head strap, I could navigate better than before and had far better opportunities to take in the Old Town scene.

The sandal-maker took a good look at my feet, sent his assistant to rummage through the stock on the top shelves at the back of the shop, and produced a display of brilliant, glitzy footwear. We spent a very pleasant hour trying everything on. With some reluctance, I passed on a pair of high-heeled sandals with huge fake rubies embedded in the heels. They added three much-needed inches to my height, and Zawadi giggled that they imparted a very interesting sway to my walk, but realism interfered. I'd already come close to breaking my neck just trying to manage the bui-bui in flats; in these puppies, I probably wouldn't make it down the block.

"You can wear them when you go to *mzungu* places like the Royal Court Hotel," Zawadi suggested, "or when you go home to America."

Very true. And Lensky's eyes tended to light up in a very interesting way whenever I wore my high-heeled black patent leather sandals. It would be – scientific – to find out whether the ruby-heeled gilt ones affected him the same way. I left that shop with both my old American sandals and the new high-heeled ones in a plastic bag. On my feet I was sporting modest flats whose scalloped red straps were stamped with gilt elephants.

Zawadi's veils went up and down, back and forth, as we sashayed to the perfumer's store that was to be our next stop. "Oh, there's my cousin!" she would exclaim as we turned a corner, and like magic the headdress flipped into place while she exchanged prolonged but modest greetings with a young man. Half a block farther on we would meet somebody else she knew, but this time she would drop the veil entirely. "It's all right, Saliya," she didn't exactly explain, "he's my *cousin*."

Too bad I wasn't an anthropologist like Victor. It seemed to me that the rules about wearing the veil in Mombasa were complex enough to be worth a dissertation in their own right.

On the way to the perfumer's Zawadi explained that everybody who was anybody in Mombasa had her own personally blended scent. We wouldn't be bringing my perfume home with us today; this was a preliminary sitting, where the designer would dab samples of various scents on my skin, wait a few minutes, and observe how my personal bodily spirits reacted. "The old women think it's a kind of magic, but it is actually very scientific," she told me.

It was also *slow*. I wasn't in training for this sort of thing; at home I don't spend a lot of time on stuff like cosmetics and hairstyling. The perfumer's stall had a generous shaded area out front, with chairs for customers who liked that sort of thing and plenty of squatting space for the more traditionally minded. From a social/anthropological standpoint, it seemed to serve the same function as the beauty parlor where my mother got her Greek hair tamed into a bulletproof helmet once a week. Women could get out of the house, spend hours in the shade chatting with their friends, give the gossip of the day a good stir and put it back in the pot newly enriched. And husbands didn't dare complain because everybody knew that a quality perfume job couldn't be achieved in a hurry. At least so Zawadi and the other girls at the perfumer's assured me.

After a quick introduction, Zawadi started chattering to a chance-met friend while the perfumer got down to work dabbing one of my wrists with jasmine, orchid and citron essence, all of which I liked. The inside of my elbow got sandalwood and cedar, which I thought were kind of heavy until he got hold of the other arm and laid on the really heavy stuff like patchouli, musk and civet.

It took forever; each little sample required a wait of several minutes before he sniffed my skin and made notes in a little leather-bound notebook. I squinted at the notes, but they didn't look like writing so much as a series of occult symbols. Zawadi explained that his notes were encoded to prevent anybody from stealing his trade secrets. Apparently being a perfumer in Mombasa was a cutthroat profession.

Even though Zawadi kept assuring me that our time there was well spent, it seemed to me that she was getting more and more nervous as the perfumer went on with his work. She glanced out at the sunny street every few minutes, and her chatter with her friend got more and more shrill and strained. I asked if she was going to be in trouble for spending too much time shopping with me, and she assured me again that everybody understood you couldn't spend too much time getting a good, professional perfume job. But there was a fine line between her eyebrows now, and her eyes kept flickering towards the street.

Finally, just as the perfumer announced that his research was done and that he would have my own personal scent compounded and ready for me in a few days, Zawadi stood up and waved at someone across the street.

Yet another young man.

"Saliya, this is my cousin Khamisi," Zawadi announced, practically hauling me out of the perfume shop while I clutched at my bui-bui. "What a coincidence to see you here, Khamisi!"

Khamisi was about my age, medium height with a pleasant enough face sporting a thin mustache, and dressed in Western-style shirt and pants. "Show some respect, Zawadi!"

Zawadi giggled and explained that technically Khamisi was her uncle, not her cousin. "I bow before your white beard, *mzee*!" They went through the same semi-formal ritual that Zawadi had done with the other two 'cousins,' inquiring about a long list of relatives by name and exclaiming, "Thanks be to Allah!" after the assertion that each one was well. This time they did it in English, rather than Swahili, which was nice of them, but the greeting formula still didn't mean a lot to me. And I didn't think I was picking up any lover-like overtones between them. Though I wasn't totally sure about that; breathing in all those scents had left me feeling a bit light-headed. I really wanted to go home and wash all the samples off.

"Yes, I think that is a very good idea," Zawadi said when I suggested it. "Khamisi will walk you home; I should be getting back now."

"Oh, he doesn't need—" I started, before realizing that unless I could casually slip out of their sight to teleport, somebody did need to take me home. Somewhere between the sandal shop and the perfumer's I had become completely turned around, and I had no clue how to navigate the maze of narrow streets back to Prajapati General Merchandise and the apartment above the store.

"It will not be improper for him to walk with you," Zawadi assured me, "everybody knows that *wazungu* have different rules for their women. In fact, perhaps it would be best if you do not wear the bui-bui on the way back. If everybody can see that you are *mzungu*, they will think nothing of Khamisi's escorting you."

It was almost noon, and the tapering streets cut off any possibility of a cooling sea breeze. I was *fine* with the idea of shedding my yards of black nylon. I stepped into the shelter of the perfumer's stall to take off my bui-bui and roll it up, stuffed it into the plastic bag with the sandals, and thanked Zawadi for a most entertaining morning.

On the way back to the apartment I found out what the real point of the morning's excursion had been.

Khamisi wasn't Zawadi's boyfriend.

He was the connection to Omar al-Zanji I'd asked for.

Via the Rashiduni.

Khamisi promised to wait on Grand Mosque Road while I ran up the back stairs to see who else was home. He probably thought I was worried about being caught by my husband with a strange man in our apartment; actually, of course, it was Victor I wanted to avoid. I wanted to hire Khamisi to spy on the Rashiduni for us, and Victor would probably throw seven kinds of fits about that notion.

Either he wasn't home, though, or he was in his room transcribing interview notes. I told Lensky and Ben to grab chairs and wait in the big bedroom at the back. (Two degrees of separation from Victor seemed a prudent minimum.)

Khamisi had a strange expression when I led him up the stairs and invited him into a room that was dominated by an outsize bed, but he relaxed when he saw that there were already two other men there. Not only that, but Lensky had had the forethought to snag an extra chair for the visitor.

"Khamisi, this is my husband Brad."

"Biradi." Khamisi nodded.

"And our friend Ben... um, Benjamin." Seemed like his full name might translate better into Swahili. It had more vowels.

"Binyamini."

I settled down on the end of the bed, facing the men, to get as comfortable as possible. I'd have preferred to sit crosslegged, but the skirt of this respectable dress was so short I'd have wound up flashing the guys. I should have hung on to the bui-bui.

"Khamisi knows some people in Jeshi-la-Rashiduni," I announced to start the ball rolling.

"Whose side is he on?" Lensky demanded.

I gave him a quelling look – at least, that was the intent. I'm not actually very good at quelling the man. "And he speaks fluent English. How about we pretend to have some manners here?"

Lensky's blue eyes flashed at me in a way that suggested trouble later, but he took my suggestion, imitated a relaxed pose and started over with something more like polite chit-chat.

Khamisi told us that he had been approached by the Rashiduni, that he did not sympathize with them but that he had not actually said so; it was not wise, he said, to insult those people. Especially in his situation.

He'd already told me everything except that aside about 'his situation.' I wondered what it was that made him feel especially vulnerable to the terrorists, but Lensky passed over that in favor of general chatting about the Rashiduni presence in Mombasa, their interactions with Khamisi and other people in Old Town, and Khamisi's life plans.

"Until – certain problems – are resolved," Khamisi said tightly, "I can make no plans."

He said that he did not know many details about the Rashiduni organization, but he could confirm that Omar the Zanzibari was their leader. "*Inshallah*, I might be able to learn more…"

Lensky exhibited more self-control by not actually drooling over this hint. It took another half hour of polite conversation to establish that Khamisi was being actively courted by the Rashiduni, that this situation put him in some danger already but that he might be willing to flirt with the leadership a little more. Lensky indicated, obliquely, that there would be significant financial rewards for anybody who brought him useful information. Khamisi indicated, obliquely, that such rewards would be more than welcome for a man with aging parents to support and student loans to pay back.

"Student loans?"

"Georgia Institute of Technology," Khamisi said. "Chemical engineering."

I propped one hand under my chin to keep it from dropping, and reminded myself not to make patronizing assumptions about the "natives." Next thing, I'd probably learn that Zawadi's two years of American college had been spent at Sarah Lawrence.

Clearly Khamisi couldn't just drop in to the apartment whenever he had something to report; that would be bad for us and possibly fatal for him. He and Lensky spent some time arranging a communications system involving inconspicuous chalk marks on Old Town walls and the display of my bright orange beach towel at a window overlooking Grand Mosque Road.

They did stall for a while on the matter of how to convey information. Lensky was used to setting up a system of dead drops, places where an agent could leave a report and he could collect it later so that they were never seen together. But Khamisi felt that the packages Lensky had used in Europe wouldn't work in Mombasa. "You cannot leave a soft drink can on the street; somebody will pick it up to sell to aluminum recyclers. The same thing will happen to an empty food tin. Anything made of metal is valuable to somebody."

"That explains a lot," Lensky murmured. He later told me that he'd been trying to make a low-tech perimeter around the terrace with trip wires around the edges, strung with empty cans that would jingle if anybody touched them. But the cans had kept disappearing...

They explored other options without finding anything mutually agreeable. A hollowed-out piece of rock might work, but it would have to be a sample of the coral on which the island was built. It would take time for Lensky to find suitable rocks and get the CIA office to prepare them as containers. It would also take time for Lensky to familiarize himself with Old Town and find good drop sites. And the danger to Khamisi, if any of these classic systems didn't work, was extreme. He could not assure Lensky that he hadn't been followed from his encounters with the Rashiduni leaders; a *gentleman*, he said with a disdainful sniff, did not keep looking behind him like a frightened girl.

But he sounded a lot like a frightened girl when we discussed having him write detailed reports to leave at a dead drop.

"The perfumer's," I said when a discouraged silence settled on the bedroom.

"Is that where you've been all morning?" said Lensky, startled. "I wondered why you smelled so…"

"Flowery? Delicious? Seductive?"

"Actually…"

I decided to let him off the hook. "Samples. Don't worry," I said, waving my left hand and inadvertently assaulting him with another cloud of musk and patchouli, "I'm going to wash them off. The thing is, I have to go back to get my personally designed scent. And I can keep going back and asking for adjustments. I'll just tell the guy my husband doesn't like it."

"Well, *I* cannot hang around a perfume shop like a girl!" Khamisi said, sounding indignant.

"No, but it's in the middle of a busy market with lots of other places you can visit. Look, when you have information, you can chalk a number on the wall at one of the places you and Brad were talking about. One of us will check the walls regularly and at the time represented by that number, I'll go to the perfumer's. All you have to do is wave at the shop and look excited about seeing someone there – it shouldn't be hard, I bet there's always a bunch of girls out front – then you come over and we step out of sight behind the side curtains for a moment."

"I fail to see what good that will do," he objected.

That was because I hadn't told him. I could see the light dawning on Lensky and Ben, though. How to put this? "Ah, Khamisi, you know about *jini?*"

"Of course," he said, "they are described in the Koran. But you should say *majini*, that is the plural."

Oh, great. Another language snob. Mr. M. was bad enough, the way he insisted that *djnoun* was the proper Arabic plural. Of course it had to be something totally different in Swahili.

"Grammar aside," I said, "you know that *majini* can transport themselves from one place to another in the flickering of an eyelash? And that they frequently take the form of a serpent? Well, Khamisi, I happen to have a djinn of my very own." I stepped over to the wardrobe, reached up on my tiptoes and lifted Mr. M. down for Khamisi to look at.

Credit where credit is due; our new agent turned the color of sour milk when Mr. M. lifted his head and complained about having his nap interrupted, but he didn't faint.

"This djinn," I told him, "can transport us from the perfumer's shop to this apartment, and no one will see our passage. You can report verbally in perfect safety, and afterwards we will send you to whatever place you choose."

After Khamisi left, Lensky asked me if I hadn't been a touch patronizing.

"You have to put things in a cultural context that people will understand," I told him.

"That's why you blathered on about djinns and pretended that Mr. M. would do the actual teleporting? Wouldn't it have been simpler to tell him the truth?"

"In my experience," I said, "people like that have a great deal of trouble understanding pure mathematics."

He blinked. "Thalia, I do believe that's the first racist thing I've ever heard you say."

"Oh, not *Africans*," Ben and I said simultaneously. "*Engineers.*"

12. Acting like newlyweds

Once we'd wound up Khamisi and set him in motion, there seemed to be depressingly little more we could do to continue the search for the stolen children.

"Is that how it usually is in the field?" I asked Lensky. "Moments of progress interspersed with long periods of nothing happening?"

"Thalia, that's how *life* usually is," he said. But he rubbed his chin thoughtfully. "And yes, a lot of field work is like that too. But in a case like this, where there's a very present threat, we would normally be putting more resources into the investigation – a *lot* more. We'd have people finding and surveilling this Omar al-Zanji, running down his contacts in Mombasa, getting at his cell phone and tracking his online presence. The trouble is – well, for one thing, Harrison is already out on a limb with the Company just for sending us all the way to East Africa. You already know that the DDO – the Deputy Director of Operations – is not a fan of the theory that there's been paranormal activity involved here. The official Company view is that the strike originated in the US and that the children are being held somewhere near Langley."

"What about the video?"

"The Rashiduni may claim credit, but so could any other group. Nothing in that video proves that they really do have the children." Lensky sighed. "There aren't many more strings Harrison can pull to get support for us."

I gloomed over that for a while. "If we could just find out where Omar is staying, *I* could do camouflaged surveillance. Or Ben and I could take turns."

Lensky spread his hands. "It comes back to waiting for a report from Khamisi."

We were hot, edgy, and frustrated. And, of course, we didn't know that the next move would be Omar's.

Lensky handles this kind of waiting almost as poorly as topologists do. After we spent the rest of the day twitching around the apartment in between hourly checks of the walls where Khamisi might leave a message, Victor came up with a suggestion to get us out of his hair.

"Ma Prajapati," he said over breakfast, "has been asking me why the honeymoon couple never does anything together. Why don't you two go out and do things to support your cover story while you're waiting? Buy tourist junk—"

Brad failed to conceal his shudder at this reminder of my beautiful, hand-carved African mask.

"—see the sights, go to the beach," Victor concluded with an expansive wave of his hand that just happened to coincide with the disappearance of the last of the *mahamri*.

"He's got a point," Brad said. "Maybe I am losing my edge after all; it's not good tradecraft to completely ignore your cover story. Let's go see some sights and try to act like a couple of newlyweds."

I considered pointing out that we *were* a couple of newlyweds, but decided it would be interesting to find out what Brad's idea of putting on a good act was. It consisted mainly of kissing me in public at every opportunity. He picked me up and perched me on a cannon at the old Portuguese fort for a snapshot and a kiss, posed with me in front of the monster "elephant tusks" for Ben to take another picture, bought some local sweets resembling deep-fried sugar pretzels and nibbled them from my lips.

He didn't lose the plot until we turned down a street in Old Town and discovered the art factory.

The street was lined for blocks with men hacking at dark wooden blanks and turning out African-styled sculptures.

"Look, Thalia," Ben said, grinning, "there's your authentic mask! Only this one's only two feet tall."

"And this must be the keychain version," Lensky said, picking up a six-inch mask. "Or do you think it shrank in the laundry?"

The proprietor of those two masks joined in, pointing out copies of my mask in every size from three inches to the four-foot version I'd been so proud of. The guys had a wonderful time.

"You're enjoying this so much, I'll just leave you to it," I told them, stalking down a side street while they laughed and pointed. Oh, good; there was that shop Victor hadn't let me explore, the Mvita Boutique. I went into the cool, shadowy interior and bought a couple of things – the best was a piece of Masai beadwork, about twelve inches by six and fringed with tiny chains – before they caught up with me.

At least my new purchases would be easy to pack.

Lensky made amends for his part in that little episode by sweeping us off to a seafood restaurant Khamisi had recommended. Their lobster Thermidor was even better than the Royal Court Hotel's version. I resumed calling Brad by his first name, and even moved a little closer so he could pat my knee under the table.

"More sightseeing?" he asked when I'd reached the point of wanting to lick the plate. "Back to the apartment for a siesta? Or the beach?"

"Beach would be okay with me," Ben allowed. "I've got some super-powerful sunscreen back at the apartment."

Brad gave him a Look. "You are not invited. Honeymooning couples don't usually have an extra man trailing around with them, haven't you noticed? Tradecraft positively requires Thalia and me to spend some quality time alone together."

Ben grumbled that he hadn't noticed his presence inhibiting Lensky that morning, but he cheered up when reminded that Mombasa boasted a crocodile farm called Mamba Village. "Oh, *reptiles*," he said with the kind of anticipatory smile I reserve for things like lobster. (*Cooked* lobster. If it's still swimming around in the water waving its claws, it's Marine Life and Ben can have it.)

Going to the beach was a *lot* easier now that I had a spot to teleport to, and there was the added advantage that we would totally frustrate anybody who might try to follow us. After sending Ben off with the address of Mamba Village I slipped into my new bikini, pulled a loose Africa-print coverup over my head, and zipped Brad and me straight to a blind corner between shops that I'd noted on the previous visit.

"That's pretty," he said, looking at my cotton shift with its pattern of red zigzags around purple diamonds. "I haven't seen it before?"

"I just bought it this morning, while you and Ben were snickering at me in the Street of the Carvers."

"You've got to admit that was pretty funny."

"If you keep on about that damn mask, I'll go back and change into the other thing I bought in the boutique. A twelve by six inch piece of Masai beadwork."

"I think I'd just as soon reserve that for a private viewing."

After he bought himself a swimsuit and a towel, we wandered down towards the water and claimed a patch of white sand. I slipped out of the coverup and turned to ask his help with sunscreen application, but the man appeared to have been turned into a statue.

"I definitely haven't seen *that* before," he said. His blue eyes were very wide and very dark.

I glanced down at the triangles of dark gold fabric. Okay, there was a lot of skin on view as well, but it wasn't like any of the territory was unfamiliar to him. And after my previous beach visit, it was starting to look nicely tanned. "Don't exaggerate. You've already seen everything you're staring at apart from the actual bikini."

"That costume," he said, "illustrates the vast difference between mere nakedness and seductive near-nudity."

"Oh, come on. This is a perfectly respectable swimsuit."

"It's more than a few square inches short of 'perfectly respectable.' Did you wear this the other day? When you and Ben went to the beach?"

His tone was veering from awed to censorious. I started feeling defensive in spite of myself.

"You *told* me to go to the beach with Ben. You practically had the hotel van shanghai us. *And* you told me to buy whatever I needed. Don't get all squinchy-eyed now just because you couldn't be bothered to check out the results!"

"And did Ben help you apply sunscreen to the copious acreage now on display?"

"Only the back. I can't reach everywhere, you know. You'll have to do it for me now." I plopped the bottle of sunscreen into his hand and lay face down on the big orange beach towel, hoping to cut this profitless discussion short.

The feeling of Brad's big hand moving in circles over my back, spreading the cool lotion, was... quite different from getting Ben to apply the stuff for me. That had been strictly practical; this was something else. After the first few slow, sensual passes over my back, I decided that he could do this for me any time. We didn't necessarily have to go to the beach first.

He seemed to be enjoying it too. At any rate, after he'd taken his time applying sunscreen to every uncovered inch of my back and thighs, he invited me to roll over so that he could continue his attentions on the front.

"I can do that part," I murmured out of the delicious languor he had induced.

"But we'll both enjoy it more if I do it."

No argument there. I allowed him to continue lavishing attention on my breasts and stomach until a nagging sense of responsibility forced me to sit up.

"What's the matter?"

"You. You're even more fair-skinned than Ben. You'll look like an extra-crispy potato chip if you don't protect your own skin."

"Or... let you do it for me," he suggested with a grin, passing over the bottle of SPF 20 kazillion sunscreen.

It was occasionally difficult to remember that this was a family beach, but eventually we managed to achieve a good distribution of sunscreen without getting in trouble for public lewdness.

"You're not to come here with Ben again," Brad pronounced after I'd got his shoulders and chest properly anointed. I'd taken my sweet time, just like he had; if a thing's worth doing, you know...

"Sez who?"

"I don't want him ever, *ever* touching you the way you were just doing with me."

"Don't worry. With Ben it's all about avoiding sunburn. Strictly practical. He might as well be painting a wall." *Efficiency* was Ben's watchword when performing such menial and boring tasks. Though I supposed he might have found the job less boring if he'd been working on Annelise.

"All the same."

"If you come too, you can do my sunscreen."

"I plan to. I'm not outsourcing that job to anybody ever again." That statement was accompanied by an intense blue stare that made me feel short of breath.

What with one thing and another, we were approaching a level of heavy breathing that was incompatible with the 'family beach' standard, so I waded into the water to cool down. Brad followed me.

Of course, no matter what the label says, no sunscreen is really proof against rolling waves of salt water, so eventually we had to re-apply it. This time I tried to use conversation to dilute the sensual effect of his big-knuckled hand massaging my spine and spreading lotion. There were things we needed to discuss.

"I think you've had more fun this week than you ever had in Austin. Spreading disinformation, evading surveillance, recruiting Khamisi as an agent. You want more, don't you?"

He didn't deny it, though he tried to sidle around the implications. "It's certainly been a change of pace. But I'm not selfish enough to want children put in danger just so I can run around being a field officer again." His hand skipped over the strings holding my bikini top on and massaged the back of my neck. I tried to concentrate despite the move. Trust Brad to redefine *that* as an erogenous zone.

"No, of course not, that's not what I mean. But there's enough trouble in the world to keep you fully occupied without wishing for more."

"You maniacs at the Center for Applied Topology certainly find enough trouble for yourselves." His touch became more of a gentle squeeze.

"Are you deliberately missing the point?"

"How would I know? Point me at it and we'll find out." He shifted location again, pouring lotion onto the backs of my thighs, and I tried not to purr.

I pillowed my face on my crossed arms. "I think you're happier as a field officer than you have been since you were posted to the Center."

"You've got a very strange definition of happiness. I myself would have put our wedding day somewhere near the top of my list of peak moments. Have you forgotten that already?"

"By no means." It had only been a little over a month. I would forever treasure the memory of Lensky wearing a traditional Greek "wedding crown" wreath of pearls and porcelain roses, staring straight ahead while a tiny vein jumped at his temple. And I totally melted when I remembered him holding me close at the end of the ceremony, and the love and tenderness I'd seen in his eyes. "But there's *personal* happy and then there's *career* happy. The more I see of you in this environment, the more trouble I have believing you feel truly fulfilled in Austin, riding herd on a bunch of topologists."

"That's not all I do there." His hands stopped moving over me.

"No. You also fly around the Southwest interviewing professors and executives who've recently traveled to global hot spots, getting their perspective and persuading them to act as your agents. Not exactly a thrill a minute."

"I also get to help break up terrorist cells in the United States. Destroying the network that hired Sandru Balan was *extremely* satisfying." He slipped one hand under my face and bent to kiss my cheek. "Thalia, stop looking for trouble where there is none to be found. I'm a grown-up; I don't need every single moment of my professional life to be a thrill. What I *do* need is…"

I turned so that I could see his face. He was staring out to sea.

"What you need…" I prompted.

"Oh. I need *you*, Thalia. I need to know that you're as safe as possible despite the complete lack of caution with which you insane topologists pursue your research. I need to know that I'm doing my job and protecting you and the rest of the Center."

It was very sweet of him to say all that, but I took it with all the salt in the

Indian Ocean. Brad just wasn't the sort of man to be satisfied with a career as a glorified bodyguard. And if I knew that much about him, he had to know it too.

What we found when we got back to the city, though, put the whole conversation out of my head for quite some time.

13. Child soldiers

"They've released *what?*"

"You heard me. Another video. And this one is... worse than the first one." Ben was slumped over the dining table, looking ill.

Lensky went white to the lips. "The children?"

"I think they're all right... physically anyway. The guy who's talking claims they're in this video. I suppose Omar felt he needed to prove he had them. But I don't know what they look like, and anyway it's hard to follow on the phone screen."

"*What did he do to them?*"

"You'd better see for yourself." Ben passed his phone to Lensky, who stabbed his fingers at the screen, then swiped them across, then scowled and complained that the screen was too small to make out details. "You should have called me immediately," he grumbled.

"I tried," Ben said. "Funny thing about that: you and Thalia both left your phones in the bedroom."

Little patches of red appeared on Lensky's white face.

"It doesn't make any difference," I said. "Does it? We'll need to use the CIA computers to get a good look at this."

Lensky looked at the screen and groaned. "It's after six."

"So? Since when do you guys punch a clock?"

"I've never been able to get hold of Finch this late." He dialed anyway, got bumped to voice mail. "I don't dare leave a message about this on voice mail.

He's gone slack." He stopped and shook his head. "No, that's not fair. Finch had no reason to expect we'd need him after hours."

It seemed to me that if Nelson Finch had had the slightest respect for Lensky, Harrison, and the current crisis, he would have volunteered to work twenty hours a day to help find the missing children. I bit my lip. It wouldn't help anybody for me to start bickering with Brad about his dear old buddy Finch.

I did think of something that might help, though. "What about Mr. Prajapati?"

Lensky and Ben both stared. "What about him?"

"He seems to have everything you can imagine tucked away somewhere in that shop downstairs. Who knows, maybe he's got a laptop we can borrow. Or," being more realistic, "he'll know where we can get one."

"Borrow a computer – Thalia, you're brilliant! No, never mind Prajapati; we'll go use the Royal Court Hotel's business center. I *knew* I had a good reason for not checking out of there yet."

First we had to get respectable again – Brad and I did, anyway; Ben seemed to have navigated the crocodile farm without becoming any more disheveled than usual. It didn't take long to shake the sand out of our shoes and throw on respectable clothes; then Ben and I took Brad's hands and said, '*Brouwer.*'

That maid didn't need to make such a fuss about our arrival in the room. What was she doing in a guest's room so late in the day, anyway? I bet she'd been pretending to dust while watching a soap; the TV was on. Oh, well. I expect she's calmed down by now.

"I thought the point was *not* to frighten the locals by popping out of thin air," Brad complained.

"We do our best."

The business center had wi-fi, computers with nice big screens, and, best of all, privacy. There'd been a couple of dapper gentlemen tapping away at computers when we entered, but they decided to leave after Lensky started prowling up and down the room. He frequently has that effect on people, even when they don't know about the Glock on his hip or the snub-nosed derringer in his ankle holster.

I had a belated thought. "I'm surprised Nelson Finch isn't available. After he sent us this video, he had to know we'd want to use the resources at his office to analyze it."

"Oh, he didn't send it," Ben, bent over a keyboard, informed me. "Jimmy DiGrazio did. I'd asked him to put some virtual trip wires out on the Internet, let me know if anything related to this case turned up."

I should have thought of that. Asking Jimmy, I mean. Just because our colleagues were on the other side of the world didn't mean they couldn't help. This *was* the twenty-first century.

On a full-size monitor, the video was grainy, dark and jerky. It seemed to have been shot outdoors with a hand-held camera, maybe at twilight. What it showed, though, was mesmerizing. Tiny figures marched in lines, threw themselves down on their stomachs and shot rifles nearly as tall as themselves – presumably at the targets which the video showed flying apart in splinters, but I had my doubts about that. Anybody could take one video of child soldiers shooting and another view of targets being shot to pieces and splice them together – I mean, not that *I* could, but I was sure Jimmy DiGrazio would have been able to do it.

"Pause it! That's Sam Harrison," Brad said hoarsely, tapping the face of a tall, thin boy frowning over his rifle.

"You're sure?"

He handed me his phone. "I was at his birthday party last year. And Steve sent me a slew of recent pictures. And now – oh, God! He's been dragged into some kind of child soldiers' training camp."

I glanced at the pictures on his phone. Yes. Tall for his age, with brown curls over eyes the same gray as his father's; even without these pictures I might have been able to pick out Sam as Steve Harrison's son.

"He doesn't seem to be completely with the program," I said when they restarted the video. To me, the boy's movements said *complaisance*, not *enthusiasm*.

Brad exhaled. A long, shaky breath. "You think not?"

I cast my mind back to my kid brother, who had never had much interest in sports but whose height and coordination had inspired innumerable gym teachers and coaches to pursue him. "I'm sure not. He looks like Andros did when the sixth grade coach forced him to try out for basketball. He's just going through the motions."

"He's only just finished third grade…"

"All the same."

Another shaky breath. "You could be right. He's a good kid. Almost as sharp as Linda, you know?"

Brad considered his niece Linda to be the best, smartest, most talented child in Texas, and she regarded him in a similar light. I just hoped this happy relationship would survive her upcoming teen years.

"They may not have had time to completely indoctrinate him," Brad mused now, squinting at the grainy images. "God, I hope not! It'll kill Steve if we get him back and he's turned into a brainwashed little warrior against America."

"We'll get him back," I said with absolutely no basis for that other than the need to stabilize Brad, "and they haven't brainwashed him, no matter what the claims on that damn video." There was a voice speaking over the shots and yells in the background; a smooth, creamy, satisfied voice with what I now recognized as a strong Swahili accent. The speaker claimed that all three of the kidnapped children had seen the light and had embraced their true destiny of fighting with the Rashiduni to bring down the foreign imperialists. They would be raised as good Moslems and some day, when their training was complete, they would strike at America.

"He's lying."

"If he can keep them long enough –"

"We aren't going to let him do that. *You* aren't going to let that happen," I corrected myself.

"What about the other two?" Lensky muttered. He squinted, reversed the video, ran it forward again at half speed. "There, that's Bobby Navarro." He indicated a younger boy, a blond, who was running forward and throwing himself down in the mud to slide even farther, shouting something unintelligible. "*He* seems to be quite enthusiastic."

"He's – what? Five years old? He doesn't know what it's all about. Of course he likes running and yelling and playing in the mud, he's *five*," I said with somewhat more conviction than I actually felt. My principal concern right now was Brad's psychological state, not the children's. We could worry about the children's degree of indoctrination once we actually had them back, and our chances of getting them would only decrease if Brad went into a guilt fugue about what had already happened. "What about the little girl? Rosie Jamison? I didn't have the impression this bunch were looking for women soldiers."

"No. You must have missed the part where Omar – or whoever that is, talking – said that her destiny was to marry a leader of the Rashiduni, to be a reward for extraordinary service. I got the feeling *he* was the extraordinary leader he had in mind."

"Ugh. But – she's only six, right? He'd have to wait a few years." Like ten, at a minimum.

"The Prophet," interrupted a croaky voice down at floor level, "married his last wife, Aisha, when she was six years old." Mr. M. rose and hovered over my shoulder. "But," he continued, "the marriage was not consummated until she was nine."

I felt sick. Brad grabbed my shoulder – the one Mr. M. wasn't using. "We will have *all* the children out of there before anything like that happens. That is a promise." He leaned over the table and squinted at the video again. "We need to get hold of Khamisi. Maybe he can figure out exactly where this children's training camp is. I'm betting on one of the offshore islands, but it would be good to know which one, and exactly where on the island."

Getting hold of Khamisi was impossible at night and not easy the next day. Ben grumbled that the man should have given us a cell phone number. Didn't he know what century this was?

"Says the man who refused to get himself a cell phone until Annelise talked him into it last year."

"Cell phones," Lensky said, "are too easily compromised. The classic techniques really are the best."

The classic technique in question required me to fork over my new orange beach towel so that we could hang it in the window overlooking Grand

Mosque Road to get Khamisi's attention. Then Lensky drifted down that street to another, looking as inconspicuous as a square, blond man in a Swahili neighborhood could hope to look, and chalked a "10" on a graffiti-covered cement wall that too many cars had already scraped. My part of the job was to show up at the perfumer's at ten o'clock, in the hope that Khamisi would have got the message. If he didn't, Lensky said grimly, I'd just have to return once every hour.

"I'll stay there for a while, wander around to the shops in that square and keep checking at the perfumer's," I decided. "It'll be less disruptive than trying to teleport there repeatedly; somebody would be bound to notice eventually." Under our original protocol, of course, Khamisi would have been the one requesting a meeting and I'd only have had to go at the time he indicated. We hadn't really given enough thought to making it work the other way.

In the event, I only had to wait long enough to have a mango milk shake at the dairy bar, pick out some cute little glass bangles like the ones Fadiya had worn, overpay for a handful of sickly onions at the vegetable stall, and buy a raffia hold-all for the stuff I was accumulating. Khamisi turned up, looking pale and worried, just three-quarters of an hour after the time we'd been shooting for, while I was debating the merits of an orange-and-blue striped coverup over a more sedately traditional blue-and-white one. I grabbed my purchases and drew him behind the billowing shades at the side of the perfume shop.

"What took you so long?" Brad was *pacing* again, in the apartment.

"What do you want?" Khamisi asked. "Do you think I can make new information overnight?" He was even paler than he'd been in the market. I thought he had been so shaken up by teleporting that he hadn't even noticed I'd forgotten to bring Mr. M.

"Onions?" Ben asked. "You're going to take up cooking?"

"I was running out of things to buy."

"The Rashiduni have put out a new video," Lensky told Khamisi. "We want you to look at it and try to figure out where it was made."

Ben and Lensky hadn't wasted their morning; they'd bought a laptop and had paid Mr. Prajapati for access to his wi-fi.

Khamisi asked us not to hover over him while he worked, which seemed reasonable enough. The guys took chairs out onto the terrace and sat in the shade of the big tree that rubbed against the side of the building, talking in undertones. Me, I decided to be a nice traditional little woman; I brought Khamisi a cup of coffee and then sat down very quietly behind him, in a good position for over-the-shoulder peeking. It worked. Evidently Khamisi's nervousness wasn't enough to override the invisibility of women in his world.

He studied the video intently, running it over and over, stopping at various points and stepping through the frames with infinite patience. One spot in particular seemed to affect him strongly; he went pale when he first saw it, and replayed the surrounding frames half a dozen times before moving on. Finally he made a number of screen shots and tapped his phone.

"I am not sure… I do not know the islands well," he apologized when he had finished and Brad had come back inside. "I will show these pictures to some people I know."

"Natives of the islands?"

Now Khamisi flushed dark. "And… others who may know. Do not send for me again; I will notify you when I have more information. This may take several days."

Lensky took down his cell phone number, promised not to use it except in dire emergency, and let him go with that unsatisfactory resolution.

"I probably will not use his phone in any case," he told me. "As I said, cells are too easily compromised."

"Can I see the video again?"

"Why?"

"He seemed extremely interested in one particular spot. Around 5:14."

Brad tapped the computer screen, swiped, and tapped again right at 5:10. We studied the next ten seconds of grainy footage several times.

"There must be something in the background that could narrow down the location," he sighed, "but damned if I can pick it out. But that's got to be it; none of the children we're interested in appear in those ten seconds."

Some older children and possibly some very young teens did appear, though, going through similar maneuvers to what Sam Harrison and Bobby

Navarro had done. And I wondered if 5:14 might hold a clue to why Khamisi was being so extremely cooperative. He was taking some terrible risks for not very much reward, and I didn't think it was just because Zawadi liked me.

I didn't have a chance to run my extremely shaky theory by Brad, though, because Nelson Finch banged on the front door just then and shouted at us to let him in. Brad headed for the door; I tapped the computer and shut off the display.

"About time!" Finch was sweating and looked somewhat less dapper than he had at the hotel. "It's too damned hot today to keep people waiting at your door, Lensky."

"Kind of hot for a casual visit, too," Lensky said. We had already acclimatized to a way of life in which nothing much happened between noon and 4 p.m. "What brings you this way, Nelson? Why didn't you call first? We might not have been in."

"This time of day," Finch said, "everybody is home in the shade." He shrugged off his suit jacket and dropped it over the back of a chair. "I just took a fancy to see what kind of a setup you'd rented. Christ, couldn't you find anything with air-conditioning?"

"It's convenient to the part of town where we're working," Lensky said. "And it's easy to do an SDR between downtown and here, as I trust you've noticed?"

Finch brushed off that question and demanded a beer.

"SDR?" I murmured to Lensky when we were in the kitchen.

"Surveillance detection run. Remember how we got to the apartment? Very basic tradecraft. I'm sure Finch can do it in his sleep." He took the bottle out to Finch. Just as he set the beer down, somebody else banged on the door.

"Oh, for –! Victor," he called, "it must be some of *your* friends. Everybody *I* know in Mombasa is already here!"

"Except Khamisi," Ben said, coming out of his room.

"Khamisi?" Finch looked up.

Lensky waved one hand. "Nobody important."

Ben bristled. "What do you mean, nobody? He's the first useful asset we've acquired!"

Ben had been spending so much time with Lensky, CIA-speak was rubbing off on him.

There was a rather heated discussion going on at the front door. In Swahili, so I couldn't really eavesdrop.

"You've recruited an asset?" Finch repeated. "You should have run the name by the office first. We have a list of people who aren't to be trusted."

Seemed to me a list of people who *could* be trusted would have been more useful, not to mention shorter. But – as Finch would doubtless point out if I said anything – I wasn't a highly trained field operative, and he was.

"If you're talking about Khamisi bin Ali bin Abdallah, the old Sheikh's grandson, you're making a mistake," Finch went on after a lengthy pull at his beer. "I know your buddy Victor Salvez uses that family as informants, but there's a bi-ig difference between anthropology and our work. I wouldn't trust any of them with sensitive material."

"Perhaps you are forgetting," said Lensky, tight-lipped, "that the flow of information usually goes the other way. I don't give Khamisi sensitive information – that's what I pay him to give *me*."

Not that we'd had anything like that from him yet.

Victor stomped into the living room then, looking as ruffled as I'd ever seen him, and complained that he couldn't work when idiots kept showing up at the front door and demanding to see the apartment.

"I had to tell him six times that I'd rented the place from Prajapati and he'd need to go through him, and he didn't go away until I told him one of the friends I'm sharing the apartment with has a gun!"

Lensky compressed his lips. "Not the ideal way to get rid of importunate visitors, Victor. Have you forgotten that the point of working through you was to keep a lid on the Company's involvement?"

"I didn't say anything about you being CIA. And if you're so picky, you can deal with the next intrusion. In Swahili, and good luck with that!" Victor stamped out again, probably congratulating himself on having had the last word.

Finch shook his head, laughing quietly. "It *has* been a while since you were in the field, hasn't it, Lensky? I can't say I congratulate you on your choice of cutout – or your first asset. You'd really better run everything through the office from now on just for your own protection. I'm sure I can find some better people for you to talk to."

"If you really want to help, you could—" Lensky started.

I was afraid he was about to mention the latest video, so I kicked him and interrupted. "That's very good advice, Mr. Finch, I'm sure he'll bear it in mind from now on. It's so kind of you to offer to help us find agents."

"Think nothing of it," Finch said, tilting his chair back and taking a long pull on his beer. "It's not as if there's a lot of business of world-shaking importance going through the office right now. The Company's not what it was when we started, Lensky. There's no room, any more, for initiative and – and *style*. It's been strangled by nervous-nellie bureaucrats, always looking over their shoulders for fear the media will get hold of something that can make them look bad."

Over a second beer he expatiated on this theme, complaining that not only the CIA but all of America had become soft and nervous and useless. "If those with power are afraid to act, those with courage will take it from them," he declaimed with the air of somebody stating an unvarying truth. "America will have nobody to blame but herself when she goes under to younger, stronger nations with the courage to act on their convictions."

"I haven't seen a whole lot of countries that I'd call stronger than the United States," Brad said mildly.

"Ah, that's because you're only looking at the surface of things. What good is it to have more divisions than the enemy, if the politicians are afraid to use those divisions? A real man can't get ahead in America any more, Lensky. And certainly not in the Company. They've succumbed to fear. You know what that ass Taylor said the other day? 'Whenever the guns come out, the CIA gets in trouble.' I tell you, the Company's rotting from within. They prefer to operate in the shadows and leave the real action to others. You should get out before it's too late."

"Are you planning to do that?"

"Never – never tell anybody your plans." Finch banged his empty bottle down on the table and glared at us. "Never apologize – never explain. Duke of Wellington."

"Can I help you get back to the office, Finch?"

He heaved himself out of his chair. "No need. I can find my way around this pissant little town. Not much more than a wide place in the road!"

"You should have let me whisk him back," I said when the apartment was quiet again. "I think he was followed coming over here, and that's what attracted our pushy visitor that Victor had to get rid of."

Lensky sighed and sat down at the table. "I wanted to. Never thought I'd see Finch drunk on two beers, but maybe he'd started before he came over here."

"He was slurring a bit, towards the end."

"And misquoting. Badly."

"What, the Duke of Wellington didn't say, 'Never apologize, never explain?'"

Lensky gave me a tight-lipped smile. "No. It was John Wayne in *She Wore a Yellow Ribbon*."

Lensky is an aficionado of old movies, and as I may have mentioned, his world view frequently reflects them.

"I'm very much afraid you may be right about Finch," he went on now. "He has gotten stale here. But there's no way to prevent him from being just as careless again – and right now I am not sure how he'd react to a demonstration of your particular abilities."

I brought him a beer. I seemed to be serving a lot of drinks today, but never mind; he needed it.

"If he was followed, Victor's crack about my carrying will just have confirmed that this is a CIA house. I'm afraid this apartment won't be good for much longer, Thalia. I'd like to keep it another couple of days, though; if we move without telling Khamisi, it might spook him. And anyway, re-establishing contact will be a bitch."

"I might be able to reach him through Zawadi."

"Who?"

"The girl I went shopping with, who introduced us? A granddaughter of Mama Aesha's? She went to Sarah Lawrence," I added before remembering that this was just my imaginative gloss on her two years of college in America. It didn't matter, did it?

"That reminds me," said Lensky, after another restorative pull at his beer. "You kicked my shins before I could tell him about the new video – okay, I took the hint, but what gives? If we can't share information with our own people, what chance do we have here?"

"I don't know, exactly," I confessed, "but his insistence on our running everything through his office bothers me."

"Just territorial maneuvering," Lensky dismissed my concern. "Happens all the time. Harrison sent us straight here instead of contacting the local office and asking them to request our help. Finch probably feels we've stepped on his toes, coming in like this." He finished the beer.

"Maybe. Or maybe you're insufficiently paranoid where some people are concerned. I didn't like the way he dismissed Khamisi."

"Ah, you and Finch just rub each other the wrong way. I've noticed that from the beginning." He caught me by the waist and drew me down onto his lap. "I hadn't meant to mention Khamisi by name, but that's not because I don't trust Nelson; it's just good operational security. Don't worry about Finch. He may have spent too long in this backwater and become a careless son of a bitch, but there's no harm in him. If he weren't a good guy, don't you think I'd have seen something wrong during our training at the Farm?"

What I thought was, one, that maybe Finch had changed in more fundamental ways than Brad was willing to consider; and, two, that he wasn't worth a fight with my husband. "Do you want another beer?"

"I'd rather have a late siesta… with my wife." He nuzzled the back of my neck and I forgot about any number of things I'd meant to think about.

I didn't even notice that Ben had quietly left the apartment.

14. Thief-wiring

We didn't come out again until after the evening call to prayer.

My first sight of the living room gave me a nasty shock. Ben's body was sprawled out across the coconut matting.

At first my heart thumped painfully; then I saw that he had flung one arm over his eyes and his fingers were twitching.

"What happened to you?"

He removed the arm and peered up at us. I repeated myself with more feeling when I got a good look at the bruises and cuts on his face. "*What happened to you?*"

"They broke my glasses," he informed me. "And don't go like you've been worried sick about me. I've been back here for *hours* with nothing to do but not listen to the sounds emanating from your bedroom."

I could feel my face turning almost as red as the unbruised portions of his. "Next time read a – oh, right. They… *Who* broke your glasses? And why?"

"We didn't exactly have a lengthy philosophical discussion about it."

It seemed Ben too had felt there was something off about Nelson Finch. When Finch left the apartment, Ben had generated camouflage around himself and followed him.

"I didn't really expect him to do anything but go home or to the office," he confessed, "and then I planned to come right back here." He'd certainly spent enough time in the apartment to use it for a destination; he could have teleported back from anywhere in the city.

But instead of the expected moves, Finch had walked through the fringes of Old Town and on into a part of Mombasa that, although furnished with street signs and sidewalks, was in other respects considerably less savory than our own neighborhood.

Lensky sucked in his breath when Ben mentioned the names of the major streets he'd crossed.

"Majengo. That is *not* a good part of town, Ben."

By now we were all seated around the table, making further inroads into the beer supply. Well, Lensky and I were, and Victor was nursing an open bottle that he seemed to be using mostly to cool his hands. Ben was holding a bag of ice cubes over a swollen eye that looked worse by the minute, and he said he felt too queasy to drink anything but water.

"So I learned," Ben said grimly.

"But you were using camouflage?" I asked. "You should have been all right."

"That's what I thought too," he said. "I also thought that if Finch could go for a stroll there, it must be at least sort of an okay neighborhood."

Both those beliefs had turned out to be inaccurate.

Finch had paused at a street corner to talk to a group of men who were lounging in the scanty shade of a couple of mango trees. Ben wasn't sure whether they were Arab or Swahili. Not, he said definitely, pure African. By now we'd all seen enough of the blue-shadowed blackness of pure Africans to recognize people with a more blended heritage.

Of course, 'blended' described approximately sixty percent of the population of Mombasa, so it didn't really narrow things down much.

They looked like a tough bunch, Ben said. He'd certainly felt intimidated and grateful for his camouflage. But Finch had seemed quite at his ease, exchanging jokes and, eventually, passing out money.

"He runs his own assets," Lensky said. "Any field officer worth his salt would do the same."

"What, right out on the street in front of God and everybody?"

The guys ignored my interruption.

"These fellows," Ben said, "are not what I'd call assets. Not in the old meaning of 'assets to society,' anyway. If I were you, Lensky, I'd worry about the company your friend keeps."

Ben's quiet surveillance had come to an abrupt end when a little boy on an antique bicycle rode into him.

"You know how hard it is to maintain camouflage when you're being jostled," he said to me. "Suddenly I couldn't keep picturing the set of open covers that I'd envisioned projecting a background image over me."

"And you couldn't get it back?"

"It all happened so fast," Ben said defensively. "The kid and I both hit the sidewalk, he started wailing, Finch looked around and saw me. He pointed at me and shouted something, and the next thing I knew, I had my arms over my head and his native buddies were kicking me and stomping on my glasses. The only thing I could think to do was to teleport back here."

"Thank God you did that." At some later time I'd bug him about remembering to raise a shield. This was the second time in a couple of weeks he'd forgotten to protect himself against violent thugs. And these people sounded even more dangerous than those high-spirited wannabe-rapists we'd tangled with in Germany.

"You're sure Finch recognized you?" Lensky asked. "He couldn't just have been startled by somebody appearing out of thin air?"

"*No*, I'm not sure. I'm just telling you what happened. If you want an official CIA interpretation, go ask your buddy Finch what *he* thinks he saw, and why he sicced those guys on me." Ben was veering from defensive to aggrieved, and I couldn't blame him.

"It doesn't look good," Lensky said in response to a look from me. "But you can't expect me to condemn an old friend unheard!"

"No. Of course not. Only... could you just not tell Nelson Finch about the video or anything else we've got? For a couple of days anyway?"

A deep sigh. "Thalia. That video is our key to getting complete and total CIA support. When Steve Harrison sees it, he'll put an army of operatives in this city. You can't expect me to bury it!"

"No. But if you do what Finch demanded, and pass everything through his office... I'm afraid it might *get* buried. Could you contact Harrison directly with the video? Make sure he knows about it?"

Lensky sighed and rubbed his face with the palm of his hand. "Yes. Right. I'll…" He glanced at the laptop. "I'm not sure how secure Prajapati's wi-fi is."

"Not at all," Victor said cheerfully. "All the neighbors have probably figured out how to tap into it, and anybody else can do so easily enough. Didn't you notice that his password is 'PASSWORD'?"

"Damn. I don't want to go back to the Royal Court Hotel, not after the way you two terrified that maid."

"I'll call Jimmy," Ben volunteered. "If we give him Harrison's contact info, he can send the best-definition version of the video he's been able to find directly to Langley."

Lensky nodded. "That'll do… for now. Dammit, I can't figure out why they haven't already seen it and contacted me!"

I could come up with more than one hypothesis to account for that. One was that the people at Langley weren't *looking*, that Harrison's boss had squashed his belief in an East African connection. Another was that too many people, including those at Langley, had fallen for Nelson Finch's desire to be at the center of all communications in this part of the investigation… and that Finch had already buried the information.

But why would he do that? Territorial disputes, rivalry with his old Farm buddy, a desire to be the star of the show… nothing I could think of would account for Finch's doing something so nakedly destructive. Probably I'd been around Brad so long that his paranoia was rubbing off on me.

When I woke up screaming in the small hours, though, I knew that what wakened me hadn't been a bad dream or a paranoid fantasy. Mr. M. had the evidence to prove it.

Brad crashed through the bedroom door, gun drawn, and flipped on the lights. "*Thalia*? What happened? Are you all right?"

I was shaking; I sat up, pulled the discarded sheet around me and tried to take in the situation. Brad was wearing only his boxers. He hadn't been in the bed when I woke up. Sitting up, brooding? Probably. I stored for future reference the fact that he could get to his preferred weapon at light speed even when practically naked.

Ben was behind Lensky, peering over his shoulder. And Mr. M. was zipping around the room at head height. He had something gripped in his beak that interfered with actual singing, thank God, but he still managed to buzz a wordless song of victory.

"Something... poked me. Here. Sharp." I pointed at my right thigh, now covered by the sheet.

"A dream?" Ben hazarded.

"A bug?" Lensky suggested, lowering his weapon.

Mr. M. dropped his trophy into my lap and said, "A thief."

I picked up the twig he'd dropped. It looked like the tip of a bamboo fishing pole, but instead of hanging from a string at the end of the pole, the fishing hook was attached to the bamboo by tightly wrapped wires.

"Oh!" Brad put down his gun, sat on the bed and gave me a hug. "Somebody trying to get through the thief-wiring. He must have seen me leave and thought the room was empty. You probably scared him more than he scared you, Thalia."

"I doubt that!" My heart was hammering and I was having trouble making sense of what was going on. "Thief-wiring?"

He waved at the decorative iron grille behind the bed. "That ironwork? It keeps people from reaching a hand through. Small-time thieves like to stick a fishing pole through the window and, well, fish for valuable trinkets. They're usually not violent."

"Oh, good, then that's all right."

Brad scowled at the thief-wiring. "No, it's very far from all right. Dammit, I *knew* that terrace would be a magnet for thieves; I should have made Finch give me some decent alarms, instead of trying to improvise my own system. I should have insisted Prajapati put heavy shutters up. I should have..."

Now that his arm was around me, I'd stopped shaking. "It's *all right*," I repeated. "No harm done, and we can talk about shutters in the morning, or whatever you think needs to be done." I thought back on our first days in Old Town. "All those artistic iron grilles that I was admiring? They're really low-tech home security systems, aren't they? That's why you grinned every time I pointed out a new pattern. You rat. You could have told me!"

"Ah, I didn't want to make you feel bad. You were ticked off enough after we stumbled across the Street of the Carvers."

He didn't leave the room again. He turned the lights out, Mr. M. coiled up on the bureau in a state of high alert, I snuggled up to Brad, and eventually I got back to sleep.

In the morning I awoke to the banging of a hammer and a very dim room. Lensky was tacking flattened cardboard boxes to the window frame.

"I didn't feel right about demanding expensive shutters from Prajapati when we're going to move out anyway as soon as I can set up new protocols with Khamisi," he explained. "These should do for a couple of days, just to discourage voyeurs and small-time thieves. I'm afraid it'll make the room kind of dark, though."

Better than the alternative. If I needed to find anything I could always turn on the overhead light. And I could still read in here; all my reading matter was stored on a Kindle with a backlit screen. The e-book format works fine for fiction. (It's not always so good for mathematics involving lots of diagrams and drawings, which is why I was missing my topology library. Those books were way too heavy and expensive to lug overseas. *Lectures on the Topology of 3- Manifolds* alone had set me back more than my Kindle Paperwhite.)

Later, Mr. M. told me that it hadn't been just my screams that scared off the thief. "Just before he woke you, a wave of cold air startled him and made his hands shake. That was how he came to touch you with the end of his fishing pole; I think he would not normally have been so clumsy."

Cold air.

"TheSila?"

Mr. M. inclined his head. "I, of course, was aware that she was watching."

"You didn't tell me?"

"She did no harm, and possibly some good. There was no need for her to interfere with the thief's explorations; I believe she does not wish you ill."

That was not terribly reassuring. I wasn't all that happy with the concept of even a benevolent djinn watching Brad and me acting like a couple of newlyweds.

"Can she see through the cardboard?" I nodded at the newly covered windows. The dim light made me feel as though I was sitting at the bottom of a well, not in a second-floor room overlooking a pretty little rooftop terrace. And the cardboard closed off the breezes that made this room comfortable. Oh well, it was only until we found something better and gave Khamisi our new address.

Mr. M. was not entirely sure that TheSila couldn't see through cardboard, but he thought it unlikely that she could do something that was beyond even his advanced skills.

Oh well, it was only another couple of days, etc., etc.

They were a tense couple of days. In no particular order:

-Ben made a series of telephone calls to his optometrist in Austin and managed to have his prescription sent to a Kenyan optometrist who would make him a replacement pair of specs immediately... for an African value of "immediately." The guy was in Nairobi, so Ben couldn't even go visit his office and pressure him in person.

-Lensky and I did not talk about whether Finch could be trusted.

-Victor decided to stay with a friend until we vacated the apartment and, for preference, his life. The glamor of CIA work seemed to have disappeared once it threatened his research plans. I couldn't blame him.

-Ben stole my Kindle, because he could set the font big enough to read without glasses, and complained because I had selfishly loaded it up with the kind of things I liked to read. He said he was drowning in romantic suspense and lightweight fantasy. "Fine, I've just bought *Euler's Gem*," I told him. That was more in the genre of popular mathematics than serious stuff, but Dr. Verrick's honors course in topology hadn't gone into the history of the field; I had quite enjoyed reading about Euler, Catherine the Great, polyhedra, and the origins of topology. "Or check out the Kipling anthology. I've got lots of stuff that isn't goopy romance; you're just not looking."

-Lensky and I continued not talking about Nelson Finch.

Finally there was a chalk mark at one of Khamisi's locations. I teleported to the perfumer's at the indicated time and picked up both Khamisi and my own personally blended perfume. A successful trip.

Well, reasonably successful. We were all disappointed to learn that Khamisi still hadn't identified the spot where the training camp video had been made. We couldn't really complain, though, because he had gotten himself into potentially serious trouble through pushing Omar al-Zanji's second-in-command for more information about the camp.

"Who exactly is this guy?" Lensky wanted to know.

"Like half the Swahili men in Mombasa, his name is Muhamed. The Rashiduni do not use their family names, so he goes by a nickname: *Anakijua*, 'The one who knows,'" Khamisi said, "and he claims to know everything about the camps and forces of the Rashiduni. It took me a day and a half to get to talk to him, and then he told me such information was not for those who were not fully committed to the cause. I told him that Al-Zanji's speeches had shown me the true light and that I desired nothing more than to take their blasphemous oath – may Allah forgive me! – but he said that I must prove myself worthy of the oath." He stopped short and stared through me.

"Ah – he has something in mind? Or are you supposed to think up a way of proving yourself to them?" Lensky prodded after a moment.

Khamisi laughed, but not as though he though anything was funny. "Oh, Anakijua has something in mind, all right. You will appreciate the irony of this, Biradi. He wants me to blow up the CIA office here in Mombasa and kill both the *wazungu* field officers."

15. A modification of fire

"What, he wants to kill Brad?" I gasped. "How does he even know about us?"

"No. Biradi was not mentioned. Two men called Finichi and Talori are the targets."

"Finch and Taylor… Ben, could you make some coffee?" Lensky asked. *"And don't let Khamisi leave,"* he added in an urgent undertone before drawing me into the dimness of the back bedroom.

"You can't suspect Finch now, Thalia! His life is in danger."

"What do you want to do?"

"We need to bring him in on this. Can you take me to his office?"

I took his arm. "Picture it as clearly as you can."

We popped into the office out of thin air and startled Finch into a hasty step back. He almost tripped over his own chair, but we didn't have time for acrobatics; I grabbed his arm on the way down and he completed his fall onto the coconut matting in our shadowed bedroom.

"You—why—what?" he gasped.

"I did tell you," said Lensky, "that my wife had certain special abilities that could be a great help in this investigation, but you didn't want to hear me."

Khamisi blinked when three people came through the bedroom door instead of the two who had gone in, but he kept his composure better than Finch. Of course, he'd already been teleported a couple of times, even if he did think Mr. M. was a djinn who'd done the heavy lifting.

Lensky outlined the situation but finished by saying that of course

Khamisi couldn't be asked to do this.

Nelson Finch demurred. "If he refuses to do it, haven't we just painted a big target on his back? These people don't take well to being turned down. They might kill him on the grounds that he can't be trusted."

Khamisi's eyes were showing a great deal more white than usual.

"Tell you what," Lensky said. "Khamisi, can you make sure your bomb doesn't affect anything more than our office? Like, it won't be big enough to blow up the whole building?"

"Of course I can," Khamisi said. "Chemical engineering, Georgia Tech, remember?"

"Right," Finch said without blinking, "that's probably why they tried to recruit you in the first place; they need your skills. They've got plenty of shooters and panga gangs…"

"Panga gangs?"

"Specialize in murder by machete," Lensky said briefly. I decided I didn't really want to know more.

Finch didn't seem surprised by Khamisi's academic background, and I reluctantly revised my opinion of him just a tiny bit. If he already knew about Khamisi's education maybe he was a reasonably competent operative in his own right. Maybe it was just his bitterness, the constant catty swiping at Lensky and dismissive cracks about Taylor, that made me dislike and distrust him. And that attitude of his probably went right over Brad's head; he had too generous a spirit himself to understand that some people felt threatened by others' competence, were so insecure that they always had to put down those around them.

"Getting back to the bomb question…" Lensky prodded.

They eventually agreed that Khamisi would insist the bomb had to be a package small enough to fit under LeShawn Taylor's desk.

"That might slow them down," Khamisi said. "If they were planning to use ANFO…"

"Mix of fuel oil and fertilizer," Lensky explained quickly.

"Popular with terrorists," Finch added.

"But bulky," Khamisi finished. "God willing, they will have to procure something else, and that should buy us time."

Khamisi would tell us when it was scheduled for; Finch would take that day off. He would also give Mashika, their part-time secretary, an errand that would keep her out of the office all day.

"What about Taylor?"

Finch scoffed. "The man just casually dropped in this morning after being out 'sick' for days, and he probably considers that to have satisfied his work requirements for the week. If you insist, though, I can contact him and make sure he doesn't come into the office that day – whatever day it is. Maybe we can invent an American holiday to explain our absence."

It didn't buy as much time as we'd hoped; Khamisi reported that same evening that Anakijua had promised him Semtex. By tomorrow. The bomb would be planted at dawn on the day after.

After Lensky left to deliver this information to Finch in person – he was becoming extremely paranoid about saying anything more than 'Good morning' over a cell phone – Khamisi lingered to talk to Ben and me.

"There is still some reason to hope that the bomb will not explode," he said. "In Africa it is necessary to protect Semtex from the heat. It can lose its plasticity, get hard and even disintegrate."

"Wouldn't Anakijua notice that?"

Khamisi shrugged. "I do not think he intends to get his own hands dirty. They will expect me to assemble the package."

"In that case…" Ben began.

Khamisi started shaking his head before Ben could even finish the sentence. "They will watch me. If I fail to connect the detonator properly…"

"There are other things we can do," Ben said.

Khamisi brightened. "Your djinn? Can it disconnect the detonator?"

"Something like that," Ben said. "Give us as much time as possible between placing the bomb and the detonation, can you do that?"

He nodded. "I can insist on making the placement before dawn, when I have the best chance of entering the building unobserved. I can also insist on setting it to detonate in mid-afternoon; I will tell them that the *wazungu* are lazy and only come to the office when it is so hot they want to enjoy the air conditioning."

"That should be enough time, don't you think, Thalia?"

"Depends on exactly what you're thinking of." I had done a lot of small object manipulation, but only working with familiar objects. Playing cards. Coins. Most recently, little balls of sticky rice. The detonator on a bomb? That would be tricky, not least because I didn't know what it would look like. When last confronted with a bomb, I'd elected to teleport out of range rather than attempt defusing it. "Mr. M. likes military hardware…"

Khamisi indicated that if we were planning to consult with Mr. M., he would really prefer to be elsewhere, and I teleported him to one of the blind spots we'd selected earlier.

"Yes, at first I was thinking of fiddling the detonator," Ben said when I returned, "but I've had a much better idea since then!"

I regarded him warily. Ben's 'better ideas,' had a checkered history at the Center. There was the time he'd set the office on fire in a misguided attempt to generate light, for instance. "Just tell me this doesn't have anything to do with Riemann fire."

"I was actually thinking of a modification of that," Ben said with wounded dignity. "Don't you see, Thalia? Semtex decays in heat. All we have to do is cook the bomb after Khamisi places it."

"Why not before?"

"We won't know exactly where it is, will we? Once it's under LeShawn Taylor's desk, we can strike with surgical precision. Well, you can, anyway, you've seen the office now."

"In that case, why don't I just teleport there, remove the thing and drop it offshore?"

"Because this will preserve Khamisi's cover! Don't you see, this is already a known liability of Semtex. When it doesn't go off, he can yell at Anakijua for giving him outdated materials that hadn't been protected from the heat!"

There was a certain beauty to that notion; enough that I spent an hour with Ben and a notepad, sketching exactly how to modify the use of Riemann surfaces to produce intense local heat around the bomb package without actually setting anything on fire. If it worked, Khamisi would be off the hook in a totally undetectable way. And if it didn't work – well, Finch had promised that the office would be empty anyway.

To Ben's chagrin, I worked out the modifications before he did. He was handicapped by the fact that without his glasses, he could barely make out the relevant diagrams. He kept asking me to draw them larger until I rebelled. "I'm working on four sheets of paper taped together already."

"Yes, but the lines are too thin for me to see properly."

"*Sorry.* All I've got is a No. 2 pencil. You want nice thick lines, get me an oversized drawing pad and some sticks of charcoal."

Annelise's call couldn't have come at a better time.

"You should absolutely go to Nairobi to meet her," I told Ben.

"And leave you to do this alone?"

"At least I can *see* what I'm trying to do! I'm afraid your visualizations will be as blurry as your physical vision. I've got this, Ben. Take the express train to Nairobi. Have a couple of fun-filled days with Annelise. Get your new glasses and come back! We're not going anywhere."

Or so I thought then.

After he went off to get a train ticket, I tidied up the apartment. I picked up all the pieces of paper we'd been scribbling on, memorized the topological construct I'd need to visualize, tore up the papers and turned them into papier-maché with tap water and soap. There was nothing left, physically, to give anybody a clue to our plans.

Of course I would tell Brad about our failsafe, when he returned.

I *ought* to tell him.

He really didn't like it when I surprised him with unauthorized topological meddling.

Against that, though, I had to weigh the danger that he'd give our plan away to Finch, whom I really did not trust. That might not be a problem in itself, but Finch had already shown that he was extremely careless and insufficiently paranoid about being spied on by Rashiduni agents. And letting the Rashiduni know that we had foreknowledge of the bomb and had acted to disable it… that could get Khamisi killed.

I really didn't have a choice; the stakes were too high. Brad and I had recovered from worse rough spots in our relationship, but Khamisi would not recover from what the Rashiduni would do if they thought he'd betrayed them.

My cell phone rang then. It was Ben, calling from the Royal Court Hotel. On leaving our apartment, he'd recognized two of the guys from Majengo who'd beaten him up, loitering at the corner. He'd camouflaged himself and drifted close enough to eavesdrop; unfortunately, they were speaking Swahili, so he couldn't pick up much beyond the fact that they kept using the word *majini*. He'd decided to teleport to the hotel before calling to warn me.

"You," I said, "definitely need to make yourself scarce for a couple of days. Lensky and I will be fine; they've never seen us. Take a cab to the railroad station, get your ticket and *don't come back here*. Just get straight onto the train. Okay?"

Then I hung up and brooded. True, the Majengo thugs hadn't seen Lensky or me. But... Ben had teleported directly here from that nasty confrontation in Majengo. How had they even found this apartment? I could think of only three possibilities. One, it was pure coincidence. Two, they had a djinn of their own that had followed Ben here.

Or three, they had been pointed at this apartment by somebody who recognized Ben and knew where he lived.

16. Djinns, devils, and assault rifles

Lensky opened the door to a white-faced Finch.

"That damned fool!" Finch said. His hands were shaking. "I warned him, Brad. I sent Mashika up to Garissa to get us some district papers, she isn't back yet. He shouldn't even have been there… I suppose he thought he could stop by and pick up his mail beforehand, and then he was late getting there. The idiot. The damned suicidal *idiot*."

Lensky drew him into the apartment.

"I came as soon as I heard," Finch said. He sank down at the table and stared right through me.

"Heard what?"

"Didn't you – Isn't it on the news? My God, they *can't* hush it up. It's murder, now."

Lensky sat down opposite Finch, exuding calm and solidity. He was very good at that. "Take your time, Nelson. No, we've heard nothing." And he'd been listening to the local news all afternoon, waiting to hear about the scheduled bombing. "What do you mean, murder? Wasn't everybody warned in time? Did the blast take out other offices, or what?"

Finch drew a long, shaky breath and focused with a visible effort. "Oh, *warned*, yes, but that fool Taylor didn't pay attention. He was at his desk when it went off."

"And it had been placed—"

"Right under his desk, as we agreed. I *told* him, dammit!" Finch shook his head. "He didn't make it, Lensky."

It had been obvious that was where he was heading, but I didn't believe it yet. I couldn't believe it. I – if this was true, then I had massively fouled up. My attempt to degrade the explosives remotely by Riemann heat must have failed. *All* our plans had failed. And now a man I knew and liked, Khamisi, had caused the death of an American agent whom I'd never met, but who had been supposed to be safe and out of harm's way regardless of whether the algorithm Ben and I had developed worked out. I felt sick at my stomach, and Lensky – who didn't even know about that second plan – looked worse.

"Let me get this straight," Lensky said. "You're sure Taylor was there?"

"I wish I weren't. My God, surely they *can't* hush up something like this?"

"I wouldn't have thought so," Lensky said grimly. "Maybe State is leaning on the Kenyatta administration – But how would they have known so soon?"

Finch shook his head. "I don't know. I don't understand anything. I was at Taylor's house just last night, after your asset sent us word of the timing. I *told* him not to go to the office today. God, Lensky, I knew the man was sloppy and practiced bad tradecraft, but I never realized he was this stupid!" He shook his head again. "It's – beyond belief. I'm going back now, somebody has to secure any documents or other materials that weren't destroyed. I just – needed to see you, first."

"Can I help?"

"No! I came to warn you, you have to exfiltrate immediately! If you stay here, if they connect you with the office, they might work the other direction and find Khamisi through you. It'll set our work here back twenty years if the CIA office in Mombasa is found to have been blown up by our own asset. And worse, if you don't get out... Lensky, you can't risk an African jail. You can't risk it for *her*." He jerked his head at me.

Lensky accompanied Finch down to the street. When he returned he told me that he'd seen the man into a tuk-tuk and had given the driver the address of a coffee shop near the office.

"I've never seen anybody lose his nerve so fast."

I had had time to think while Lensky was out of the apartment. "We should have gone with him. Let's go to the office building now."

"Thalia, we can't do that," Lensky said firmly. "I appreciate your wanting to take care of Finch, but you heard the man. We are at the center of this; if the police start looking at us, that may lead them to Khamisi. I don't want to see the boy arrested for a murder he never meant to commit. We've already failed him by not clearing the office as we promised."

Actually, I wasn't thinking about taking care of Nelson Finch. I was thinking that I did not believe him. What, there'd been a bombing in downtown Mombasa, a bombing that claimed the life of an American case officer, and the Kenyan government had immediately clamped down on *all* news organizations to stop them reporting on it? Our own government wasn't anywhere near that efficient.

"You're – we're not going to run away, are we? Leaving Khamisi to fend for himself? And Ben?"

"No, of course not. Finch momentarily lost his nerve. Trust me, Thalia, there's no way the Kenyatta administration is going to arrest American citizens on mere suspicion."

"You think they're that much better behaved than our own government?" A branch of which had recently drugged me, thrown me into a windowless cell, and pepper-sprayed me, all in the name of the greater good.

"No, but I think they need America a lot more than America needs them. You know that new desalination plant they want to build on the north coast?"

"Um, no, why?"

"Well. It could help avert a famine, come the next drought. But it's not cheap, and they're hoping to get the US to help pay for it. Uhuru Kenyatta is counting on that and other American-financed infrastructure projects to consolidate his hold on power; there were… questions… about the integrity of the last elections. So, no, he's not about to do anything stupid while the new aid package is being negotiated."

Brad had more faith in the ability of governments to avoid being stupid than I had. But since I found the idea of giving up and running away, not to speak of abandoning those kids in the training camp, deeply distasteful, I wasn't going to argue with him. Besides, I had other things to do. "I suppose you're right," I said, and took myself and my phone to the dimness of the back bedroom. Thank God we still had access to Mr. Prajapati's wi-fi! I tapped the phone and scrolled through local, national and international news sites. None of the sites I visited had been blocked by censors. None of them had anything to say about a fatal terrorist bombing in the heart of Mombasa.

I went back and searched the largest sites on "Mombasa," "Bombing," "Terrorism," and "Rashiduni." I found nothing but one weeks-old article arguing that al-Shabaab, not Jeshi-la-Rashiduni, had been responsible for terrorizing the residents of some island called Kisiwa cha Shetani.

What *had* happened, then? Closing my eyes, I built the image of overlapping grids and surfaces that I'd used to reach my awareness into the bomb under LeShawn Taylor's desk early that morning.

I saw… nothing.

Could I possibly have got everything wrong?

Would it have worked better if Ben had been able to check the math?

Could I go to the site myself and see what had happened?

I didn't know what would happen if I tried to teleport into an office that no longer existed because it had been blown sky-high by Semtex, and I was not eager to make the experiment. But I did have a pretty fair idea of what would happen if I tried to go there now by conventional means. It would mean a knock-down drag-out fight with Brad, for starters. And if I explained my private reason for doubting Finch's story – the 'failsafe' plan I'd kept from both him and Finch – that wasn't going to do my relationship with Brad a lot of good, was it?

I chewed my nails, indecisive and confused, until I heard Brad's cell phone ring. A moment later the bedroom door swung open. "That was Khamisi. The usual place. Can you bring him here?"

Lensky might disapprove of using cell phones for clandestine communications, but they were a lot more efficient than strolling around town looking for chalk marks on walls. In the somnolent heat of late afternoon, the perfumer's was closed and the market around it was almost empty. I took Khamisi's hand and whisked us back to the comparative coolness of our apartment.

"Are the Rashiduni happy with you?" Lensky asked as soon as we stepped out of the air into the living room.

Khamisi's grin was a bit shaky. "No, of course not. They are furious. I pretended to be equally furious; I pounded the table and demanded Anakijua's head for giving me decayed, useless explosives. If I had really wished to blow up your offices," he said, "I *would* have been angry. The man is incompetent. Allah only knows how long that Semtex has been knocking about Africa, stored in the sunshine most likely. It was so heat-degraded that the 'explosion' was about as impressive as throwing a brick."

I leaned my head back against the chair and closed my eyes, weak with relief. It had worked. Riemann heat had ruined the explosives – unless, as Khamisi believed, Africa had already taken care of that for us. Either way, I was not responsible for a terrorist bombing in the heart of Mombasa.

Then my eyes flew open again. "Wait, you mean *nothing happened?*"

Khamisi's hands described an eloquent arc. "As I said – as impressive as throwing a brick."

"Finch was just here a couple of hours ago," Lensky said. "He described it as something more. He said that LeShawn Taylor had been killed."

Khamisi shook his head. "Biradi, I was there, across the street. There was a very small thud and a little smoke, no more. The black man from your office came running outside. He was angry but not hurt."

"Brad, I've been looking for any mention of the bombing on local or national news," I put in. "There is nothing."

Lensky's eyebrows almost met. "But why would Nelson have told us the office was destroyed and Taylor killed?"

"Perhaps to inspire us to run away?" I thought back to what had been said. "Maybe he told us what he thought had happened. He knew when and where the bomb was supposed to go off. He'd have had no way of knowing the explosives were a dud. Maybe he wasn't anywhere near the office. Maybe he just assumed it had gone off as planned."

"Then how – what made him think Taylor was in the office, if he'd warned the man himself last night?"

I could think of only one explanation for that, and it was not going to go over well with Brad.

"If," I said slowly, "for whatever reason, he did *not* warn LeShawn Taylor to stay out of the office today, then he might assume he would have been killed when the bomb under his desk exploded."

"And he would feel guilty as sin for not having made sure Taylor understood the warning," Brad said. Neat! With a little twist of wording, he'd turned a suspicious omission into a simple misunderstanding, so he still didn't have to see the danger in trusting his old friend Finch. "He was probably desperate to see that we didn't suffer as well."

Khamisi's eyes met mine. I had the feeling he found this interpretation as unlikely as I did.

"He wanted us to exfil immediately – ah, leave town," Lensky translated for Khamisi.

"Ah. Yes. We must do that, of course."

"What? Why?"

"I know where the training camp is," Khamisi said. "After I fought with Anakijua over the bad bomb, I took the oath of loyalty." He shivered. "It is an evil oath, *haram* and *shirk*. I hope Allah will count it in my favor that I meant no word of it."

Mr. M. decided to join the conversation. "The Prophet, peace be upon him, said, 'Verily, Allah knoweth what is in the hearts of men as well as that which comes from their lips, and the vows of the heart shall weigh against those of the lips as gold weighs against a feather.'"

"Did he?" Khamisi said. "I do not know that *hadith*. Is it verified? From whom came it?" He seemed more concerned that he might be discussing an apocryphal tale of the Prophet than that he was having this theological discussion with a turtle head attached to a metallic snake body. I suppose his ability to freak out had been temporarily overloaded.

Mr. M. drew himself up and began a long chanted exposition of the sources for his quotation, only to be interrupted by a pounding on the front door of the apartment.

This time it was Mr. Prajapati, coming to warn us that a hostile mob was gathering in the streets as people left the mosques. There was talk of djinns and devils and he had heard people saying that the *wazungu* who lived over his store were evil magicians. He intended to pull down the steel shutters at the front of his store before taking his wife to a good Hindu neighborhood, and he thought we too should flee before the mob reached here.

"I'll help you close up downstairs," Lensky said, and headed down the narrow stairs at the side of the building. I was close behind him, and Khamisi followed me.

No, I wasn't selflessly dedicated to saving Mr. Prajapati's store. While that might be desirable, it wasn't anywhere near the top of my priorities. I intended to grab Lensky and teleport us both to some place safe. And I don't know why Khamisi was joining the stampede into danger, unless he had figured out that I, and not my 'jini' Mr. M., was the key to getting us out of there alive.

At least – I should have been the key. Turned out that galloping downstairs to the street was a very, very bad idea.

There were already too many people in the street, but they seemed to be still in the milling-around-and-talking-trash mode. I rounded the corner of the stairs, headed for the door Lensky was already disappearing through, and… the world went away.

When I blinked, I seemed to be back in our cardboard-darkened bedroom. A whole family of African drummers had taken up residence in my right temple, and my vision swam. Lensky was bending over me with a glass in his hand, and my face was wet.

Nothing computed.

"Thank God! You're back with us."

"*Alhamdulillah*," Khamisi breathed from the doorway.

"I told you she was not seriously injured," Mr. M. croaked from somewhere out of my sight.

"Where?" I creaked.

It was indeed the back bedroom. After the half-brick hit me, Lensky had thrown me over his shoulder and charged through the store, out the back, and up the back stairs. Then he'd alternated throwing water at me with grabbing vital supplies out of Prajapati's and enlisting Khamisi's help to drag them upstairs. The pillows were soaked; I must have been out longer than I'd thought.

A noise like a hundred overturned beehives rose from the street in front of the apartment. I grabbed Lensky's sleeve. "We have to get out of here. Come on!" But when I tried to visualize the construct that we used for teleportation, the intersecting two-dimensional shapes in a black and empty three-space, the bright shapes wobbled in my mind and became attenuated clouds of points, then curling ribbons... I put one hand to my aching head and groaned. "Can't quite do it yet. I should be able to any minute though." I hoped. Oh, I hoped. Could traumatic head injury have permanently destroyed the quirk in my brain that turned topological theorems into real-world actions?

If so, the rising noises outside suggested I might not live to regret it. Not long, anyway. "The back stairs?"

"No," Lensky said. "There's another crowd on Grand Mosque Road." I stifled a second groan.

He patted my hand. "Just rest. Let me know when you feel like you can teleport." He disappeared in the direction of the living room.

Lying down with my eyes closed didn't really help; it just allowed me to focus on the relentless pounding in my head and the churning in my stomach. I made my way out of the bedroom and down the hall, touching one wall for balance.

Lensky and Khamisi were sitting on the floor in the middle of a pile of trash, doing something with empty glass bottles. The room smelled like a gas station. It didn't help my symptoms any. And I couldn't make any sense at all of what they'd scavenged from Prajapati's. I looked dubiously at a bag of tampons and maxi-pads. "Ah, Brad, I have enough feminine supplies already, and I don't even use these brands."

"Wound dressings," he said, pointing at the pads.

"And these?" I picked up a package of tampons.

"You can stuff one into a bullet hole. To stop the bleeding," he explained at my blank look.

Oh, so that would be a bullet hole in a *person*, not in a wall or anything. I had hoped we wouldn't actually encounter that particular problem.

"And Superglue is good for closing the edges of a wound."

Something else I would have been happy never needing to know.

Looking much too cheerful for a man in a potential war zone, Lensky set

Khamisi and me to creating Molotov cocktails. "You poke some Styrofoam down the neck of a bottle, pour a little gasoline on it, you get a grand inflammable sludge," he told us. "Experiment with the proportions, figure out what works best. When the bottle is full – well, partly full, you don't want the stuff actually oozing out – dip a rag into the sludge and stuff it into the neck of the bottle."

"What rag?"

A good question. Just like empty tin cans and scraps of paper big enough to write on, rags were valuable commodities in the poorer parts of Mombasa.

"Well, there's that red and purple coverup of Thalia's."

"There is *not*!" I might be a tad woozy, but I wasn't ready to let him ruin one of my few souvenirs. "Give me a knife, I'll cut up one of the sheets."

Lensky produced a six-inch piece of black ceramic from his other ankle – I mean, the one that wasn't already wearing a derringer. He snapped his wrist and a blade slid out with a menacing *click*. "Gravity knife. Have fun, Thalia!"

He was certainly having the time of his life; he couldn't stop grinning. While Khamisi stuffed Styrofoam down bottles and I ripped a sheet into strips, he went back to our bedroom and dragged out a flat metal box that I didn't remember seeing before. He punched the combination lock on the top and flipped the lid open to reveal two long, black, ugly shapes.

"Those things were under our bed? And you didn't bother telling me?"

White teeth flashed at me. "You'd have slept better if you'd known?"

"Okay, you win. No, I would not have slept better knowing I was inches away from a couple of assault rifles." I blinked and looked away. My vision was still messed up. Those long shiny barrels couldn't really be undulating like snakes, could they?

"Assault rifles? That's a meaningless term," he told me, watching my face while his hands slid and turned things on the weapons. Black bits moved over other black bits and fitted into place with quiet clicks. Apparently he didn't need to look at what he was doing. Those stories about field-stripping weapons blindfolded must have been true. "To be precise, these are fully automatic AK-74Ms with built-in aiming optics, 30-round magazines and GP-34 under-barrel grenade launchers." He sounded as if he was describing the charms of an old girlfriend – one I would not have liked.

Not, I thought, something he would have picked up in Prajapati's. "Did Nelson Finch get you those things?"

Another flash of teeth. "The one thing I can definitely say in Finch's favor is that he inspired me to reach out to nonstandard channels."

A typical Lensky non-answer.

I blinked and realized that the illusion of undulating barrels hadn't been entirely due to my concussion. Mr. M. was sliding all over one of the rifles, loving it to pieces. He had long been agitating for grenade launchers to be retrofitted to the mechanical part of his body, and our engineer had been putting him off by claiming he wasn't heavy enough to withstand the recoil. Right now, I was just glad she'd never fitted him with a trigger finger.

"Leave it alone," Lensky told Mr. M., "these have to go to people who can handle them. You'll cover me?" He looked at Khamisi, who shook his head and backed away. At last, I'd met a man who wasn't seduced by the Romance of the Gun.

And it had to be at a time when we could really use another shooter.

Lensky gave Khamisi a stern look. "Time to man up. If I have to go out on the street—"

"You're not going out on the street!"

"Shut up, Thalia." Back to Khamisi. "Even if I only throw bottles out the window, I'll need somebody to cover me. And if they storm the back terrace, you'll have to take over in the front while I defend the terrace. We can't expose Thalia; she's still our best ticket out of here. So it's up to you and me to hold them up until she recovers enough to teleport. Well?"

Khamisi gave a somewhat wobbly nod and bent to pick up the rifle that Lensky slid towards him.

"At least he knows not to point it at us," Lensky muttered, watching Khamisi's tentative handling of the thing. "Thalia, have you got all the bottles prepped?"

"You," I said with a wave at our newly constructed stock of Molotov cocktails, "are enjoying this. Aren't you?"

"Ahh, now, I wouldn't say that exactly."

But I would. His eyes were sparkling, his movements were deft and assured, and his hands were moving over that ugly black killing machine with the sort of caresses I preferred to see reserved for me.

I closed my eyes and reached for the blackness of the in-between. Still wobbly, dammit. Lines and shapes and bright individual points swooped around my inner vision almost randomly, blurring in and out of focus.

The shouting outside was punctuated now with thuds and crashes. What were they throwing?

"Front room," Lensky said. "Khamisi, cover me." He filled his hands with wine bottles.

"You're not going outside!"

He grinned and saluted me with a handful of Molotov cocktails. "Not yet. Have a little faith in me, Thalia." For a square, solid man, he was remarkably graceful as he moved through the apartment, hands full of bottles, crouching past windows to present the smallest possible target. Khamisi trailed behind him, holding the rifle awkwardly. I hoped he would remember that he wasn't supposed to shoot my husband in the back.

A moment later I heard the sound of shattering glass from the front of the building, followed by yells and screams from the crowd. Brad slithered back to the living room to report cheerfully, "That's given them something to think about… How are you feeling, Thalia?"

"Still dizzy."

"Well, don't worry. We've got plenty of ammunition! Watch the back, and call me if they get on the terrace." He oozed back towards the front room, this time carrying the second rifle.

I heard a stuttering rattle from what had been Victor's bedroom. That would be Lensky and Khamisi shooting out, right? Not somebody shooting them… I felt an almost physical force tugging me that way. I needed to see Brad. But he'd given me a job to do…

"Mr. M., can you go see what's happening at the front?" He undulated off and I made my way back down the hall to our bedroom. How was I supposed to know if anybody was on the terrace? Brad had been much too thorough with his improvised shutters of flattened cardboard boxes. I pulled one corner away from the wall. A tack popped onto the floor and a sliver of light showed through the opening. I knelt on the bed and put one eye to the crack. The terrace faced west, and the setting sun stabbed directly at me. My eyes watered. But there was nobody on the terrace.

Not yet, anyway.

They came when the sun dipped behind the westernmost buildings of Old Town and plunged us into the sudden tropical night: a rush of bare feet, a rustle of robes, half-smothered exclamations.

17. Island of *Shetani*

I didn't have to shout for Brad; Mr. M. peeked over my shoulder and zipped back to the front room, an undulating silver blur on the coconut matting. A heartbeat later, I felt Lensky's reassuring bulk behind me. "Get back." As I left my observation post on the bed, he ripped another slit in the cardboard with the tip of his rifle and sent a series of short bursts out onto the terrace. I heard a scream, a rush of retreating feet. Brad was laughing under his breath.

Well, great. My loving husband was having the time of his life. By now he'd probably corrupted Khamisi; if I retreated all the way to the other end of the apartment, would I find the peaceable chemical engineer hurling flaming bottles and firing into the crowd with the greatest of ease? Most likely. Even Mr. M. was zipping back and forth through the apartment, buzzing, "Praise the Lord and Pass the Ammunition."

Men.

I had learned a couple of things from watching Brad shout at the television set about all the errors in the spy shows and shoot-em-ups he liked to watch when there weren't any classic movies on. One, eventually everybody has to reload. Two, "plenty of ammunition" is not the same as "an infinite supply of ammunition."

So, as the member of the team who wasn't busy shooting anybody, it behooved me to get back to exercising my particular skills before we ran out of ammunition.

I really prefer to do mathematics in a quiet, well-lit space where nobody is screaming or trying to kill me. However, my fellow topologists and I have had our differences of opinion, some of them rather loud, so I wasn't unfamiliar with the concept of working through noise. And the things we'd been involved in since Lensky and his agency took an active part in our lives had not exactly been peaceful. I took a moment for a confidence-building review. I'd successfully teleported in all manner of difficult situations, and I had the informal reports to document it: while being held at gunpoint (*A Pocketful of Stars*), grabbed by thuggish protestors (*An Opening in the Air*), threatened at gunpoint again (*An Annoyance of Grackles*) and dodging German bombs in the streets of London (*A Tapestry of Fire*). Surely I could get Brad and Khamisi and me out of this latest tight spot?

Well… I'd never actually teleported while recovering from a slight concussion. But the key word there, surely, was 'slight.' I sidled into the living room and found a strip of torn sheet that hadn't been stuffed into a bottle. Soaked it in the kitchen sink and wrapped it around my aching head, feeling a bit like Sydney Carton at his studies. Not *that* much like Sydney Carton, though, because I had no intention of doing a far, far better thing and sacrificing myself for the sake of my comrades. Our situation was kind of the reverse of his: we all needed me alive and functional if we were to get out of this. I sat down and leaned back against the chair, consciously relaxing my muscles, feeling the soothing coolness around my temples, breathing slowly and regularly.

Closing my eyes, I put one hand in my pocket and felt the tiny electrical tickle of an infinite set of points of light dancing against my palm. I reached out through them to a sense of the universe around us. I breathed, "*Brouwer,*" in the hope that habit would strengthen my visualization. For a long moment there was nothing but the ordinary darkness behind my closed eyes. Then the greater vision became clear: absolute blackness surrounding me, infinite space, two surfaces shimmering with color and touching at just one point. Yes! I could do this. Now to collect Khamisi, Brad, and Mr. M. How was that going to work, when both guys were now firing almost continuously from opposite ends of the long, narrow apartment?

We'd have to be fast, that was all. And I'd have to go the minute I grabbed them. I unwound the strip of wet sheet and dampened the top part of my bui-bui instead, stepped into it, tucked the bottom part into my waistband and tied the head strings firmly. The cool, damp cloth felt good when I tucked it down over my forehead. Then I asked Mr. M. to tell Khamisi we were ready to go. He needed to drop his rifle and *run* to the back bedroom where Brad and I would be waiting for him, because now that the rioters had found the terrace we couldn't afford to leave that end of the apartment unguarded for a minute. The front was slightly more secure, at least it would be if Khamisi had been discouraging anybody from rushing the stairs.

I felt modestly proud of myself for that bit of tactical analysis.

There couldn't have been more than a few seconds to wait in the dark back bedroom, but it felt like forever with the rifle fire spattering in my ear and the damp bui-bui clinging to my face while I held the visualization steady: two glowing surfaces, a single point of identity, and our destination warped across the curve of the upper surface. Then Mr. M.'s metal scales wrapped over my shoulders. I put an arm around Lensky's waist, grabbed Khamisi's elbow, and concentrated. *"Brouwer."*

The in-between buffeted me in an unfamiliar way, as if it had developed the ability to create storms without matter. I felt pulled this way and that, couldn't afford to slacken my concentration on the Brouwer visualization to figure it out; poured stars and all my thought towards the image of our destination. White walls and hard-packed earth, crouching, dark-clad figures... The brilliant images and dark backdrop of the in-between faded and the courtyard of Mama Aesha's compound became solid around us.

"Nani anakuja?"

"Khamisi!"

"Saliya? Kwa nini umeja..."

The babble of Swahili coming from all sides was too much for me. I sagged against Lensky and he guided me to an empty kitchen chair. I thought it was the same one where I'd put in my time scraping coconuts and acquiring merit with the women of the family. Behind us, I heard Khamisi talking rapidly and sounding authoritative. The women stopped crowding us and gradually retreated, looking nervous.

Oh. The guys hadn't dropped their weapons after all, had they? I briefly resented having wasted mathemagical energy on teleporting those things. A boy appeared and gestured that Khamisi and Lensky should give him their rifles. And, much to my relief, someone closed the heavy spiked door that I had only seen standing ajar, and lowered a hefty plank of wood across it.

"I thought we were going to the hotel!"

Brad. That explained why this very short jump had been so difficult and draining. Not only was I recently concussed, not only did I have two hulking guys to carry with me, but one of those guys had – consciously or not – been trying to steer me in a totally wrong direction. I opened my eyes enough to scowl at Lensky. "You wouldn't have held on to your rifles long at the Royal Court Hotel."

"We didn't get to keep them for long *here*," Lensky said with a pained glance at the interior doorway through which the kid had vanished. "And – where *is* 'here,' anyway?"

It hadn't been that long a jump, but I had the shakes. "I need something to eat."

Khamisi said something else in Swahili – several somethings else, actually – and Rifle Boy reappeared, carrying a plate of sticky candies. Mmm, jellabies – those sweet, deep-fried twisty tubes that Brad had bought me on the one day when we were trying to be a normal couple. Eating those was like mainlining sugar. I began paying attention to my surroundings.

Zawadi was not here, which made things slightly more difficult – or not; I didn't really feel like being our spokesman. No, I was more than willing to leave that task to Khamisi while I leaned back and explored the feeling of sugar and energy revitalizing the wrung-out dishrag I'd felt like minutes earlier.

"This compound belongs to some of Khamisi's family," I explained to Brad during the occasional pauses in the rapid-fire Swahili debate going on all around us. "I've visited here before. They're good people. They aren't with the Rashiduni. Nobody will be looking for us here – and even if they did," I said, thinking about that massive door, "this place, unlike our apartment, was built for serious defense." I still wasn't sure about the function of those nasty-looking spikes on the outside of the door, but they did send a message. Something along the lines of "No Solicitors," but with more teeth in it.

Eventually the impromptu Unexpected Visitors Debating Society broke up and Khamisi updated us on the arrangements. We would all three spend the night here, but he and Brad would be together and I would have to go in with the unmarried granddaughters. Very early in the morning we would leave here, quietly, and take back alleys to a place where we could get a dhow to the island where the training camp was located.

Apart from the notion that there were any streets this deep in Old Town that *weren't* back alleys, I was fine with this program. Brad was not quite so happy. He didn't like having to let me out of his sight, and he didn't like being separated from the rifles. In the interests of a harmonious marriage, I refrained from asking which of these two things bothered him most.

Dinner happened about then, so we would have been separated in any case. To my everlasting regret, the convention about serving men separately deprived me of seeing how Lensky would cope with the two-fingers-rice-ball convention. I, however, successfully deployed my skills at small object manipulation to get myself a healthy sample of numerous dishes this time. My head still hurt, and the women told me with sign language that I had an impressive goose egg on the right side of my forehead, but there was nothing wrong with my application of topology now. They had this one dish of greens cooked with onions and tomatoes that would have made a veggie-lover out of anyone. And the things these people did with coconut milk... But I digress. We ate, we retired for the night, and approximately five minutes later by my internal reckoning I was scrubbing my sleepy eyes with a cloth dipped in cold water and putting on my bui-bui for the trek through the streets.

I wasn't up to noticing much at this hour, but I did see that Khamisi and Lensky were lugging two shabby but heavy suitcases whose contents shifted strangely as they moved. It wasn't hard to guess what was in them. I oozed up beside Brad and lowered my veil a couple of inches. "Do those suitcases hold what I think they hold?" I mouthed.

"Shush. Khamisi says we won't be able to hire a boat if anybody knows what we're carrying." He eased the handles of his suitcase over to the other hand. "Too bad you didn't think to rescue the gun case too."

"Whine, moan, complain. My hands *were* rather full at the time. Too bad *you* didn't think about the gun case. Anyway, wouldn't that make it too obvious what you were carrying?"

"There is that." He shifted the suitcase again. "On the other hand, it wouldn't have come this close to falling apart on a short walk to the old harbor."

The waterfront: a sense of salt in the warm, heavy air, birds swooping and crying overhead, long rays of morning light passing over rickety wooden piers. In the echoes of the morning call to prayer, ragged boys danced and cartwheeled and tried to take our hands. "*Jahazi, mashua, ngalawa?*" they called. "*Mnataka kuona pomboo?*"

One especially energetic kid danced right up between Brad and Khamisi and tried to grab their suitcases. "*Mtaona pomboo mengi, bwana!*"

"*La! Hatutaki pomboo!*" Khamisi snapped.

The boy fell back before us, his mobile little face expressing surprise and disbelief. "*Hamtaki?*"

"He cannot believe that we do not wish to see dolphins," Mr. M. croaked into my ear.

Dolphins?

I wouldn't mind seeing some dolphins.

Maybe we could come back?

"*La! Nenda!*"

"*Wazungu wanataka daima pomboo.*" The boy folded his arms like someone expressing an immutable truth: white people always want dolphins.

"These white people," Khamisi told him, "do not want dolphins. They want to go to an island."

An older boy darted up, speaking a singsong English. "Ah, Wasini Island tour, very very good, only twenty thousand Kenya shilling!"

"No."

"Ok, because you are Swahili, for you and friends only, special price. Ten thousand shillings for each."

"That's even more, and we do not want to go to Wasini Island!"

"Why not? Wasini is the *best* island!" He launched into a catalog of Wasini Island's virtues which Khamisi cut off with three words.

"*Twenda kwa Usirudi.*"

The waterfront got very quiet.

One of the men who'd been watching the interchange, grinning, turned around and began washing down the deck of his little boat.

Two others seated themselves, arms folded, looking past us.

It must have been my imagination, but it seemed to me that even the seagulls stopped screeching.

"*Kisiwa cha shetani,*" somebody muttered. "Island of devils," Mr. M. translated quietly.

"What is the matter?" Khamisi demanded. "I am looking for a *man* to carry us, not a little girl who is afraid of shadows!"

"It is too far," another man muttered.

"No farther than Wasini."

"Yes, but there are *polisi* on Wasini. They do not want the *wazungu* frightened away. No one goes to that other place."

"What are you afraid of? Pirates? The Somali pirates don't come so far south. Are the dhow captains of Mombasa all cowards?"

Argument and insults didn't get us a dhow for Usirudi. An offer of what Khamisi considered a ridiculous overpayment finally interested the proprietor of one small, shabby dhow, little more than a dugout with one slanting sail and a beat-up outboard motor. But that was only the beginning of the negotiations. Khamisi felt it important to mention that taking us to the wrong island, or taking us out to sea and throwing us out of the dhow, or attempting in any other way to defraud us, would be extremely bad luck and would definitely entail the loss of the half of the fee which would be paid on our safe return to Mombasa.

Jumanne, proprietor of the *ngalawa*, mentioned that he had agreed to that miserly fee only on the understanding that it would all be paid up front.

Khamisi said that he *might* be persuaded to pay sixty percent of the exorbitant fee now, but that Jumanne should know we happened to have a *shetani* of our own which would take any attacks upon us very poorly. On cue, Mr. M. croaked a few bars of the Marine Corps Hymn and flashed his lasers at the dhow owner.

They eventually reached an agreement at seventy-five percent down, the rest upon our safe return.

"Usirudi!" one of the others called mockingly as we boarded the little craft. "I'll comfort your wife when you don't come back, Jumanne!"

The three hours of sailing south on a tiny dhow should have been a romantic experience of blue sea and steadily lightening sky, white sand beaches to our right – sorry, I never can remember whether that's starboard or port – and clusters of coconut palms around whitewashed buildings. I'll have to go back and take that tour of Wasini some day; wondering whether the dhow owner is going to throw you overboard to avoid landing on the "island of devils" takes all the romance out of the most scenic dhow voyage.

We had plenty of time to talk and plan, anyway.

On the way, Khamisi explained that the superstitions attached to Usirudi Island had made it difficult for us to get passage there. It started with the name: *Usirudi* was Swahili for "you don't come back," and it got worse from there. The ghost stories and the tales of infestation by *majini* had probably been encouraged by pirates who found it convenient to scare people away from the island.

"I thought you said pirates didn't come so far south."

Khamisi grinned. "I said *Somali* pirates don't. I didn't say anything about Kenyan, Tanzanian, or Zanzibari pirates. Just because those Somalis get all the publicity, you should not assume they are the only ones operating off this coast."

Oh, that was tremendously reassuring. Even after Khamisi added that the Somali pirates got the most attention because they were the most brutal of the lot, I couldn't feel there would be any upside about encountering a pirate from some other country. But then, we weren't cruising for pleasure – something it occasionally became difficult to remember in the balmy weather, surrounded as we were by blue-green water and motoring past white beaches. We were heading south to tangle with people even worse than pirates.

I remembered the one article I'd read that mentioned this island. The writer had claimed that al-Shabaab was responsible for terroristic activities there.

Khamisi shook his head. "They may have had ambitions, but it really is too far south for a group out of Somalia to control. No, if anybody is there it will be the Rashiduni. There was a Swahili city on Usirudi once, and the remains are in better shape than most because the archaeologists have never been able to keep laborers long enough to start a serious dig there. The Jeshi-la-Amani is probably hiding out in the ruins."

"Wouldn't the buildings have mostly fallen down by now?"

"Our ancient stone towns were built of coral blocks. The most damage to them has not been done by nature, but by people taking the stones to make new buildings. The worse the location's economy, the better the ancient buildings have survived."

Oh, great. We weren't just heading for a terrorist training camp; we were heading for a terrorist training camp surrounded by an elite fighting force.

Brad took my hand. "Don't look so fretful, Thalia. There's a big difference between a bunch of African terrorists and somebody who's been properly trained."

Yes, and one of the differences was that there were a *lot* of the former and only *one* of Lensky. The man had a pathological inability to reckon the odds against him. I'd seen that in him before. I blame John Wayne.

I squeezed his hand and went back to running through my tools for influencing the situation. Teleportation was our ace card, of course; the simplest thing would be to sneak into the training camp under camouflage, grab the kids and teleport to a safe place. Trouble was, the only reasonably close locus would be Jumanne's dhow, and I wasn't entirely sure how safe that would be.

Personal shields would be useful too, but I couldn't shield Lensky or Khamisi individually; the best I could do would be to keep them close by me and raise a shield big enough to cover all three of us. I had no illusions about how well that would work once Lensky got into the spirit of the action. Too bad I couldn't tie him up and leave him in the dhow with Jumanne while Khamisi and I snuck in to get the children. I looked fretful and nibbled on my fingernails.

"At least we've only got to grab three kids, one each," I murmured.

Khamisi looked deeply unhappy. "Ah… Saliya, that is not quite accurate."

"I can hardly rescue everybody in the camp, not that most of them deserve rescuing," I pointed out. "It's going to be quite hard enough to teleport you two and three children out of there."

"Cannot your djinn help?" He nodded at Mr. M., who was comfortably snoozing around my waist.

"Even so."

Khamisi took a deep breath. "Well, then. If you cannot take more than five people to safety, Saliya, leave me to find my own way out. You *must* take Tabari with you."

"Tabari?"

"My half-brother. Our father divorced his mother two years ago. He has been angry ever since. When I came back from America, he had run away. Our father said he did not know what had happened to Tabari, but I found out." Another slow breath before bursting out with what I'd just guessed had to be coming. "He had joined Jeshi-la-Rashiduni."

"How old is he?"

"Thirteen… He does not know what he has done, he is a crazy kid; he just wanted to hurt our father."

"Rough on his mother, too."

"As I said," Khamisi repeated, "a crazy kid. He thinks that he wants to hurt the whole world – at least that is what he said when he ran away. I think he is sorry now. I think he will be very happy to come home with us – with you."

"You know he's at this camp?" But I sort of knew the answer to that also.

"I saw him on the video."

At 5:14. I knew it!

"I – we'll see what we can do."

Not that it mattered at this point, but I felt marginally less guilty than I had about getting Khamisi entangled in our problems. His troubles with the Rashiduni had started before Zawadi introduced us.

Khamisi lapsed into a brooding silence. I edged closer to Brad and laid my head on his shoulder.

"It'll be all right, Thalia. More than all right. We finally know what we're doing!"

He looked less reassuring than eager, this crazy man with his knight-in-shining-armor complex. He seemed totally confident of our ability to sneak past an army to extract four children, one of them probably kept separately from the others, from a training camp for child soldiers. Anybody would have thought he did this kind of thing before breakfast every morning.

I didn't think we knew what we were doing at all. Granted, I should have learned by now to be comfortable with that, since it was usually the case once the Center for Applied Topology got involved. Some things you never get used to.

"Too bad we didn't take time to get reinforcements," he added. Sounding marginally less insane. "I should have called Finch... I wonder if we can get a signal from here?"

"Brad! You even *try* to call that man and I will throw your phone into the ocean. Are you still kidding yourself that he's on our side?"

"I don't care how much he irritates you, Thalia, he's a Company man."

"A Company man who has tripped us up at every turn of this investigation. He claimed LeShawn Taylor had died in the bombing; we know that was a lie."

"A misunderstanding."

"He demanded everything be run through his office, yet every single thing we've learned has come from outside that office. The thugs he met in Majengo beat up Ben and could have killed him if he hadn't been able to teleport. Ben saw some of the same thugs in front of Prajapati's store; how did they find us, if Finch didn't point them there?" I thought of another thing. "And why did the Rashiduni suddenly demand that Khamisi blow up the CIA office to prove himself? Maybe Finch wanted Taylor dead. I will bet you anything you like that he never warned Taylor at all."

"He couldn't have known the bomb would be a dud."

"Right! He assumed it was successful, and he fed us both a line of garbage about what he thought must have happened. He didn't know I would make sure the bomb never exploded."

"You *what?*"

Oops.

I told him about the modification of Riemann fire I'd come up with to slow-cook the Semtex explosives until they crumbled and disintegrated.

"You didn't tell me you were going to do that."

"No. I couldn't trust you not to tell Finch, and if the Rashiduni found out, they'd have killed Khamisi."

"You couldn't trust me."

The words fell between us like stones into the sea.

18. Master of the glass

Blue smoke wafted upwards through the open spaces above Omar's head. The walls of the ancient town had withstood the ravages of time quite well; the roofs, with their long wooden supports, had mostly collapsed. He should recruit some builders and set them to renovating a few rooms before the next rainy season…

Building was boring stuff; conquest was better. When he was lord of the Swahili coast, he would make slaves of the upcountry pagans and sacrifice any who couldn't or wouldn't rebuild his cities. He breathed in the smoke from his water pipe and let it flow out his nostrils, feeling the arousal that thoughts of conquest and dominion always brought him. The *jini* formed herself out of the floating smoke and twined herself about him, and he did not push her away.

"Oh, master of the glass, what is thy will?"

He fondled her with one hand, stroked the blue glass in which he had captured her with his other hand. One was soft and yielding, the other reassuringly cold and hard to the touch. So long as he kept that bottle intact, he could order her back into it at any time. So long as he had that power, she would bend to his will as it was proper a woman should bend before a man – any woman, human or *jini* or *shetani*.

"I sent you to tell me of those *wazungu*. To tell me that they were dead or fled."

"Would it please the master to know that they are both?"

175

"How so?"

The *jini*'s laughter was low and thrilling, a promise of infinite delights. "If they fled to the ocean, should they not drown?"

"Allah! Have you given them the running-sickness?" It was one of the torments that untamed *majini*, particularly those of the ocean, loved to inflict on humans. A man would waken to the sensation of paralysis; when he was able to move again, he would run blindly, screaming, until the *jini* guided him into the ocean.

"You might say that. They are fled, and into the ocean."

"And drowned?"

"Are they *wachawi* or *majini*, to breathe water and live? In my ocean all are equal; *wazungu* drown as easily as any other men."

Omar laughed softly.

"Is the master pleased with my service?"

"I am pleased." But Omar was too drowsy from the *bhangi* he had been smoking to do more than pat her shoulder before lapsing into a dream in which he was Caliph of the Swahili Coast from Somalia to Mozambique. In his mind, the weathered gray stones around them were once again bright with white coral plaster, the pavement before the mosque covered with rugs for the men who knelt there to pray towards Mecca after he expounded the will of Allah to them and announced the punishments for those who had failed to please God through him.

The *jini* looked down at him as he began snoring. "Who would have thought such a handsome vessel would be no better than a broken pot? If you had loved me as you did at first, Omar of Zanzibar, I would have splintered their vessel and sent them to the death you desired for them. But since you are a fool, I am content that my words should delude you." True, *wazungu* in mid-ocean drowned as easily as any other mortals... but not when their boat was sound and the sea smooth as glass.

She allowed her lower limbs to revert to their serpent form and tried to wrap her tail around that accursed blue glass bottle, but even in his drugged stupor Omar wrapped his hand tightly around the thing and clutched it to his bosom. So be it! Let him suffer the consequences deserved by those who take the words of a *jini* at face value. The *wazungu* had fled Mombasa, but they meant to attack Usirudi. She could have raised storms to capsize their pitiful little dhow and drown them, but now she would not. Perhaps they would break the bottle for her.

***

Hours after we'd left Mombasa, Usirudi Island became a low outline on the horizon. We watched tensely as the boat drew into a shallow harbor with a small beach. I could see a scatter of small thatched huts in front of a forest. The village was quiet in the baking sun. A couple of men sitting on the sand were doing something with the nets spread out in front of them – mending them? In the shade of one wall, a woman crouched, cleaning fish; her right arm threw out a glittering shower of scales with each movement of the knife in her hand. An unappealing muddy path led away from the beach, past the huts and into the darkness of the interior.

The friendly greetings and morning calls of Mama Aesha's house might have been in a different world. The people here scarcely looked up at our arrival, but bent more closely over their tasks. I had a feeling that they had learned it was not safe to notice too much about visitors to their island. I pulled up my bui-bui and tucked the veil firmly over my nose and mouth.

Jumanne tied his boat up to a pier that made the ones at Mombasa's old harbor look like miracles of civil engineering construction, jumped out into thigh-deep water and waded ashore, haranguing the men with the fishing nets. Khamisi clambered onto the pier and bent to take the suitcases from Lensky, then offered me his hand onto the irregular surface.

Keeping the folds of the bui-bui modestly in place was really a two-handed job; I was grateful for Khamisi's steadying hand on my elbow as I picked my way onto solid ground. If the locals were watching, I hoped I was getting props for keeping my eyes modestly lowered. The fact was that the bleached driftwood of the pier, held in place by ropes here and nails there, demanded my total attention if I was to reach the sandy beach in one piece.

We might have to move a little faster on the way out... oh, to heck with it, I could just teleport us from the training camp back to this boat, couldn't

I? As long as nobody moved the boat… maybe the pier itself would be a better locus, actually.

Mr. M. was concealed under my bui-bui with strong instructions *not* to move, talk, or, God forbid, sing until we had left the village. Seeing him moving and talking would be sure to freak out people so superstitious that they called their home "Island of Devils," and as for his singing, well, that usually upset anyone within earshot. Children would cry, birds fall out of the trees… you get the picture.

Khamisi told me in an undertone that Jumanne was bargaining for the right to leave his boat at the pier and for a meal to be served to the crazy *wazungu* who had paid him for a tour of the ruins on the island.

"How do you fit into the picture?" I whispered to him.

Khamisi grinned. "I am the guide for the crazy *wazungu*, of course. He probably thinks that I am charging you an exorbitant fee for this trip and that he got only a small share of the money."

I didn't really care what Jumanne thought, I just hoped he would finish his bargaining quickly. The beach was hot in the mid-day sun and the only shady place had a strong smell of fish. I sat on Lensky's suitcase, pulled the bui-bui closer over my face and imitated a well-behaved woman. Or an inanimate black sack. The two seemed to be indistinguishable in the Swahili worldview.

Food, when it came, was also not much like what came out of Mama Aesha's kitchen. There was a lot of cornmeal mush, a reasonable amount of greens cooked to a limp defeat, and some chunks of fish swimming in a thin, tasteless sauce. I applied my small object manipulation skills to the stiff cornmeal mush, which served as a utensil for picking up bits from the other two dishes, and ate as much as I could get past the bui-bui. It wasn't easy, but I had made the mistake of coming out here with no food stash. I needed to ingest calories now so that I'd be able to do some heavy-duty teleporting when the time came.

The path to the ruins turned out to be even more unpleasant than it had looked at first glance. The beach where we'd landed was slightly higher than much of the island; the path took us down into a swamp where we had to pick our way through a tangle of mangrove roots in black water. "Do I want to know about snakes in the islands?" I murmured to Khamisi.

"The villagers are pretty good about chasing them out of their territory."

"That would be very reassuring if this looked more like a village street and less like a *black, stinking swamp.*"

Lensky, ahead of us, choked.

"I suppose for you," I said under my breath, "this is almost as much fun as being back on the Farm, doing a training exercise."

"Oh, more," he breathed, "in real life the odds aren't stacked against us nearly as much as they were in those exercises."

Considering that we were going up against a terrorist army, I differed with his interpretation. But we were supposed to be approaching quietly, so I shut my trap and concentrated on keeping the hem of my bui-bui out of the water. After all, I was having it easy on this part of the journey; I didn't have to carry a suitcase full of an AK74-something with optical thingies and underslung grenade launchers, or whatever it was Lensky had said in his loving description of the rifles.

Eventually – not nearly soon enough to suit me – the path rose again, and the boy who'd been drafted to guide us held up his hand for total silence. We moved forward slowly, inch by inch, until I could see dark grey weathered stone shapes beyond the mangrove trunks. He stopped and pointed downwards. There was a deep trench immediately in front of us: a straight line cut through the jungle and down into the coral rock, with smooth sloping sides. It looked firm, regular, and distinctly un-African.

"Army Corps of Engineers?" I whispered to Lensky.

"Archaeologists," he murmured back, his lips barely moving. "Rashiduni ran them off, remember?"

I was suitably grateful to the unknown archaeologists for giving us such a fine place to lurk. Since they left, storms and attrition had already begun covering up the trench; once we scrambled into it, we were able to crawl under where some large limbs had come down across the cut, giving us shade and partial cover.

When I looked back, our guide was gone.

Our post was too far from the principal ruins for us to get a clear idea of what was happening there – not much, actually, it was siesta time – but it turned out that we were admirably placed to watch the training exercises. Nothing much happened while Lensky assembled the rifles, but as the sun dipped lower, we could see occasional movements outside the walls. Then, in answer to a shrill cry, a dozen boys formed a ragged line on the flat ground. A man walked along the line, handing out rifles that were bigger than some of the children who had to take them, and haranguing them in a harsh shout. In answer to shouted commands, the boys ran up one at a time to throw themselves behind a coral block, aim the rifle and fire. The first time one of them pointed his weapon straight at us, I ducked so fast I scraped my forehead on the side of the trench.

"They don't let them play with live ammunition," Lensky muttered, sounding amused.

Whatever that meant. I didn't want to get killed by dead ammunition either, did I?

"There's Bobby Navarro," I whispered, brilliantly identifying the only blond boy.

Lensky nodded. "And I've spotted Sam. Khamisi?"

"Tabari is the tallest one." He jerked his chin at a lean brown boy who appeared, to me, to be playing the same game as Sam: how to show the least possible amount of school spirit while avoiding getting yelled at by the coach. My kid brother Andros was an expert at that –

Oh. Oh, *shit*. This wasn't a game. The man I'd been thinking of as "Coach" yelled at Tabari, grabbed him by the ear and jerked him into the middle of the practice ground, then kicked him behind the knees to force him down. He shouted something at the other boys and they came forward slowly, eyes wide. Khamisi was cursing under his breath. "Coach" took the rifles from the boys and handed out sticks, pointed at Tabari's kneeling figure and shouted an order. Khamisi's body jerked. "They will kill him! I have to – Give me a rifle!"

Lensky moved sideways, smoothly putting himself between Khamisi and the weapons. One big hand fastened over the back of Khamisi's neck. "Cool it. They are not going to kill him now – but they certainly will, if they catch us."

I could tell when Khamisi's body relaxed because Lensky's hold loosened at the same time.

And so we watched, through an improvised screen of fallen branches and trash, while the other children in the training camp beat Tabari bloody with their sticks for his failure to show appropriate enthusiasm. But when the call to prayer rang through the sky and "Coach" allowed them to stop, Tabari stumbled to his feet and followed them back into the ruins, limping. Khamisi was cursing now, regularly, monotonously.

"You two have thrown away the best chance we will ever have!" he upbraided us, furious, but still very quiet. "We had all three of the children within sight, and but one guard—"

"There are *four* children," I said. Also quietly. "You are forgetting Rosie Jamison."

Khamisi spread his hands. "We will never be able to rescue her. She is not with the child soldiers. Better to take the three we can find."

"You missed some guards," Lensky told him. "I spotted three rifle barrels behind that tumbledown wall. You would only have gotten yourself killed if you'd run out there, Khamisi. That wouldn't do Tabari any good."

"Instead, I watched him beaten, and did nothing!"

"Thanks be to Allah that you had that much sense. Do you think Tabari would have escaped beating just because you threw your body in front of him – and got shot for your pains?" Lensky's face looked hard as I'd only seen it once before, hard as a statue's. "Listen well, Khamisi. *I* am in charge of this operation. Can I trust you to follow orders, or do I have to kill you myself?"

Khamisi was breathing hard. "You can't risk shooting me! They would hear."

Forgetting Swahili mores, I grabbed his arm and shook it. "Khamisi, don't be stupid. He probably knows six ways to kill you without making a noise, and in five of those you wouldn't even see it coming!" I hate it when people underestimate Brad.

"Four."

"Huh?"

"Offhand, I can only think of four ways to kill him that he wouldn't see coming," Lensky said, very matter-of-fact. "The other three, he might notice something, but don't worry, he wouldn't have time to make a noise."

Khamisi slumped back against the wall. "You people are assuredly mad, and you are probably all *majini* and *shetani*, and *I* was mad to come here with you."

Mr. M. popped his head up over the waist vee of my bui-bui. "Well, good," he said cheerfully, "I'm glad we have all that cleared up."

He volunteered to scout the ruins for us, saying happily that the Swahili seemed to be extra-afraid of snakes because they thought that the Djnoun took the forms of serpents, and anyway he could camouflage himself as well as any topologist, and furthermore he still had his personal weaponry with which to defend himself.

"I think I should go with you," I said.

"On no account," said Mr. M. "My task will be infinitely harder if I must conceal you as well as myself." I was perfectly able to camouflage myself without his help, but before I could point that out he continued listing his objections.

"You are large—"

Well, from his perspective, I suppose.

"—and clumsy, and noisy when you walk. *I* have the advantage of a naturally lissome and athletic body which takes up very little space and can move very quietly... Do we have any coffee?"

"We do not."

"A pity..."

I thought it was more of a saving grace. When caffeinated, Mr. M. frequently sings. Aesthetic considerations aside, our chances of infiltrating the training camp unnoticed would rapidly approach zero if even one of our number roared into action with a spirited rendering of "The Fall of Idols." (We're hoping he'll get over his recent fascination with Morbid Angel and other death metal bands. So far, all efforts to redirect his attention have failed.)

19. Classical methods

It was after dark when Mr. M. returned, and we were all tired, hungry and thirsty. If we didn't move soon I might not be able to teleport at all.

He reported that the three boys and the other child soldiers all slept in a large room at the edge of the ruins. The room's doors and windows were long gone, but there was a guard on duty. Rosie Jamison was not there; he thought she might be in Omar's personal quarters.

"Did you figure out where those are?"

"One room was guarded by the djinn. Being unsure of her allegiance, I felt it wiser not to converse with her."

"Well, *duh*. She belongs to Omar."

"Between a human being and one of the Djnoun," Mr. M. said pedantically, "the question of who belongs to whom is debatable. On our last encounter with her, TheSila did you no harm. She even frightened away the thief who awakened you. Still, I felt unwilling to take the risk of open contact. As for the guard on the boys," he said, admiring the moonlight on his silver scales, "the man on duty now is a user of *bhangi*, and in addition he seems more concerned with preventing the children from leaving than with watching for intruders. These amateur groups are *so* slipshod. Nabû-kudurrī-usur would have had his head."

"Don't worry about the guard," Lensky said, "he's mine. Thalia, you will have to carry one of the rifles until I neutralize him. Then we can ask the boys where Rosie is." He slipped the Glock out of its holster on his hip.

"Ah, wouldn't it be better to 'neutralize' him from a distance with the rifle?"

"In this light? Anyway, we don't want to alert them with gunshots."

"Lensky, I've heard you fire the Glock. It's not exactly silent."

"That's why I'm not planning to shoot the guard." Lensky hefted his pistol thoughtfully. "It may have been a mistake to go with this polymer frame. Right now I could really use a nice solid steel pistol. Oh well, too late now."

Oh.

I decided to shut up and do what I was told. It would be a nice change for Lensky.

Never having been inside the ruins, of course, I couldn't teleport us directly to the children. All I could do was keep camouflage over us and try not to fall over my own feet while we oozed silently towards the battered walls of grey coral blocks. Well... sort of silently. It might be more accurate to say we rustled, thumped, and sidestepped our way to the opening in the wall that Mr. M. indicated. At least I didn't have to fight my way through the hampering folds of a bui-bui this time. We'd decided that it wouldn't really help if anybody caught sight of us, and my concentration was better put to use keeping up camouflage around us all.

The guard's presence was announced by a powerful whiff of pot. He had evidently indulged to the point of drowsiness before coming on duty. We weren't so impolite as to disturb him; a single blow from Lensky put him out for the duration.

Most of the children were sleeping soundly, presumably exhausted from a busy day of pretending to shoot, decapitate and disembowel infidels. One long form twitched and moved restlessly. Tabari, still in pain from that beating? Khamisi went down on one knee and put his hand over Tabari's mouth until the boy's eyes opened and went wide with recognition. He mouthed something at Tabari, got a nod of response, and lifted his hand.

Lensky had already spotted Sam Harrison on the far side of the room. He moved out of my camouflage space to reach him, stepping between sleeping children with that incongruous grace he displayed in combat situations. Just as he reached Sam, one of the smallest boys moved in his sleep, tossing back the fabric that had been over his head, and I recognized Bobby Navarro's blond head gleaming in the broken moonlight that came through the remnants of a roof. I went past Tabari and knelt beside him, dropping camouflage so as not to scare the kid. "It's all right, Bobby," I whispered, "we're here to rescue you."

The boy's eyes opened and widened just as Tabari's had done. Only I hadn't put a hand over his mouth, and I was too slow to stop him when he gasped and screamed.

"*Wazungu! Majini!* Help!"

The room erupted with shouting children, and I heard people running towards us. *Shit.* And we were spread out across the width of the room. I hauled Bobby to his feet, nearly dropping the rifle. Khamisi took him from me and threw him over his shoulder, then shoved me towards Lensky. He had evidently grasped that we all had to be touching for me to get us out of there.

I fell over another child and grabbed Lensky's arm. Behind me, I could feel Khamisi reaching for my elbow. I had to trust that he had Bobby and Tabari, and that Lensky was still holding Sam.

The pier, the pier made of crooked bleached driftwood, the pier in moonlight instead of afternoon sun. I croaked, "*Brouwer,*" and the habit of long practice helped to form the two surfaces in my mind, glowing against infinite blackness and touching at just one point.

We were on the pier.

The boat wasn't there.

And someone was shouting in the village. Just our luck, I'd forgotten to raise camouflage again as we teleported and some idiot had been sitting up in the moonlight to see our extremely untidy arrival on that pier. I disentangled myself from Bobby Navarro's legs and Khamisi's arm, pulled the rifle sling over my head and handed it to Khamisi. Seemed like time for somebody who knew how to use it to carry this thing.

Counting heads: Tabari, Khamisi, Bobby, Lensky, Sam. And Mr. M. was coiled around my waist. Good, I hadn't left anyone behind.

Except Rosie Jamison, of course.

"Majini! Shetani!" More Swahili followed, apparently amounting to, "Kill them!" according to Mr. M.

Oh, dear. Why couldn't these people react to the sight of teleporting devils by hiding in their huts? They were way too excitable.

Lensky fired a very short burst at the villagers. (*"Over their heads,* Thalia," he corrected me just now. "Killing anybody would have been an unnecessary complication.") Then he shoved his rifle at Tabari.

"You two," he said to Khamisi. "Hold them off for a few minutes. Try not to use too much ammo. Thalia and I *will* be back for you."

"What?" I asked.

"We're going back for Rosie."

"Hadn't we better take Tabari to show us where she is?"

"We need him here. Unless you want to ask Sam Harrison to take a rifle?"

"But – how are we going to find her?"

Lensky's grin would have been terrifying if we weren't on the same side. "Classical methods."

Seconds later we were just steps from the outer wall of the ruins – I'd been paying attention to the terrain; it wasn't hard to teleport the two of us back there – and Lensky was holding his gun against the neck of a terrified guard while I relieved the man of his weapons. My hands were shaking; I wasn't sure whether it was cowardice, or overdoing the applied topology. Maybe both.

"Now," he breathed, "you are going to tell me where Rosie Jamison is."

Mr. M. translated.

The guard's eyes rolled up and he sagged, whispering something to himself.

"He is praying," Mr. M. informed us. "He has no idea what you asked him." He addressed the terrified guard directly. "*Msichana mzungu wapi?*" and snapped at the answer. "More prayers! Useless!" He added something else in Swahili and the guard moaned and tried to slither down to the ground. Mr. M. said a few more words in a voice like a whiplash and the man started babbling.

"As I thought," he told us, "the child sleeps in the quarters reserved for Omar. It seems we will have to deal with TheSila after all."

"Did he tell you enough?" Lensky asked. "Can I knock him out now? I would rather not try to drag him with us."

We left the guard unconscious, gagged, and tied up with bits of his own unsavory clothing. For his sake I hoped there were no snakes on the island; he hadn't personally done us any harm, and he *had* pointed us towards Rosie.

"Only after I promised that Lensky would shoot him in the kneecap and cripple him for life," Mr. M. told me.

We stopped outside a stone house that was in slightly better condition than most. Blue flames flickered up out of the ground between us and the walls. I concentrated on keeping our camouflage up while Mr. M. engaged the djinn in discussion. It didn't sound like they were speaking Swahili; maybe it was Arabic. I wouldn't know. All I knew was that after several increasingly tense minutes, the cold flames parted to let us through.

Beyond the open doorway the room was black. I tripped over something on the floor, threw out my hands to save myself and came down, hard, on something soft and yielding. Softer than the rocks I was expecting to land on, anyway. The man's body thrashed under me; I tried to get up, slipped, and my elbow came down on something even softer than the rest of him. There was a gurgling, choking noise.

"Nice move, Thalia. Encourage him to stay down, will you?" Lensky thrust something small and hard into my hand. Oh – his backup gun. I lifted my elbow slightly, allowing Omar to breathe, and pressed the short barrel against his neck.

"Rosie, it's all right. Your mommy sent me for you, Rosie." Lensky's voice was calm and soothing as he scooped the little girl up. She clung to his neck, but she was sobbing. We needed to get out of there. I tried to grab his leg, but a shadow of flame came between us.

"First keep your promise," TheSila hissed from her cold, shimmering flames. "Quickly, before he calls on me!"

"Promise?"

"He sleeps with it under his pillow."

I slid one hand under there, found something hard and cold and drew it out. Not a weapon; a glass bottle.

"Break it! Break it!" The non-flames danced higher, and the whole room grew cold. In a radiance without any visible source, the bottle shone blue and iridescent.

I had to sit up to lift it, removing my elbow. Omar's gurgles turned into something more like words. I swung the bottle by its neck and hit him in the head. Not nearly hard enough; his lips were still moving.

"No, no, break it!"

An impossible frost was forming on everything in the room. I swung the bottle again, this time aiming at the wall, and was rewarded by a tinkle of breaking glass. The flames transformed into blue flickers and vanished into Omar's mouth. His lips went slack; his open eyes gleamed in the moonlight. Lensky stooped and put one finger against the man's throat, then took my hand. "Can you teleport?"

"Of course." I'd definitely overdone it; I felt sick and dizzy. But what was one more little jump with Lensky and the kid?

The answer: it wasn't worth much. True, I was able to get us to the pier where Khamisi and Tabari were still firing occasional short bursts to discourage the villagers. But the boat still wasn't there, and I was pretty sure we didn't have enough ammunition to keep the villagers off until I recovered enough to teleport us out of there. It would have to be back to Mombasa, we hadn't put in at any of the coves or beaches on the way down. Fifty miles, over water, and somehow I didn't think the villagers were going to give us food and water to replenish my blood sugar. If I couldn't get over these shakes, I might drown us all in the escape attempt.

Lensky was firing too, holding the Glock out two-handed. While I stared stupidly and shook, while Bobby Navarro and Rosie Jamison wailed, while Mr. M. engaged in lively conversation with something I couldn't quite see clearly, he fired one last shot and holstered the weapon.

"Out of ammo," he said, very calmly.

"The riches of the New World would be fitting ornament for your beauty," Mr. M. told the quivering shape of flames and shadows.

"Thalia, can I have my derringer back?"

My hands were empty, except for the neck of a broken bottle.

"I think I dropped it when I broke this." I dropped the useless piece of glass and shoved my right hand into the pocket of my shorts. I was going to need all the help the stars could provide if I had any hope of pulling this off.

"The Daughter of Stars has fulfilled the promise which I made to you." Mr. M. was beginning to sound testy.

"Oh, well. Time to improvise, before the boys empty the rifle magazines." Lensky sounded unreasonably cheerful. He took the black ceramic knife out of his other ankle holster and began whittling at one of the loose strips of driftwood on the pier. One of the rifles stuttered into silence.

"I owe you nothing," the shadow of flames told Mr. M., "but these pets of yours *are* amusing."

A cold fire, an invisible smoke wrapped around us and I felt it drawing us northwards. I opened my hand and sent a dancing funnel of stars in the general direction of Mombasa. The sounds of people on the beach were swallowed up by silence.

20. Termination

We slid down a blue funnel of wind into someplace dark and still. The blue light vanished and moonlight revealed a dim indoor space. I took a cautious step forward. There was something like coconut matting underfoot, but this didn't feel like our apartment. For one thing, it had air conditioning.

There was movement around me and I slowly picked out the figures of my companions. Lensky, Khamisi, Tabari, and Sam Harrison were standing around me. Mr. M. was around my neck. Lensky was holding Rosie Jamison, who was still crying, and Khamisi had the little Navarro boy.

Wherever we were, it was crowded, not designed for this many people. As my eyes adjusted, I made out bulky rectangular shapes that looked like office furniture: a desk, a filing cabinet, a bookcase.

Lensky cleared his throat. "Thalia, where have you brought us?"

"I didn't. And I don't know." I might have been reaching for Mombasa, but my efforts had been augmented by a breathtaking surge of power that had nothing to do with topology. Whoever had determined our destination, it hadn't been me. And I didn't think it was Mr. M. either; he wasn't actually that good at teleporting, not that he'd ever admit it.

A switch clicked, bright light flared and I blinked. We appeared to be standing in an office, all right, and the furnishings looked similar to some I'd seen quite recently. I opened the door nearest me. Yes, the next room was Nelson Finch's office. "Brad. Do you have LeShawn Taylor's private number?"

"I – oh, yes, I guess I do. He was out of town when we got here, so I never used it. I just talked to Finch." He hoisted Rosie up a little farther on his shoulder and fished out his phone.

"Well, just this once," I said, "*please* contact Taylor first, and wait on Finch?"

"You still don't trust him, Thalia?"

"Do you?"

Lensky called Taylor at home.

Once the circumstances were even partially explained, Mrs. Taylor insisted that we all take a taxi to their home. We couldn't possibly take care of those poor, traumatized mites in an *office!*

And so, as a new day dawned in Mombasa and all fifty-seven mosques turned on their loudspeakers to inform the faithful that prayer was better than sleep, we had a brief council of war while sitting around an American Colonial style table and eating Wheaties from white plastic bowls. The younger children had been tucked up in a guest bedroom; Tabari and Sam insisted on sitting up with the grownups, but from the way their heads were nodding I thought Lensky would wind up carrying them to bed sooner rather than later.

"I cannot believe that nice-seeming Nelson Finch was in cahoots with the Rashiduni. And trying to get LeShawn *killed!*" Mrs. Taylor said indignantly. "More sugar, Thalia?"

I had already embarrassed Lensky by pouring most of the contents of the sugar bowl over my cereal. Too bad. I might not have been solely responsible for that last powerful teleportation, but I'd done plenty of paranormal work before that to lower my blood sugar, and I needed a refill *fast.*

"No, thank you, Mrs. Taylor."

"Alicia."

"Thank you, Alicia."

"I am afraid there is no escaping it," Taylor said heavily. "I've known for some time that something was wrong. Drinking, sloppy tradecraft, the usual signs that an officer is losing it. I had planned to recommend he be transferred back to the States…" He fell silent, shaking his head.

The betrayal was clearly hard for Lensky and Taylor to stomach, but it was undeniable now that they'd finally compared notes. Finch had dined with the Taylors on the night before Khamisi set the bomb in the CIA office, and both of them were clear that he had not said one word of warning to either of them.

"He *wanted* LeShawn killed," Alicia said, "and he would have been if not for you, Thalia!"

She looked as if she might hug me, or cry on me, or both. "The Semtex might have decayed on its own," I mumbled, and concentrated on spooning up the last of the cereal until she looked elsewhere. "Oh, Tsenga!" she called, and a young man appeared. While she was quietly instructing him to do something or other, Lensky tried to steer the conversation into less emotional channels.

"I was wondering, Taylor.... Can you tell me where you've been? Finch implied that you were laid up with a fever, but..."

Taylor looked as abashed as was possible for a very big, very black, very healthy man. "Yes, well, that was what I told him. I had to take some personal days and go to Nairobi, and, well, the reason was kind of embarrassing."

"Idiot," Alicia Taylor said fondly.

"You wouldn't say so if it happened to you!" Taylor protested. "Actually, it was..."

"Wisdom teeth," his wife said when he stopped there. "All four at once, and all impacted."

Lensky whistled. "That must have been fun! But aren't you, ah, a little..."

"Kind of old for wisdom teeth? That was the embarrassing part," Taylor said. "I'm forty-eight. Can you *imagine* the jokes? So, me being specially trained by the CIA in working undercover, I figured I would just keep this little secret to myself. Trouble is, the only dentist I trusted to have excavating my mouth to this extent was in Nairobi. I thought the simplest thing would be to take a solid week of personal time and claim a touch of fever. Possibly not, in retrospect, my best decision ever."

"Oh well," Lensky said, "it worked out all right in the end."

Taylor looked sad. "Yes, but I missed all the fun."

Strange definition of fun, but Lensky was nodding sympathetically. Me, I would have voted for more beach-and-shopping days and fewer crawling-through-mangrove-swamp days, but that's just me.

Tabari and Sam were about to fall asleep with their faces in the cereal bowls. Alicia Taylor enlisted Khamisi's help to get them settled in the room with Bobby and Rosie, which apparently had enough bunk beds to accommodate everybody. The Taylors' servant, Tsenga, brought in a bamboo tray piled high with wonderful things I recognized – *mahamri*, those coconut doughnut triangles, and *kachori* smelling of curry – and other things that I didn't recognize but was totally willing to try. Yes, I was tired and sleepy, but not dozy enough to pass up fresh-fried *mahamri*. I helped myself to another mug of coffee and dug in. LeShawn excused himself and Lensky, saying that they had boring business to discuss and would take it to the study. I was able to translate that – "boring business" meant "CIA secret stuff" – but it was fine with me as long as they didn't take the *mahamri* with them.

As they left the dining room I heard Taylor saying, in the rumble that was his best imitation of a discreet murmur, "Does she always eat like that?" and on Lensky's assent, saying "Amazing!"

Yeah, well, *he* should try teleporting two adult males and four children before breakfast. Even if I'd had some kind of help on the big jump, I'd burned plenty of energy during our visit to the Island of Devils.

I wondered if Jumanne had chickened out and abandoned us there or if something had happened to him and his little boat. I made a mental note to ask Lensky if somebody could check up on that. As a mere woman, I could hardly go down to the waterfront myself and interrogate dhow captains. I'd be happy to let Taylor or one of his minions have that bit of 'fun.'

Alicia Taylor had yet another spare room for Lensky and me. I made a mental note that there were some perks to being a field officer stationed in a Third World country. I was willing to bet she hadn't personally laundered the dazzling white sheets that I eventually crawled between, wearing a borrowed nightgown.

At some time during my morning doze Brad joined me. He gave me a bone-crushing hug, complained that it was too hard to locate me swimming inside Alicia's nightgown like that, and fell asleep in mid-complaint with his mouth still open.

The day was well into official siesta time when I felt perky enough to rejoin the world. The shorts and shirt I'd worn under my bui-bui had been restored to some semblance of respectability while I slept; some stains had defied the laundry, but at least they no longer smelled like a mangrove swamp. Lensky, when I found him, was in a similar semi-presentable state, and working on his third cup of coffee. Tsenga, who appeared to have powers of telepathy that the Center for Applied Topology really should investigate, brought me a very cold Diet Coke and a new kind of little triangular pastry pockets. These were deep-fried and filled with curried veggies. He told me they were called *samosas*.

While I investigated the *samosas* Lensky caught me up on the current state of affairs. The American children were already on their way to Washington, being escorted by Taylor's secretary Mashika. He and Ben and I were to leave in a couple of days, after the State Department got us temporary papers; there was, he said, no question of returning to the apartment in Old Town for anything we might have left there.

"What about Nelson Finch?"

Lensky looked so sad I regretted the question. But we did need to settle the matter of Finch. Didn't we?

"He has not returned to the office. Or to his apartment. He may have – that is, I hope he has left the country."

"Why?"

"He knows too many operational details about all our African field offices. We have agents and case officers operating in less friendly environments than Kenya. If that information got into the hands of the wrong people, their lives could be at risk. So yes, I hope Finch's activities were no more than a misguided attempt to get the promotion he felt he deserved, and that he's now content to escape. And will stay far, far away from anything involving the intelligence community in future. Otherwise." He came to an abrupt halt.

"Otherwise?" It seemed to me that trying to get your boss blown up went beyond the "misguided attempt" category and right into "attempted murder," but Lensky was looking so grim that I didn't want to push him.

"Dammit, I knew he was disaffected!" he said suddenly, pounding a fist into his palm. "That time he went off in our apartment, complaining that the CIA was washed up, that there was no place for a real man of action any more. I told myself it was the beer talking, that everybody has gripes about their job. And there's more. I brushed aside all your warnings, everything that seemed off key about him. I should have caught and stopped him much earlier."

I went around the table to hug him. "Brad, how would you have stopped him? LeShawn Taylor was in Nairobi getting his wisdom teeth removed, you had no official authority here, the Mogadishu office didn't support you."

"There are ways," he said.

Ways he probably should not, for his own mental health, be thinking about.

"He was your friend once. The only thing you did wrong was, you were too loyal to that memory to let yourself see that he had changed."

He let his breath out with a huff. "Yes. My *friend*. Now I'm wondering if I misjudged him all along. Was he a back-stabbing traitorous son of a bitch when I teamed up with him at the Farm?"

Quite possibly, in my opinion, but saying that wouldn't make him feel better now. "People change," I said. "*I've* changed since I met you."

I was going to go into more detail about that – I had something to say that would almost certainly have distracted him – but Lensky wasn't through grieving the loss of his friend yet.

"You realize he could have been working with the Rashiduni?"

Of course I did. "I wondered," I temporized. "That demand for Khamisi to bomb the CIA office? It happened right after Finch found out we were using Khamisi as an agent. Perhaps he thought it was a win-win situation. Either he'd get his boss out of the way, or our agent would be discredited with the Rashiduni."

"And that's why you didn't tell me about your plan to neutralize the bomb. As you said, you couldn't trust me."

And I couldn't stand the pain in his face. "Brad, I didn't have the *right* to trust you with that. If Finch *was* working with the Rashiduni, it could have got Khamisi killed. I'd trust you with my own life in a heartbeat. But I couldn't decide for Khamisi that he should do the same."

Finally Lensky's body relaxed slightly and he put an arm around me, returning my hug.

"I hope you were wrong about that, but I do understand why you couldn't risk telling me. The thing is… if Finch *is* working with a terrorist group, with all the information he has…"

He sighed deeply and started over. "LeShawn and I were discussing whether the Company should terminate Finch."

"Well, obviously they have to fire him!"

"*Terminate*," Lensky repeated, heavily, and this time I got it.

"Oh."

"It won't be our decision. Higher will have to make the call."

But might it be their task to carry it out? I prayed that our papers for repatriation would come through before anybody had a chance to convey *that* order to Lensky.

I had a chance to say goodbye to Khamisi and Tabari later that day. It had been decided that it was too dangerous for them to stay in Mombasa, so Taylor had made arrangements for them to go to Mogadishu. That didn't sound like a net improvement to me, but at least they were going to be housed in the CIA compound inside the fortified perimeter of the airport.

"If you get lonely there," I suggested to Khamisi, "there's a girl from Mombasa staying in the compound… a widow, now." There'd been no official confirmation of Omar al-Zanji's death, but I knew what I'd seen. "I'm sure she'd like to see somebody from her home town." And Khamisi could do worse than spend some time with a nice girl like Fadiya. I wasn't exactly match-making, just giving events a tiny push. Two people who couldn't go home… It would be pleasant to see something good come out of all this.

Just a few days later we caught a flight out of Nairobi for America, meeting Ben and Annelise at the airport. Traveling under State Department auspices was definitely pleasanter than going it on our own; shorter lines, and fewer of them, before we stumbled into Bergstrom Airport and, by mutual consent, teleported to our own places.

Lensky recovered from jet lag faster than I did, which is totally unfair considering that he's eight years older than me. I had to put up with his usual comments about the virtues of exercise, vitamins, and sobriety during the phase where he was watching the news and I was alternating between Diet Cokes and involuntary naps. Fortunately, I wasn't alert enough to be irritated.

When I did find myself wide awake and bright eyed, it was the middle of the night – some night; I had a feeling it wasn't the first since our return. Lensky wasn't in the bed. I padded out to the kitchen and found Mister Sobriety sitting in front of an open beer, with two empty bottles on the table beside that one.

"Trying to drink yourself to sleep?" I insinuated myself between him and the table, perched on his knee and put an arm around his neck. If we were both awake at this hour, whatever it was, I could think of better ways to get relaxed than drinking.

"You haven't been watching the news."

"Of course not." I hadn't been doing anything except alternately sleeping and stumbling to the kitchen for another Diet Coke.

"Terrorists have murdered an American in Mombasa."

"Not LeShawn Taylor?" I had liked the big man who was so embarrassed about his very late wisdom teeth.

"No. Nelson Finch." Lensky hoisted his current beer and drank most of it. "He was – beheaded. By the Rashiduni. They made a video."

"You watched it?" I was horrified.

"Yes. Not on TV, of course. Internet." He finished off that bottle with another long pull. "They made a statement. Said he was a traitor."

"Well, he was, but…"

"A traitor to the *Rashiduni*," Lensky interrupted me.

"How did they get that idea?"

He lowered the bottle with a thump. "Possibly from the press conference the ambassador held two days before we left, crediting Finch's undercover work with the Rashiduni for our recovery of the kidnapped children."

I hadn't been aware of that either.

"Why…?"

"If Finch had left the country, he would have been all right, and crediting him might keep the Rashiduni from going after Khamisi. If he was still in

Mombasa, hiding out with the Rashiduni and giving them information, then he had to be terminated… and this way, the CIA wouldn't be blamed for his death."

"Oh. I didn't realize Taylor was that subtle."

"Thalia… it was *my* idea."

He lifted his bottle, set it down again when he realized it was empty.

I got two more beers out of the refrigerator and sat down at the table with him. We drank to old friendships until morning light brightened the room.

A few days later, a large crate appeared on the doorstep of the condo, with a sealed envelope taped to it. Lensky opened the letter.

"Oh," he said flatly. "Well, that's nice."

"What?"

"Victor packed up the stuff we left behind and Taylor had it shipped here."

He levered the lid open onto a jumble of papers, clothes and just plain junk.

"Men," I commented over his shoulder, "do not know how to pack… Some of this is Ben's, shall I call him?"

Lensky wasn't in any hurry to sift through the stuff, with all its memories; we drank coffee and waited for Ben, and I tactfully refrained from rooting through the box in search of my souvenirs.

Once Ben got there, he and I started pulling things out of the tangle in the box. We needed a black garbage bag, large size, for all the stuff that never should have been shipped: the bui-bui Lensky tore and the one Ben never used, the tampons we hadn't needed for plugging bullet wounds… Victor had evidently been intent on erasing all traces of our sojourn from what was now his apartment. We threw our clothes into the laundry hamper as we came across them. A couple of small stacks sufficed for the things we actually wanted. My Kindle, our phones, our real passports (not that I was going to toss the fakes provided by the Company.) I set aside the deep gold bikini, the red and purple coverup, the ruby-heeled slippers and – oh, joy! that little rectangle of Masai beadwork.

"Glad to get your souvenirs back?" Ben asked, watching me grinning over that last find.

"Well, yes."

"I don't suppose you'll have many more chances to go shopping in exotic places, now."

"You think?"

"Well, if you're going to take –"

"Shut up, I haven't told Lensky yet."

"You guys really need to communicate more, you know?"

"Shut *up*."

I turned to Lensky. "Brad, I've been doing some serious thinking."

A quirked eyebrow invited me to continue. I took both his hands. "You were happier on parts of this mission than I've ever seen you here in Austin. Steve Harrison told me that you were born to be a field officer. I think he was right. And I – I think you should go back to Foreign Operations."

"Leaving you here while I'm away for months at a time?" His voice suggested that was not acceptable. I was glad to hear it.

"Well… I've been thinking about that too. You know that modification of Riemann fire that neutralized the Semtex? Ben didn't work out how to do it; he was half blind without his glasses. I figured it out. Without my colleagues, without my office, without my books. Don't you see, Brad, my career isn't like yours. I don't really need to be here in Austin; I can do research and apply topology anywhere. Including anywhere you are sent."

"Thalia?"

"If – if that's an arrangement that would be okay with you?"

He swept me into a hug that indicated total assent. It also nearly broke a couple of ribs, but I wasn't complaining. "*Okay*? Everything I could ask for in life, in one package? Thalia, Thalia, *Thalia*…"

I became aware, belatedly, of Ben making disgusted noises in the background. "*That's* your decision, Lia? And I suppose you expect me to break it to Dr. Verrick?"

Lensky relaxed his hug just a little and looked over my shoulder. "What does Verrick have to do with this?"

"He—"

"Not a thing," I said, but Ben refused to be interrupted.

"He wanted to retire and make Thalia Director of the Center, and up until two minutes ago we all thought she was going to go along with it."

"Well, you all thought wrong," I said.

Lensky's shoulders were shaking.

"Running away, Thalia?"

Oh, hell. Busted. "Running away *with you*," I emphasized.

"Well, I'm not complaining," he decided. "I still get everything I wanted."

Ben, bored, was poking at the crumpled paper in the bottom of the case. "Aha," he said now, "I wondered why they needed such a big box." He pushed the papers aside and moved a squat blue bottle that I didn't remember seeing before. I didn't think much about it; I was too concerned about what I could now see peeking out from under the packing paper. Ben lifted out the four-foot African mask. "Victor's revenge!"

Lensky started laughing out loud. A funnel of coldness formed at the back of my neck, and Mr. M. lifted his head to stare behind me.

"Interesting pets, indeed," said TheSila's lazy, smoky voice. "I think I shall like it here."

Keep reading for a first look at the next
Applied Topology book, *The Lake of the Dragon*.

The Lake of the Dragon

It all started with Aunt Alesia and the dragon's rubies, and that dance at the Austrian embassy in Paris.

Purists would go farther back, maybe as far back as the day a couple of years ago when I was concentrating really hard on the Axiom of Choice and accidentally selected several objects out of my kid brother's miscellaneous collections of plastic junk. Without touching them. You could make a case that it all started there.

But I'd been applying topology, and researching further applications of topology, for nearly two and a half years since then without ever causing an international incident. So I blame this one *entirely* on Aunt Alesia.

When Lensky and I agreed that his career would take priority for a while, because I could do my research anywhere that he might be stationed, we'd both envisioned the usual CIA overseas posting. He'd be assigned to some interesting part of the world to collect information and recruit people to bring in more information, preferably not breaking too many laws of the host country too noticeably. We'd set up house wherever he was sent and I would settle down with my books and a stack of blank notepads for a long, quiet period of research.

What we hadn't figured on was that after we successfully retrieved the hostages from East Africa, the entire Operations side of the CIA would become very, very interested in applied topology.

The CIA had funded the Center for Applied Topology from the very beginning, though at first they managed to hide that fact by passing the funds through a non-government foundation. But apart from sending Brad Lensky to pass on occasional requests and to try to keep us out of trouble, they'd left us pretty much alone. In the weeks following the bombing and the hostage retrieval, I realized that this was because most of the people in Operations didn't really believe in our paranormal abilities. They'd been too afraid of looking like gullible fools to actually *use* us.

Now, though, the careful people at Langley realized what an asset they had in the Center, and they were lining up around the block to use us. Their principal interest, to begin with, was in black bag jobs. Every field office in every capital city had a list of places they'd dearly like to bug. Other countries' embassies were high on that list, together with ambassadors' residences, military clubs, private political clubs, you name it. Up to now, they'd had to work with a series of difficult tradeoffs. How hard would it be to break into a given location, and what was the cost if they were caught sneaking around there? Everybody in this business spied on everybody else, but getting caught was not cool and sometimes resulted in embarrassing diplomatic conflicts. Putting your own ambassador on the spot could be a quick ticket out of field work and back home to a basement full of analysts.

Now they thought they could bug every place they'd ever dreamed of, for free – that is, at little or no risk. The theory was simple enough. We – the applied topologists at the Center – could teleport to any place we'd been previously, and we could take passengers. Let a topologist mingle with the legitimate embassy personnel, get invitations to parties at various embassies and other places of interest, then teleport back in the small hours with a technician who would place the bugs. Even if surprised, we could vanish before anybody believed what they were seeing.

There was just one catch. There weren't anywhere *near* as many applied topologists as there were field offices begging for our services.

To be precise, there were exactly four of us: me, Ben Sutherland, Ingrid Thorn, and Colton Edwards.

We did have an infinite set of the magic-enhancing stars that Mr. M. had brought with him from ancient Babylon, but since they could only be deployed by topologists – or Mr. M. himself, of course – that didn't solve the CIA's problem. Too, most of them were not real clear on the whole concept of infinite sets, nor did they find it easy to believe in tiny sparkling points of light that were invisible to anybody but topologists – or Mr. M., of course. The stars didn't really feature in most Company discussions of how to use us.

Lensky tells me there were some nasty scenes, and almost some blood spilled, in the initial discussions of how to divvy up the treasure that we represented. He was in most of those meetings to advise the department heads on how we could best be used, and he took the opportunity to advocate on our behalf before anybody got crazy or cruel notions.

We were going to start in European capitals, because those would be the easiest locales for our untraveled crew to begin with. Postings would consist of one topologist and one partner of the opposite sex, because there were always places a man could go that a woman couldn't, and vice versa.

This worked out nicely for us, as we all had non-topologist partners.

I, of course, was married to Lensky. Just before the diplomatic initiative got started, Ingrid had married our computer expert, Jimmy DiGrazio. Colton had a thing going with Meadow Melendez, the robotics engineer who maintained Mr. M.'s prosthetic body and built the enhancements for it. And Ben was living with his rich girlfriend Annelise, who also worked for the Center as our resident liar. She was an expert at spinning stories to convince people who stumbled across our paranormal work that they hadn't seen what they'd seen, and she looked forward to doing the same, or better, to foreign diplomats.

For our first assignments, they tried to match us with cities that would be relatively easy for us. The Swedish embassy didn't actually have a long list of places they desperately wanted bugged, but Stockholm would be a good place for Ingrid, with her parents' Swedish background, to start work. Colton was assigned to Spain because Meadow was fluent in Spanish. Ben got London, and he swore that Annelise's rich father hadn't influenced anybody to give him the easy English-language assignment. "And besides, Thalia, you got the best posting of all!"

"*Paris*," Ingrid sighed. "While I'm freezing in Stockholm…"

"Paris," Annelise echoed. "Do you realize Paris Fashion Week is just starting? Balmain, Balenciaga, Lanvin…"

"Barcelona is pretty interesting too," Colton said cheerfully. He and Meadow were being sent to the Consulate in Barcelona, rather than to Madrid, because the Catalan independence movement was heating up to boiling again after several months at a slow simmer. "I've always wanted to see Sagrada Familia and Parc Güell."

"*I've* always wanted to see *Notre Dame*," Ingrid grumbled. "The Louvre. The Louis Vuitton Museum: they're doing a temporary exhibit of that Icelandic artist's light installations this month."

"Well, you can go look at the Little Mermaid instead," I suggested.

"*Really*, Thalia. That's in Copenhagen, not Stockholm. Why they're sending a cultural illiterate like you abroad at all escapes me."

"I'm a State Department intern taking advantage of this new program to give me a smattering of overseas experience before I settle in to a permanent post," I said, repeating the line we'd all been told to use as an explanation for our joining the various embassies. In most cases the American ambassador didn't know any more than that. Officially, at least. Lensky's agency is very big on plausible deniability.

In fact, I wasn't that thrilled about being sent to Paris. Ingrid could have had it with my best wishes. I'm not exactly the person you would think of in connection with elegant Parisians; ever since graduation I'd managed to use the same little black dress for almost every occasion that demanded something more than T-shirts and jeans. Mom had forced me into ivory satin for the wedding, but apart from that my little-black-dress record was perfect.

There were going to be a lot more of those occasions now, and I had a new wardrobe (courtesy of the CIA and a fashion consultant) with which to meet them. But I was uncomfortably aware that the only reason I was starting off in Paris was because of my Aunt Alesia, whose French husband had died some seventeen years ago. She had lived with us off and on while I was growing up and had become more French every year. I'd picked up her excellent accent over years of French chit-chat over the breakfast table, and had supplemented that with two years of college French.

That wasn't a whole lot of equipment, linguistic or otherwise, with which to tackle a glittering social life in the fashion capital of the world.

"Cheer up," Lensky said when I whined to him, "you're vastly overestimating the sophistication of State Department social life. It's more like an infinitely boring desert with not nearly enough oases."

"Tell me again about the infinitely boring desert," I suggested under my breath while surveying the ivory and gold ballroom that filled the entire second floor of the Austrian embassy. Men in sober black and white were surrounded by women in a rainbow array of formal gowns, many of them sparkling with enough jewels to rival the GDP of a small country.

The CIA makeover budget did not include jewelry. Fortunately, as a mere intern, I wasn't really expected to compete in that league. My topaz-colored silk sheath with a frill of lighter gold chiffon bursting out from knees to floor was more than adequate for my official position. All the same, I could have used a modest spray of citrines, or something of the sort, to build up my morale. Too bad I couldn't wear my infinite set of stars – well, I could have, but since they were invisible to everybody else they wouldn't have much of an effect. "How am I supposed to compete with *that*?" I groused as a tall brunette wearing a fountain of rubies and diamonds whirled past. "Holy shit," I gasped as her profile came into view. "I don't believe it."

"That kind of language will certainly make you stand out," said Lensky. I ignored him. Men have it so easy; one good dark suit and they could fit in everywhere. I started after the brunette and Lensky grabbed my arm.

"Hey, when they said *mingle*, they didn't mean charge out on the dance floor and trip over people," he said.

"Didn't you recognize her?"

"Who?"

I jerked my chin towards the ruby-bedecked brunette. "Considering she was *Koumbara* at our wedding, I'd think you would remember her. That. Is. My. Aunt. Alesia." She was thirty years older than me and I was willing to swear she didn't own any rubies. What was she doing at the Austrian embassy's ball of the year? For that matter, what was she doing in Paris at all? I'd last seen her sitting at Mom's kitchen table, peeling carrots.

"Let's catch up with her and find out," Lensky suggested, swinging me out onto the dance floor with surprising competence. The man could waltz like a Viennese, something I had not previously discovered during the year and a half we'd known each other. He was even good enough to make up for my awkward steps; the month of makeover-and-training provided before the CIA threw us in at the deep end hadn't been nearly enough to turn me into an expert dancer, but it didn't matter with Lensky taking the lead.

Staying upright through a Viennese waltz was enough of a challenge without trying to look for Alesia. I concentrated on my steps. We turned, dipped, swooped and suddenly backtracked. The music ended with us standing beside Alesia and her partner, a short man with thinning blond hair whom I'd never seen before.

"Thalia, *ma petite!*" Alesia exclaimed. "What brings you here?"

"Funny, I was just about to ask the same question." Up close, I got the full impact of the rubies. The necklace consisted of gold filigree with little fountains of rubies spraying out on fine wires, each ruby surrounded by tiny diamonds. There were matching earrings shaped rather like chandeliers. Only somebody as tall as my aunt, with her long elegant neck, could have carried it off.

"Oh, Daryush and I are old friends," she said. "He was the Cultural Attaché for the Taklanistan embassy in Rome when my dear Georges was posted there, you know. And now he's an ambassador! We were just remembering those happy, happy days."

"Not so happy for all of us," said Daryush in a heavily accented voice, "since you, *ma chère* Alesia, were so devoted to that Georges of yours!" He turned to me. "All of us young men in Rome wished him at the devil, that lucky Georges, monopolizing the loveliest lady in diplomatic circles!"

"Daryush, you will shock my niece," Alesia laughed, "she doesn't know that old people like us ever loved and laughed. This is my little niece Thalia, Daryush."

He clicked his heels, bowed over my hand and just brushed his lips across the knuckles.

"And she is newly married," Alesia went on, "so you mustn't flirt with her,

Daryush. Her nice American husband would not understand!"

"But Alesia, *ma belle*, you know my heart is entirely yours!" Daryush protested.

"Do my parents know where you are, Aunt Alesia?"

She shrugged. "I may have said something about going to Paris with my old friend Solange. Or I may not... I believe, actually, I had intended to return to Austin after meeting Solange in New York. But when she was so kind as to invite me back to Paris, how could I refuse?"

The music started again. Daryush, taking my aunt in his arms, whirled back out onto the dance floor. I stayed where I was, frowning.

"Is this going to be a problem?" Lensky asked.

"Oh. No, I don't think so. You never mentioned where you work to Aunt Alesia, did you?"

"Thalia, even your parents don't know who I work for."

"Oh. Right." I have occasionally made fun of the Company's passion for secrecy, but just now it struck me as a very good thing. I wouldn't get many invitations to parties on other embassies' turf if I were identified as a CIA field officer rather than a State Department intern.

Lensky's waltzing style had attracted some attention among the diplomatic wives, so I found that mingling was relatively easy now. The wives wanted to dance with my husband, and offered me up to their escorts in exchange. It worked out reasonably well. The husbands didn't want to dance and neither did I. They fetched me flutes of champagne and little plates of snacks and we chatted amicably enough; they were so grateful that I didn't pine for the dance floor that it was easy to keep them happy. By the end of the evening I had scored invitations for cocktail parties at the Ukrainian and Polish embassies, a reception in honor of Central Asian artists at the Guimet – the Musée National des Arts Asiatiques – and a dinner party at the home of the Egyptian cultural attaché. Not to mention figs wrapped in paper-thin Parma ham, asparagus spears in puff pastry, and Sachertorte under whipped cream. Lensky hadn't done too badly himself: two more dinner parties, a concert and a museum opening.

Aunt Alesia and her date the ambassador were nowhere to be seen. Oh, well. It wasn't like Taklanistan, wherever that might be, was a country of burning interest to the CIA. I could safely leave that to my wayward aunt and concentrate on the Ukrainians, Poles, Egyptians, and whoever Lensky had scooped up.

We decided that we could skip the reception for Central Asian artists, as nobody at the embassy had any desire to bug the Musée Guimet – and if they did, they could walk in there any time; it was a public place. The concert and the museum opening also didn't offer much of interest. We'd be busy enough for the next week dealing with all the other invites.

I fell into bed with a gratifying sense of duty well done. For somebody who doesn't mingle, I thought I had filled out my dance card pretty well on this first excursion. Paris wasn't going to be so bad after all.

I thought that right up until the Friday of the following week, when we returned from our dinner party at the Israeli political officer's home to find Aunt Alesia pacing up and down the marble floor of our temporary apartment. "Thalia, you have to help me," she burst out as soon as we were inside. "The most terrible thing has happened. The Shaimak Rubies are gone!"

I blinked. "What, that..." I quickly ruled out *insane, extravagant* and *flamboyant*... "that lovely necklace you were wearing at the Austrian embassy ball? How did you lose your rubies, Aunt Alesia?"

"That's just it," she said. "They weren't *my* rubies. They were a loan from dear Daryush."

"Okay, how did you lose *his* rubies?"

"And they aren't his either. They come from the Taklanistan ruby mines that were closed over a century ago, which makes them twice as valuable because of their rarity. They are the property of the nation. And those – those *canaille* who took them are blackmailing me!"

When I was so ungenteel as to mutter *Oh shit* at the embassy ball, who knew I was prescient? Because this was a genuine *oh shit* moment if I'd ever seen one.

Also by Margaret Ball

Applied Topology series:

A Pocketful of Stars
An Opening in the Air
An Annoyance of Grackles
A Tapestry of Fire

Harmony series:

Insurgents
Awakening
Survivors

Earlier books:

Disappearing Act
Duchess of Aquitaine
Mathemagics
Lost in Translation
No Earthly Sunne
Changeweaver
Flameweaver
The Shadow Gate

www.ingramcontent.com/pod-product-compliance
Lightning Source LLC
Chambersburg PA
CBHW032121170626
46808CB00006B/2050